DATING CAN BE MURDER

A Samantha Shaw Mystery

DATING CAN BE MURDER

Jennifer Apodaca

KENSINGTON BOOKS
http://www.kensingtonbooks.com

Library of Congress Card Catalogue Number: 2001095188
ISBN 0-7582-0073-0

First Printing: May 2002
10 9 8 7 6 5 4 3 2 1

Printed in the United States of America

*In loving memory of my mom, Thelma Irene Roper.
There are few people who influence a woman's life like her
mother. I was truly blessed.*

1

Finding out that my dead husband had been cheating on me made getting revenge harder.

But not impossible.

It took a margarita-laced session with my best friend, Angel, to come up with a suitable reprisal. I sold the cheating pig's classic 1964 fully restored Mustang convertible. Trent Shaw had loved his two restored classic cars, but he'd had a special fondness for the Mustang over the 1957 two-seater T-Bird, white with red interior. Special enough that he had hidden a dozen or so pairs of panties beneath the spare tire.

They weren't my panties. In those days, I had been a full-sized white-cotton housewife. The panties hidden in the Mustang had been Cheap Slut.

I'm no longer a white-cotton matron. With the money from selling the Mustang, I got myself a brand-new pair of the latest model breasts and Tae Kwon Do lessons. A girl with a perky, recently purchased size-C chest needs to be able to protect her investment.

In short, finding those panties in the Mustang was the beginning of my new-woman makeover. After buying my two sons the newest mind-numbing Nintendo unit and a bone-shattering trampoline, I used the remainder of the revenge money from the Mustang to exchange my long dresses for short skirts. With that much leg showing, I couldn't have those dowdy gray streaks in my hair. So I went blonde.

The final phase of the margarita-induced revenge plan is how I came to be in the retro-awesome Thunderbird my panty-collecting husband never let me drive this morning. Dressed in a thigh-high pale green skirt, a tight black silk shirt and a pair of black sling backs with spiky heels, I leaned over and cranked up an old Beach Boys tune. Weaving my way through town, I headed for the second most important thing in my life—my career.

I am now a businesswoman. Sort of. The parking lot of my company is a single row of spaces facing Mission Trail Street in Lake Elsinore, California. There's barely enough room for two cars to pass each other. The suites are located in a decaying building that also houses a liquor store, flower shop, baseball card shop, beach and bike stuff, psychic reader and a jeweler that has to buzz customers in the door. Okay, maybe not real elegant, but Suite 107 is all mine: HEART MATES.

A dating service.

I bought this place with the insurance money after Trent's untimely accident. Before I had found his panty stash, each with a Post-it Note rating the wearer. Classy. When I had still believed in love, romance, soul mates, and all that. Trent and I had met at this dating service, and when it came up for sale after his death, I bought it. Let's just say that my good old white cottons were wrapped a bit tight.

Now that I had loosened the hold of my misguided nostalgia, I had plans and dreams. Building Heart Mates into a success was important to me. The fact that my married life had all been a lie, and that the entire town had known my husband was a cheating louse while I had not, meant I had something to prove. Buying Heart Mates would not be another in a long stream of mistakes.

Getting out of the car, I walked to the door. One day, when I was a success, I would own this entire building, not just a single run-down suite. Romance was an illusion— one that I meant to give my clients. The walls of the long hallways would be painted in romantic misty rose, and my clients' feet would sink into the up-to-your-ankles rose carpet. Piped in lovers' music would soothe troubled and lonely souls searching for love. A well-trained staff would move silently and efficiently, guiding prospective clients into signing with us. Heart Mates would become well known for huge mingling parties, serving wine from the local vineyards in Temecula. . . .

But all that took work. Cutting off my daydreams, I went through the door. "Morning, Blaine, any new clients?" I looked at him hopefully.

"That T's purring today. You put that premium gas in it?"

Blaine was the mechanic my husband had used. I had lured him away to work for me. He was . . . well, mechanical in all ways. Very good with a camcorder and camera, to say nothing of my car. Efficient too. As my assistant, he was top notch. The fact that he was big and brawny helped in my line of work. He wore his brown hair in a 70s feather style and gathered the length in a ponytail at the back of his thick neck. He favored jeans with blue work shirts. Guess you can take the mechanic out of the garage . . .

"You put gas in it for me yesterday, remember?" Blaine drove my car whenever possible. His primer-painted Hyundai two-door hatchback with missing hubcaps was all the reason he needed.

Nodding, he dragged his gaze from the T-Bird. "Nice suit," he commented with much less enthusiasm for my new-woman outfit. "We got one new client in the interview room. And your mother's in your office."

My sling backs caught on a loose thread of the wafer-thin, industrial steel-gray carpet. "What's she want?" I whispered as I reached for the doorknob of my office. It's actually a cubicle. The suite I leased was the size of a large bedroom. Blaine sat up front with the coffeemaker and file cabinets. There were a couple of metal folding chairs for waiting clients and a stack of magazines on a TV tray. My cubicle was on the right side of the office. A separate cubicle divided the back of the office into an interview and media room where we could videotape or photograph clients. Behind the interview room was a small storage area and bathroom. I snatched my hand back from my office door.

Blaine shrugged from behind his oak desk. "She doesn't talk to the help. She just told me to make fresh coffee and bring it to her." He glanced at the TV tray holding the coffeemaker by the Sparkletts water cooler. There was a can of Chock Full o' Nuts and a glass jar of tea bags. A jar of powdered creamer and packets of sugar, both real and fake, sat next to a stack of white Styrofoam cups.

I rolled my eyes up to the yellow water stains on the ceiling and pictured my mother holding a Styrofoam cup. I could see her perfectly manicured, pearl-pink nails against the white cup. My mother rearranged the world to suit her delusions. Styrofoam was beneath her. I could hear her lecture about providing my clients with the proper refreshments in proper dishes. Then, without any thought for logic in telling me first how to run my business then how to dump it, she would smoothly segue into why I should get out of the dating service business and into real estate. My left eye began to twitch. "I had better see the new client," I called back over my shoulder and hurried into the interview room that stretched out behind the reception area and my office.

"Chicken," Blaine said.

You bet, I thought as I opened the door. This cubicle was soundproof, or as close as we could get it, for the video-taping. Blaine was one of my better business decisions. Not only was he mechanically inclined, but he was handy too. Looking at the walls Blaine had extended up to the ceiling, I congratulated myself on trusting my instincts. I had met him a few times while Trent was alive, and he struck me as calm and capable. Restoring classic cars took training, skill, and improvisation since many parts are unavailable for classics. Those things didn't stump Blaine—he found a way around them. That was the kind of person I needed to assist me at Heart Mates. We improvised a lot here.

Closing the door to the interview room, I ran my eye over the romantic posters of couples in exotic places that covered three of the walls. The far wall was blank. A stool sat there along with the tripod and other assorted tools that Blaine used to capture the image the client wanted. Everything was in place.

I fixed a smile on my face to greet my first client of the day. "Good morning, I'm Samantha Shaw."

The man sat at an oval oak table on a single pedestal that once lived in my dining room. As he looked up from the clipboard forms he was reading, I quickly appraised him. Average. About five foot ten inches, thinning sandy-blond hair, owlish brown eyes behind John Lennon glasses, and the kind of intense look that belonged to an accountant. I pegged him for the indoor breed. Probably read Tom Clancy but had never had an adventure of his own. This was his adventure—going to a dating service. He wore a short-sleeved, button-down Hawaiian print shirt.

His arms were well developed, so maybe he worked out. Muscles like those didn't come from punching a keyboard. His left arm was in a black sling.

I was beginning to revise my opinion so I decided to read the questionnaire. Pulling out a chair, I sat down and slid the clipboard toward me. "Okay, Mr.—" I looked down at the name.

It was blank. The whole sheet was blank. I lifted the first sheet to review the security check permission sheet.

Blank.

Staring at the pages, I bit down on my lips as a thread of unease curled inside of me. Just a—a what? I was being silly. A businesswoman does not let little problems throw her. I forced my mouth to relax back into an easy smile. The guy was probably having second thoughts. Most people were leery of dating services. "Well." I gave him my best trust-me smile. "Why don't I start by explaining what we do here. You see, we're really a matching type service. You fill out these forms"—I lifted the clipboard up—"then we conduct an interview to determine your preferences, and if you want, we'll do a videotape or photograph to go in your file. When we think we have a match that fits your needs, we check with both of the two compatible clients and give out your phone numbers. The actual contact is up to you."

I took a breath to launch into the second part of my speech. "Now we also offer some exciting dating packages that you can purchase. Our Temecula wine-tasting package is the most popular, Mr.—" I looked down at the blank page and said, "What is your name?"

He stood up.

My fleeting moment of unease gave way to a different kind of anxiety. I couldn't afford to lose another client! Especially with my mother in my office. Panic tested my cool businesswoman exterior. "What is it you are looking for, sir?"

He came around the table and stopped when he was standing over me. "I want the money."

I stared up at him. From where I sat in the chair, he seemed taller than I had first thought. His complexion was pasty white; that, combined with the glasses, had made me think of an accountant. But his voice didn't sound like a soft, fact-spewing accountant. He sounded low and threatening. I inhaled sharply, catching a big whiff of stale cigarette smoke mixed with cinnamon gum. What was going on? What money . . . Wait, I knew!

"Are you from the IRS?" Standing up, I explained myself. "I only just got that notice of an audit! I fully intend to cooperate!"

The man narrowed his brown eyes behind his glasses. Leaning closer, he stared into my face. "Funny. Funny can get you dead, Samantha Shaw. Ask your husband."

"But he's already dead!" Trent had died from a peanut allergy when he ate some homemade candy. What possible connection could he have to this guy? Trent had been handsome, smooth, charming slutty women right out of their panties. This man was pasty white, with hard marble eyes and a cheesy Hawaiian shirt.

"I know." His voice took on a low menace and he dropped his gaze to my chest. "Nice rack. Where'd you get the money for that?"

Hey, I'd dealt with a room full of women at PTA meetings eyeing me and whispering behind the chocolate chip cookies after I'd had myself enhanced. I wasn't taking this crap from an amateur.

Straightening up to my five foot five—with heels—height, I sucked up my one hundred twenty-nine and three-quarter pounds into the best posture I could manage. "You ever hear of sexual harassment?" I was picturing slapping the IRS with a whopper of a lawsuit, and I desperately wanted to believe he was from the IRS.

Because if he wasn't from the IRS, and he wasn't one of the polyester-suit lounge lizards that gave dating services a bad name, then I was in trouble.

Just in case, I widened my stance and said, "I know Tae Kwon Do." The truth is that I'm only a yellow belt and have trouble balancing on one foot. There were six-year-old kids passing me up in rank.

Recovering, he stepped closer. "You have something that belongs to me. I want my money or you and your kids will be visiting Trent in hell real soon."

"What money!" And what did Trent have to do with this? He'd been dead a year now. The mention of my kids scared me. Hell, this guy scared me. The feeling that I'd been ignoring since I saw the blank interview forms broke out of my control into full-blown terror. "I don't have any money!"

Good old charming Trent, it turned out, had left us a bank account with worthless zeros and a lot of debt. I'd been forced to wake up to reality and sell the house, ripping my two sons from the home they'd been born in. We'd all moved in with my grandpa in his small three-bedroom house. But the boys and I—we'd survived. We were making the best of it. Now, somehow, this man was threatening us.

What money? I'd used Trent's life insurance money to buy this place, and it wasn't producing any golden eggs.

Suddenly he reached into his black sling and pulled out what looked like an electric razor. I had a sudden vision of myself bald. Was this guy here to shave my head? My heart started bouncing in my chest. I forgot every self-defense move I'd learned except how to scream. I opened my mouth and the world went black.

* * *

I came to sprawled on the floor by my dining room table with my mother and Blaine standing over me. Where was I?

"Maybe a seizure?" My mother's voice interrupted the jerking and twitching of my arms and legs.

"Never heard of a seizure that makes someone write on themselves with a permanent black marker," Blaine replied.

Opening my mouth, I almost choked on my tongue. My muscles were not responding to my commands. What happened? Where was I? I was pretty sure I was not in my dining room despite the table. No, I remembered now, that house was gone. There had been no room at Grandpa's for anything except bedroom furniture. I had Trent's fancy oak desk in my office at Heart Mates, the big oak dining room table in the interview room, and the rest I had either sold or stored in Grandpa's garage. Which brought me back to where I was—on the floor of the interview room at Heart Mates.

"She's coming around." Blaine hunkered down by my side. "Boss? Can you hear me?"

"What happened? I feel like a truck ran over me."

Blaine's brown eyes looked up and down me as if I was a car. The diagnosis sprang out of thick lips. "Stun gun." He nodded his head, satisfied. "Judging by the message written on your skirt, I'd say you annoyed someone."

"What! This skirt is from Nordstrom's!" I struggled to get my arms, which were quivering like flopping fish, under me, to lever myself up on my elbows. Big black letters floated like spots before my eyes. "Tell me I'm not seeing that!" I heard myself wail.

"It's a short message. Guess he ran out of material," Blaine commented.

"Couldn't have been the IRS then. They're real pros at

fine print." Clearly I was not dealing with an electric razor-wielding IRS agent. "What does it say?" I was having trouble getting the room to hold still. Reading, even large black letters on my pale green skirt, was way beyond my abilities.

"It says 'Bring the money to the arcade at Mulligan's nine o'clock Friday night, or die,'" Blaine said.

Too many thoughts fought for attention in my brain. Mulligan's was a small miniature golf and go-cart park that also had a big arcade. Why there? And what money?

"Your skirt is so short that they wrote the 'or die' on the bare skin of your thighs," my mother announced in a sharp voice. "Really, Samantha, a lady always wears panty hose. It's going to take a week to get that marker off."

With that, my thoughts focused on one thing. If I held my breath, would I pass out again?

"Let me see if I understand this. An electric razor-wielding IRS agent attacked you?"

A banger of a headache was shortening my temper. "Detective Rossi, why are you here? How did I rate a detective? Is there a serial stun-gunner who writes on women in permanent marker on the loose?" I looked down at my legs and wondered if my thighs would look fat in the pictures the officer had taken.

Detective Morgan Rossi was a good-looking man. On the far side of thirty, he had a killer grin that dimpled his otherwise hard cheeks and pale blue eyes. He wore pressed jeans with a blazer—I could see his black shoulder holster lying starkly against his white shirt. He filled up the sturdy oak arrow-backed chair.

My husband had been good-looking. Good-looking men were trouble.

Leaning back in the matching chair across the oak table, I closed my eyes. "Do you think this guy was some kind of nut? What money does he think I have? This place..." I sipped at my cold coffee and didn't bother stating the obvious. I wasn't going to be winning the local newspaper's *Businesswoman of the Year* plaque anytime in the foreseeable future.

"You tell me."

Two things crossed my mind. First, women confessed to this man. Yessir, he just oozed charm that made you want to confide in him. And second, I didn't know what the hell to confess since he was talking money. "I don't have any money!"

Detective Rossi nodded and wrote something down in a small spiral notebook with a Bic pen.

My gut clenched. "You don't believe me." Suddenly, this seemed serious. Way serious. "I mean, this guy was a wacko, right? Has some sort of grudge against dating services? Maybe he used this service before I bought it and wants his money back?" I was babbling, but my whole life was tilting over.

Again, dammit. Wasn't learning that Trent had been cheating on me all the years I played the patsy/loyal wife and mom enough? Then the notice in the mail, all in accusing red ink, telling me my check for the house payment had bounced. My headache hammered beneath that humiliating memory. Trent had been dead less than two weeks when I discovered there was no money in our checking account. I'd been left with less than two hundred dollars in our savings account and a stack of incoming credit card bills from Trent's high living, car payments, utilities—it didn't begin to cover it. Checks bounced all over that month.

Rossi flicked a blue-eyed glance at me. "We'll check it out." Standing up, he said, "By the way, we'll need that skirt."

That snapped me out of my memories. I blinked. "Now?"

He pulled a Ziploc bag out of his jacket. His killer grin made a slow crawl over his mouth. "Now."

I was no longer in the mood for the Beach Boys. With the radio off, I struggled to breathe as the summer sun cooked me inside the T-Bird. Navigating the fifteen-minute drive through town on automatic pilot, I glanced in the mirror to see Detective Rossi's white Toyota Camry behind me.

At least it wasn't a police cruiser with screaming sirens escorting me home to confiscate my skirt.

My *ruined* skirt. What kind of thug writes on a woman's skirt?

The kind who meant to get his point across. It was hard to miss thick black-marker words on your skirt and thighs. This thug wanted his money.

Taking my eyes off the two-lane Lakeshore Drive, named for the manmade lake spread out on my left, I glanced at the upside-down words on my lap. *Bring the money* . . . Clearly he thought I had money. His money. Probably not money he'd earned by an income-tax-paying job.

The stun gun told me that he would use whatever means necessary to get it.

I was in trouble.

Pulling into the dirt lot in front of Grandpa's house, I parked the car. I just wanted to change my skirt, give Rossi the marker-stained one and try to figure out what was going on. Nodding to Rossi when he got out of his Camry, I hurried up the porch steps. I could feel him right behind me. Did he think I was going to escape through the back door?

I was almost to the front door when I realized that I had more trouble. The door was slightly open, about a two-finger width.

Alarmed, I stopped dead on the wood porch.

Before I could say anything, Detective Rossi slammed into me from behind, knocking me through my opened front door. Sprawled on the twenty-year-old brown shag carpet, I fleetingly thought that if whoever broke into my house fired a gun, at least I was a flat target.

"Nice thong."

The last thing I wanted to do was show the local police my fanny. However, before I could think of a graceful way to get up, a pair of strong hands hauled me to my feet. I teetered on my heels and glared at a grinning detective. "My front door was open."

His grin faded. "You locked it this morning?"

"Grandpa locked it when he took the boys to school. He always locks the door."

His blue gaze was searching the living room while only half listening to me. "Where's your grandfather now?"

I checked my watch. "On his way home from Jack in the Box." It was a morning ritual. Grandpa dropped the boys off at school, then had coffee with some cronies at Jack's. Grandpa was a retired magician who had a new career in gossip.

"Stay here." Rossi pulled his gun out of his holster. He started moving through my house, just like on those cop shows.

I followed him past the brown-and-tan checked couch and love seat into the dining room that opened to a kitchen. His shoes squeaked on the yellow linoleum. So much for stealth, but I suspected that my less than digni- fied entry had clued in any robber. Grandpa's computer on the big oak rolltop desk was humming in time with the screen saver. Rossi moved between the desk and the glass table to the sliding glass door leading to the patio and grass backyard decorated with a big round trampoline. "Door's secure," he said and moved through the long kitchen, then went around the old white refrigerator into the hallway.

I kicked off my sling backs and hurried after him. He went into TJ and Joel's room first. This time I hit the center of his back with my chin.

"Christ, I told you to stay put!"

"It's my house." Well, Grandpa's house. I looked into my boys' room. It was larger than most bedrooms. A set of bunks stood against one wall, with a couple of desks. The walls were covered in Nintendo and skateboarding posters. "Everything looks okay," I said and stepped back. The thought of some intruder in the kids' room made my stomach churn.

Right across the hall from the boys' room was a large bathroom that sported wet towels and dirty socks, but no intruder.

The next room was Grandpa's. There was a neatly made double bed. His dresser had pictures of my grandma, who had died just before Trent. "Grandpa moved into this room after Grandma died," I explained.

The last room, the room Grandma and Grandpa had shared for decades, was mine. Detective Rossi blocked my view, but I saw his shoulders stiffen. "What?"

Slowly, he turned his body so I could see. My double bed was in its usual corner slot next to a small dresser. The rest of the room held my desk, electric typewriter, a metal filing cabinet and several bookshelves crammed with books.

The big bulletin board above my desk where I kept my calendar and deadlines was tossed onto the floor. In its place was a message scrawled in black marker: "Bring the money, or you'll see Trent in hell."

I stood frozen to the floor while Rossi checked out the bathroom that opened off the room. He came back out. "I'm going to call this in."

"The boys! What if he has them!"

Slipping his gun back into the shoulder holster, Rossi grabbed both my shoulders and fixed his blue stare on me. "Calm down. Tell me the name of their school and I'll check it out. Falling apart will only make things worse."

I glared at him. "Does that speech really work?"

He shrugged. "Sometimes. Now don't touch anything." Then he went to use the phone in the kitchen.

The stun-gun thug had been in my house, in my bedroom. A creepiness slithered over my skin. Hugging myself, I shivered.

"Okay, the boys are in school. I had the secretary physically check to make sure they were there."

"Thank you."

"You're a reader." He moved past me to study the books on my shelves. I hadn't moved from the spot in the hallway. "Romance?"

When he went to my desk and typewriter, I had calmed down enough to actually think. *Uh-oh.*

"What's this?"

He was looking at the sheet of paper in the typewriter. I pretended to think he meant the machine. "I'm not on real friendly terms with computers."

" 'Three stars? Sexual tension starts off with a bang, then fizzles?' "

My face heated.

When Rossi turned to meet my gaze, I refused to flinch. "I write reviews of romance novels."

"Ah."

The glint in his blue eyes darkened the color to a crackling fire. What was it about men and romance novels? They fell into three groups. The smallest group read and enjoyed them. Then there were the ones who were threatened by them. And the final group—sexual heat sprang from the mere thought of them. I sighed and turned to go into the kitchen.

I knew he was following me by the static electricity sizzling in the carpet from his tread behind me. The coffeemaker was on the short end of the L-shaped kitchen. Filling the carafe with water, I went through the motions. A knock came from the front door, but I knew it had to be the additional officers Rossi had called. I stood at the kitchen window over the sink while Rossi let the officers in and led them through the house.

Their voices drifted to me while I noticed that the patio needed to be hosed down and the redwood picnic table could use a good scrubbing. The trampoline far out in the yard looked bare without TJ, Joel and their various friends jumping on it.

What money?

Dammit, Trent, what did you do?

Tears threatened. He did whatever he damn well pleased, and I knew it. I had gone into the marriage loving Trent with all of my being. Grand feelings of how we'd both gone to a dating service searching for our soul mates—what a crock. I'd been searching for my soul mate—and Trent? I think he'd been searching for the witless woman who would keep his life running smoothly while he played. And I'd thought he'd seen past my plainness to my inner beauty. The years had killed my romantic dreams and left me just existing. But I was not that woman anymore. I got out cups, sugar and milk.

"They're gone." Rossi squeaked into the kitchen.

"Would you like some coffee?" I poured out two cups into the white with orange flowers Corelle mugs and transferred everything to the glass-topped table. Rossi sat down and pulled his little notebook out of his shirt pocket.

"In your statement about this morning, you said your attacker mentioned that you could get dead like your husband?"

"Yes." I was fighting a surreal feeling. Adding cream

and sugar to my coffee, I stirred mindlessly. It was like a terror-filled nightmare where something was chasing me, but I couldn't see it. I just knew that if it caught me, it'd be bad. Real bad. "And that if we didn't get him the money, the kids and I would be visiting Trent in hell."

"How did Trent die?"

"An accident."

"What kind of accident?"

I looked up at him. The romance novel-induced sexual heat was gone. His blue eyes were flat and cold. Business-like. "He was severely allergic to peanuts and ate some chocolate that had peanuts in it. By the time the para-medics got him to the hospital, he was dead."

"Where?"

"A hospital in Orange County."

He stopped writing and looked at me. "I mean, where did he get the chocolate and where was he when he ate it?"

"Oh." I sipped some of my coffee. Ugh! I hate cream and sugar in it. "I don't know really. It was homemade. It was analyzed, but all they found was traces of peanut, like someone had dipped peanut-butter balls and caramels in the same batch of chocolate. There was nothing wrong or suspicious about the chocolate."

He nodded. "No inquiry? The police didn't try and find out who made the candy?"

I leaned back. "I doubt it. It was an accident. Trent knew better than to eat something homemade like that."

"Where was he when this happened?"

"Visiting a vendor in Orange County. One of the chain drug stores that was one of his customers."

"Customer? What did Trent do?"

Do? He cheated on me, left me broke with two boys to raise by myself and apparently owed someone money. Wasn't that enough? "He was in distribution."

"Sales? And what, exactly, did he sell?"

I hesitated. Thing was, I'd never been ashamed of what Trent did. I'd believed his lines about public safety, and how he cared so much about people. He didn't judge their actions, he just performed a community service that kept people from paying too high a price for any lapses in judgment.

Suddenly, with Trent dead and all that had happened— God, had I always been so gullible?

"Sam?"

Rossi's voice prodded me from my thoughts. I faced him and lifted my chin. "Condoms. Trent was one of the top salesmen for the Gladiator Condom Company."

2

An hour later, Rossi had left, while my grandpa and mom had arrived. I had escaped to my room for a few minutes. Picking up the bulletin board that had been tossed on the floor, I leaned it up against my paperback-stuffed bookcase. Then I looked up at the black-marker words on the wall over the desk.

I didn't want to think about the thug having been in my bedroom. It was easier to think about paint. I was going to have to paint over that mess.

My mother's voice pierced through the walls from the kitchen. "I told you to sell this dump! I could get you good money for this place. Then you'd be able to live in a nice senior complex!"

I closed my eyes. My mom and grandpa were at it again. I could visualize Mom with her hands on her hips, trying to convince her father to see the world her way. I knew they loved each other, but Grandpa and Mom had two different views of happiness. Mom truly thought Grandpa would be happier selling the house he'd built and spent so many happy years in with Grandma. She believed new and shiny was better than old and lived in.

Grandpa's voice was gruff and scolding. "Your mother

would turn over in her grave to hear you talk like that, Katie girl."

"My mother would see the sense in it! You are just enabling Samantha. I enrolled her in a real estate class that starts this Saturday. It's time for her to grow up! She's failing at the dating service, and now she's gotten mixed up in some kind of trouble."

I leaped off of the bed. *She what?* I hate real estate! My headache pounded deeper into my brain. But Grandpa's next words made me smile.

"She is a grown up. And I like having her and the boys here with me."

God, I loved him.

"Dad!" Mom's frustration echoed right into my hammered brain.

The clatter of dishes hitting the Formica counter was a sign that Grandpa was getting worked up. He dropped his voice to anger. "Besides, it's her husband who left her the trouble."

Uh-oh. Grandpa would never forgive Trent for what he did to the boys and me. Leaving us broke and forced to sell our home. While my mother saw it a different way—she wanted to believe Trent would have fixed everything if he hadn't died. In my mother's world, having a man made everything right. I had to put a stop to this. Besides, I needed some Tylenol. I left my bedroom and headed down the hall toward the kitchen.

"Trent was a good husband and a good provider."

My mother was launching into her standard defense when I rounded the corner into the kitchen. She sat on the other end of the kitchen at the table. Her face was flushed, but her blond wedge cut remained perfectly in place. She caught sight of me and stopped.

Grandpa stood at the sink with his back to me. I nodded to my mom and went to the cupboard next to the sink.

"Trent Shaw darn near killed Sam's spirit. . . ." Grandpa stopped talking when he saw me next to him, stretching as high as I could on my bare toes to reach the Tylenol.

Whenever Trent's name came up in one of Mom and Grandpa's raging battles and I walked in, they both got silent.

As if the entire elementary school up the road hadn't heard them. Sheesh.

Uncapping the bottle, I dumped two pills into my hand.

Grandpa handed me a glass of water. In his seventies, his face was stamped with character. His blue eyes had faded, but the lines around them crinkled easily with laughter. His thinning gray hair was combed back over his round head. There was something both comforting and magnetic about him. He called it *stage presence.* As a magician, he had to know how to carry himself to make the audience trust him.

"Thanks, Grandpa." I took the glass and washed down the pills. "Uh, Grandpa, I'm thinking about putting in a security system." Actually, I'd already made some calls. But I thought I'd ease Grandpa into the notion.

"Good idea, Sam. We have to protect ourselves." Real anger burned in his gaze. His house had been invaded and his family threatened.

I laid my hand on his arm, but my mother cut off what I was going to say.

"A security system?"

Both Grandpa and I turned to look at her. She stood up from the table. Her brown eyes twinkled as the calculator in her brain clicked. Walking a few steps toward us, she waved her hand dramatically. "This area's the type. Oh, yes! Custom homes must have a security system."

Grandpa and I both looked around the kitchen. Custom? Grandpa had this house built thirty years ago in the middle of nowhere off a dirt road. They had lived in a trailer on the land before that. The dirt road has turned into Grand Street, and a new elementary school popped up less than a mile away in the middle of modern tract homes. Directly surrounding them was a smattering of custom homes and a very nice Lutheran church.

But this house was, as standards go, strictly one hobble up from a run-down trailer. My mother hailed from trailer trash and resented it.

Grandpa said, "Katie girl, all the years of my magic couldn't change this place into anything more than a custom cracker box."

My mother turned away in a huff of Opium perfume. "Really, Dad. It's the land that's valuable. This is a custom area. We could sell this acre you own and the new people would build themselves a beautiful home and use this as a guest cottage."

I choked on that. "Mom, this is Lake Elsinore!"

She sniffed. "Yes, dear, and how many times have I tried to get you to move to Temecula?"

Lake Elsinore was the poor relation to the wine country community of Temecula. A small town of about twenty-eight thousand in population, it had a man-made lake in the center that was shallow and regularly spawned fish kills and green algae slush that slithered up on the shores. It gave split-pea soup a bad name. Lake Sushi. But the town had its charms for me. Surrounded by hills, on a clear cold morning the beauty was breathtaking. Most of the people were good, the hearty kind of good that stuck, and the small-town politics were as amusing as any hockey game. Punches got thrown, folks were slandered, and lawsuits were filed. Few people in Lake Elsinore bothered with the big-city facade of civility. We sneered at them. We also had a cool minor league baseball stadium that gave the town hours of entertainment on its controversy alone. The name of the team was The Storm.

My kids loved it here. That was good enough for me.

I heard a knock on the front door. Quickly I looked at Grandpa. "Uh, about that security system. I called Gabe and he's putting one in." I escaped the kitchen and went to answer the door.

Gabe Pulizzi stood on the porch. All two hundred pounds of him tightly packaged over a spread of more than six feet. His black eyes rolled over me. "Babe."

I hated when he called me that. "Thanks for coming." I stood back and let him in. He was carrying boxes and wires that I presumed made up a security system. As a private detective, Gabe knew loads more about that stuff than I did. He had on a loose-fit Reebok shirt, shorts and flip-flops. Dumping the stuff on the floor, he slipped his mirrored sunglasses down a bumpy nose. "No problem." He ran his dark gaze down my length and back up. "Tattoos?"

"Huh?" I looked down at the white shorts I had traded for the skirt Rossi confiscated. "Oh." I flushed when I read "or die" upside-down on my thighs. "Permanent marker. Doesn't come off real easy."

He gave me a look that meant odd for anyone but me.

Gabe was younger than me by a few years and always made me antsy. He was from a world of danger that I would never understand. Trouble was, I tended to sort of be attracted to that kind of thing. "Listen, Gabe, I've got a little problem. I'm wondering if you could do some investigating for me?"

"It'll have to wait, Sam. I'm leaving tonight."

I hadn't realized how scared I was until I heard those words. I dropped my gaze to the scars on Gabe's right leg. He'd been a cop on the mean streets of Los Angeles until some bank robbers in full body armor decided not to surrender. They'd had no problem killing civilians to illustrate their point. Gabe had gotten between one of those civilians and a bullet, ending his police career. "When will you be back?"

"Hard to say. Got a call for a skip. Could be a while." He started messing with the wires and boxes, attaching them to the front window.

I had found Gabe in the yellow pages under *Security*. I wasn't sure exactly what all he was into, but for me, he did background checks on clients for Heart Mates since I didn't want to supply serial killers and rapists with victims. He also did some bounty hunting, but I think he only did that in cases he took an interest in. He wasn't real specific and I didn't ask. I tried to keep our relationship professional.

Of course, Gabe calling me *babe* wasn't exactly professional. We were developing an odd kind of friendship. He was teaching me to be street smart, and I was amusing the hell out of him.

At a loss what to do next, I told him the whole story while he wired the alarm system.

"You got a gun?"

"No." I didn't like his reaction. "But maybe this guy is just a nutcase?" I decided to revert to denial. I'd done denial for a good ten of my thirteen years of marriage. I was naturally proficient at it.

Standing, Gabe looked at me. He wasn't Detective Morgan Rossi handsome, he was more like bad-boy dangerous. Thin lips, nose that had been broken, eyes that had seen life, and all arranged so that women just had to tame him. "Come on, babe. This guy wants something and he thinks you have it. He may even have killed your husband to get it."

"Trent died of a peanut allergy."

"I made some calls before I came. The cops were investigating Heart Mates before your husband died. They had some information that the dating service was a front for drugs, but no evidence."

"Drugs?" I gasped. I knew about drugs, sure, but . . . "Is that why I got a notice of an audit from the IRS?"

"Could be."

"You think Trent was involved? In drugs? Trent wasn't into drugs." I knew that. Didn't I?

"Doesn't mean he didn't sell them."

I opened my mouth, then closed it. Going to the kitchen, I got out two bottles of beer, opened them, and headed back to the living room.

"Samantha! It's not even lunch time!" my mother said from the table.

I ignored her and handed a bottle to Gabe. "What do I do?"

"Get a gun." He drank a quarter of the bottle, set it on the floor and went back to fiddling with the wires.

"But I hate guns!"

He shrugged. "Then get a dog. A big dog. And maybe some defense spray . . ."

"Gabe?"

"Yeah?"

"How much time have you got before you leave to chase your skip?"

Three hours later I was back in the living room staring at Gabe's idea of a dog.

When I think of a dog, I sort of think of Lassie.

This was Lassie's nightmare. A German shepherd on steroids, it had feet bigger than I did. Gabe stood in my living room with the dog sitting by his leg. Every thirty seconds or so, its lip drew back on one side revealing a set of incisors that could chew glass. I started shaking my head. "I have children!"

"Ali here loves kids."

Love kids? For what, a Scooby snack? I blinked the paint fumes out of my eyes and sneaked another look at the beast. "Ali? It's a girl dog?"

"She's a sweetheart." He reached down and scratched the dog's pointed tan ears.

I have to admit she would scare away the bad guys. I was just worried that she might not be able to tell that we were the good guys. I had spent the last hour painting over the permanent marker in my bedroom while Gabe had been out searching for Godzilla's idea of a lap dog. The boys were due home any minute.

"Listen, Gabe, I appreciate this, really I do. And the advice—" I waved at the yellow tablet on the coffee table. I had written notes on everything Gabe told me about self-defense and investigation. "But the police . . ."

The sunglasses slid up. "Didn't tell you shit. They are using you, Sam. They have an agenda. You need to take care of yourself. Ali here will help you."

"Uh . . ." the words died in my throat when the front door burst open. TJ and Joel rushed in, then stopped. "Mom, Gabe's truck is—Cool!" They both dropped their backpacks and charged the dog.

"No!" I yelled, prepared to hurl my body between the beast and my babies. But before I had the chance, Ali let out a single bark, dropped to the ground and rolled over on her back. TJ and Joel rubbed her belly. "Is he yours?" TJ asked first, gazing up at Gabe with the standard hero worship.

"She. Her name is Ali. She's yours," he added.

"Gabe," I said, but I was wearing down.

"Let's take her out back!" Joel jumped to his feet and raced for the slider door.

"Hey, maybe she can jump on the trampoline!" TJ added.

Before I could step in, the boys and Ali were hauling through the kitchen and out the door.

"Sam, she's well trained and sweet natured. She won't hurt them, but she'll tear the throat out of anyone who does."

"Yeah?" My brain was clicking now. Gabe was an ex-cop and had access to all kinds of information. "She was trained as a police dog, wasn't she? Why didn't she make the cut?"

"You know, when you actually make yourself analyze a situation, you're very good at it."

I tried to ignore his praise and focus. "You didn't answer my question."

"It's no big deal. Ali's a little too friendly and she, uh, has some quirks."

I crossed my arms over my chest. "What kind of quirks?"

Grandpa came into the house and nodded to Gabe. "Nifty security system. Hope Sam doesn't break it."

"Barney." Gabe nodded in Grandpa's direction. "Brought you a dog to fill in if Sam does break it."

"We were just considering the idea, Grandpa," I said hastily.

Grandpa slow-stepped to the opened slider. "That the one? On the trampoline? 'Cause if it is, I don't think TJ and Joel are gonna give it up."

I sighed and went over to the window. Through the glass I could hear the boys laughing as they were throwing a ball up in the air. Ali was leaping up to catch it, then bouncing wildly.

"You got a dog?" Angel's voice rang out through the opened front door.

I turned around. "Guess so," I said doubtfully. "How come you're not at work?" I asked, surprised. Angel, my best friend from high school, was fearless and loyal. Well, unless you cheated on her like her ex-husband had. Angel held a grudge for a long, long time. I had to grin at her.

"Your mom told my mom at the beauty shop that you were attacked and threatened at Heart Mates. She said that you were getting out of the dating game business now to go to real estate school. And that, from now on, you'd be wearing longer skirts. My mom rushed over to Wal-Mart on her lunch break to tell me." Angel dropped her gaze to my legs.

Angel had long, slender legs that made me wish my attacker had blacked out my entire thighs. "Did you mention to anyone at work that you were leaving to rush over to talk me out of real estate school?" On the night Angel and I plotted out my revenge on panty-boy Trent, we had made a pact. We both had been in less than wonderful marriages or careers, and we were going to change that.

The career thing wasn't going real well for Angel, but she did have tons of dates. Being gorgeous and outgoing gave her an edge in that department.

Gliding into the room, Angel threw a halogen smile at Gabe and slinked past him in her halter sundress. She had on wedged sandals and perfectly polished toenails that matched her copper hair. "Never crossed my mind. You hate real estate."

I grimaced. "I'm not going to that school. I'll pay my mom back." Just as soon as I paid the lease this month on the building for Heart Mates. And the phone bill. I didn't even want to think about the IRS.

Dropping into a chair, Angel flung her white canvas bag on the table. "You got a mystery on your hands. Sounds more interesting than wearing a blue smock behind a cash register."

I got out a box of Triscuits, pizza sauce and some cheese to make the boys a snack. Would Ali want a snack? How much did she eat? "That's your second job this month."

Gabe wandered into the kitchen and poured himself some old coffee and drank it room temperature. I knew better than to ask. Grandpa sat down by Angel. His milky gaze gleamed. "We're gonna investigate."

I pulled a couple of sodas out of the refrigerator. Getting the Triscuit pizzas from the microwave, I set it all on the counter. No need to call the boys; their food radar would bring them in. "Grandpa, this could be dangerous. The police—"

Gabe reached past me and set his coffee cup in the sink. His dark Italian eyes settled on me, tempting my libido out of retirement. "The police have their own job to do. You gotta know what you're up against. Find out, Sam. You got two damn good reasons not to put your head in the sand."

The warning buzzed through me like a shock. Translation: *Lose the housewife wimp and get some balls.* That was something Trent's last little lingerie gift in the wheel well of the Mustang had given me—guts. Squaring my shoulders, I stared back. "Damn straight. No one's going to threaten me or my kids."

"We're gonna be private eyes!" Grandpa announced, getting up from the table to fire up his computer. "I haven't had this much fun since my last magic show."

"Cool!"

"Awesome!"

TJ and Joel stood in the doorway with a perky-eared Ali panting between them. TJ was going to be a handsome, slender man like his father, while Joel had the stockier, muscular build that I had. Somehow they'd both inherited their dad's blue eyes, though Joel had my pre-dyed brown hair.

"You're gonna be a private eye, Mom?" Joel came in first, heading for the food. "That's, like, way better than finding dates for losers." He picked up his plate and soda and plopped down by Angel.

"Gramps, whatcha doing?"

"Getting some PI stuff. Gabe told me what to buy. They will mail it to us with no questions asked just as long as we have a credit card."

TJ's eyes widened. He forgot his snack and hustled over to his grandpa's side. "Like night-vision goggles and listening devices? Hey, Gramps, Joel still has that Sonic Ear eavesdropping toy you bought him. Think we can use that?"

I groaned out loud. But I caught the warning shooting out of Angel's eyes—let them get involved with the fun stuff to keep them distracted from the fact that their dead father may have been involved with drug money.

New plan. I put the second batch of Triscuit pizzas on the table, got out some extra sodas and recovered my yellow tablet. "Where do we start?"

TJ turned from the computer to snag a couple of crackers and pop open his soda. "That's easy, Mom. You start with whoever threatened you enough to make Gabe go out and get you Ali. Is he the reason you have marker on your legs and paint in your hair?" He wrinkled his nose, inhaling the fresh paint smell permeating the house from my bedroom.

I stared at my oldest son. He was suddenly too old and much too sharp. I hadn't wanted my boys to know their father was panty-scum, but TJ pretty much had it all figured out. The good news was that Grandpa had been in the boys' life from birth and was a good male role model. A bit eccentric, but at least he was there.

Trent had mostly been gone. On business trips, or at classic car shows. Grandpa took the boys when he went to conventions with the professional organization of magicians called the Multi-national Magic Makers, or the Triple M. He performed at their schools and took an interest in their lives.

"You're right, TJ. Some lunatic wrote on me at work today. But I'm going to find out what's going on."

"Me and Joel want to help, Mom." TJ crossed his arms stubbornly over his chest.

I would die first before I let anyone hurt my sons, but I understood TJ. Too much of his life had been out of his control. We'd had to sell the house he was born in. He'd lost some friends—not many, but a few. "Fair enough. First, you let Gabe give you quick instructions on our new security system and on Ali." The dog responded to special commands, and taking care of her would give them responsibility. "Then when I come up with stuff you can help investigate, you're in. Deal?"

TJ's glance slid up to Gabe behind me, then back. "Deal. Come on, Joel." They went off with Gabe.

"They'll be all right, Sam," Angel said.

"Yeah." I rubbed my head, still fighting the low-grade throb left over from the volts zapped through my body. Retrieving my yellow pad, I sat back down and looked at the notes I had taken. "If the police were investigating Heart Mates before I bought it, that seems like the place to start. Perry Wilkes was the owner, although I never saw him. I dealt with his realtor. My papers on the sale are at work. But I can get his address off them and maybe drive by. See if I can get a glimpse. If it's him"—I lifted my gaze to Angel—"then I can tell the police and make this whole thing go away."

Grandpa looked back over his shoulder at me. "Do you want a hundred thousand, or a two hundred and fifty thousand volt stun gun? The two-fifty takes two batteries, but the one-hundred only needs one."

I groaned and rubbed my temples. "Don't mention stun guns to me."

He swiveled his head back to the screen and clicked the little mouse. "Well, then, how about defense spray? They got a new foam that sticks to the face of the guy you shoot it at. We can order you a key chain defense spray, or . . . hey! They got a decoy fountain pen! You gotta have that, Sam!"

I smiled at the back of Grandpa's nearly bald head and tried not to think what might happen if he got a hold of that fountain pen. "I'm not going to need all that stuff."

Angel leaned forward and said, "Sam, this could get dangerous. How about I give you my gun?"

"Cripes, what is it with everyone and guns! I am not carrying a gun."

Angel leaned back in her chair. "Why would the guy who sold you this business wait almost a year before coming after you for this money?"

Nothing was adding up. If Trent had some money, where would it be? And where would he have gotten it? I shook my head. "I don't know. But I have to start somewhere."

The phone rang. I jumped, knocking over my soda as a flash of thirteen-year-old hormones raced past me to answer it.

"Yeah, Mrs. Simpkins, she's here," TJ said.

I whirled around in my chair and waved my hands back and forth, mouthing the word "no." Alarm fizzled hotly through my body until I felt a case of hives begin on my arms.

"Mom!" TJ groaned and rolled his eyes.

I looked around the table. Grandpa ignored us, Angel gave me a sympathetic gaze and Gabe grinned bad-boy sexy and said, "What's up?"

"Linda Simpkins." I had to bend over and put my head

between my legs. "She's the PTA president and took over from me as team mom when the boys stopped playing soccer."

I couldn't even look at a soccer ball or banner without having a panic attack.

"Want me to tell her you're dead?" Gabe suggested.

I lifted my head out from between my marker-stained thighs and glared at him. "Don't laugh. You don't know." I shook my head. He'd never had to make twelve dozen cookies in one night, redo an entire team banner in four hours or call parents the night before a game and convince someone to bring snacks. All he'd ever done was patrol the streets of Los Angeles.

But right now, he was staring at me with those sexy Italian eyes, his thin lips twisted into a smirk. Standing up and praying I wouldn't pass out on the floor, I grabbed the phone. "Linda, how nice to hear from you."

"Fake smile." Joel elbowed TJ and snickered.

I turned my back on them. I did *not* have a fake smile. When I hung up, I was nearly drenched with sweat—the sweat of relief. Linda had heard that I'd been attacked and just wanted details for the next PTA meeting.

Hey, been there, done that. I figured by Wednesday night they'd all be assuring themselves that I had gotten what I deserved for having my boobs done.

"You're one strange female," Gabe said, amusement dancing with another kind of spark in his gaze.

Maybe, but Gabe wanted me in his bed. That always made me feel better. One day, I might just crawl in and see what he had to offer.

Dressed in a T-shirt and fading black marker for bed, I looked in on the boys. Ali was on the floor, her head resting between her huge paws. She opened one eye to glance over me, then went back to sleep.

I had to smile. We'd only had Ali for a few hours, and already she belonged to the family. TJ and Joel had lost too much without me taking away their chance at a cool dog.

Looking up to the top bunk, I resisted the urge to go in and cover my baby. Lying on his back, Joel had kicked off the covers with his preteen legs and arms at odd angles. He wore an old T-shirt of Trent's that he had confiscated when we packed up the house to sell it and move here. It tore at my heart. Joel slept with a piece of his dad that he had saved when so much of our lives was lost.

On the bottom bunk, TJ had the sheet neatly folded down to his waist. He favored his side so that he faced the door. In sleep, his maturing face relaxed into a reminder of the chubby-cheeked baby I'd brought home from the hospital. TJ wore his own gym shorts; his anger at his dad prevented him from seeking the comfort of his father's castoffs.

Both the boys missed having their own rooms, and they had drifted from a few of their friends. But they were adjusting. I was so proud of them both.

And worried.

What have you done, Trent? In the quiet of the night, as I stood gazing at my two sons, I had no doubt that he'd gotten the kids and me in serious trouble.

But what really pissed me off was that I should have paid more attention. I had been too busy playing the role of perfect wife. Too busy believing my life was a romance novel come true. Trent and I dated for only a few months before we got married, at a big wedding that I thought was about celebrating our love.

Crap. What a load of crap.

That wedding had been to show Trent's bosses at Gladiator Condoms what a stable kind of guy he was. And to show the rest of Lake Elsinore what a successful guy he was. That was the beginning of things to come. Every time

Trent did something lavish, I rewrote it in my head to fit into my idea of romance. If I couldn't rewrite it into something noble and romantic, like Trent going away more and more often on business trips, spending lavishly to buy himself clothes, cars and other high-ticket items like his stupid cigars, then I ignored it.

Leaving the boys' door cracked open, I went to the kitchen and got a bottle of beer. I took it with me to finish the critique that was due tomorrow on a historical romance novel set in Ireland.

I started writing critiques when the boys were babies. It was my secret life. Maybe it was a way to escape when I didn't want to face how empty my marriage had become. If Trent wasn't home, I could put the boys to bed, then work on my critiques. I had a purpose. Lord knows I didn't do it for monetary compensation. The money almost paid for the paper and typewriter ribbon. Even after my own version of a romance-novel life shattered, I still kept at it. I'd been burned, and signed off men as lovers. I was building a career woman's life to take care of the boys and myself.

But what kept drawing me to these novels were the heroines. No matter what happened to them, they kept fighting. They had problems and flaws and bad hair days, but they never gave up. They went out and did the very things that scared them the most.

That's who I wanted to be.

Typing in the reasons why this particular novel lacked sexual tension, I froze. Was that a footstep? One of the boys going to the bathroom? I cocked my head, listening.

I had my back to the door of my bedroom. The fine hairs on my neck stood up. I heard the creak of my door opening wider. Grandpa?

Terror raced through me. I couldn't hear over the pounding of my heart. I tried to tell myself just to turn around and look when something furry touched my arm. My "Aaahhh!" came out as a squeak.

Whipping around in my chair, I didn't see anyone until I dropped my eyes in time to catch Ali hauling ass out of my room with my bottle of beer clamped in her teeth.

Hysterical laughter bubbled in my throat. I doubled over, desperate to breathe and not throw up.

Some guard dog Gabe got me. She'd stolen my beer.

3

Driving Blaine's primer-paint Hyundai was less conspicuous than my T-Bird. I left my assistant a happy man,
planning a slew of errands in my Bird. No problem; it
wasn't like we had clients knocking down the doors.

I was thinking we should advertise. I even had a slogan
in mind—*Get Hot With Heart Mates.*

Swinging a left off Lakeshore onto Clement Street, I
dismissed the Circle K and video store on the right for the
gated apartments on the left. Fortunately, those apartments were not the right address. I was wearing sheer midnight panty hose today beneath my black leather skirt to
try to camouflage the fading permanent marker on my
thighs. My sleeveless white sweater, I hoped, kept anyone
from noticing my legs, but I was pretty sure climbing a six-
foot wrought-iron gate would draw unwanted attention.

I made a slow turn left onto the next street. There were
the apartments—or were they townhouses? It was a cluster
of green-trimmed beige buildings, four or five units,
mostly with two-story apartments. A parking lot was in the
middle. On both sides were patches of grass that led to a
two-foot wall to keep kids from the street.

It was pretty quiet at nine in the morning. A lone

woman was sweeping her front stoop in a pair of purple stretch shorts and a Cowboys T-shirt. The Hyundai was at home in the parking lot. It bucked and burped happily as it idled.

This was almost too easy. The apartment I wanted was the corner unit, a one-story deal on the right side of the lot. But . . . now what? Knock on the door and if it's the guy who attacked me with a stun gun and permanent marker, then ask him not to do that anymore?

Okay, I really should have thought this out. Surveillance. That's what Gabe would do. But I would look a little obvious sitting in this small parking lot staring at the corner unit. Maybe I could just drive by a hundred or so times and see if he came out?

Maybe it's not the man who attacked me in the apartment. Or maybe it is.

Drumming my fingernails on the steering wheel, I thought about it. Ring the doorbell and run? Nah.

My mind was slipping back to thinking about advertising for Heart Mates when I saw something.

Did the door to the apartment just move? Leaning closer, I stared out the front windshield. There was a vertical wedge of light coming out of the apartment. The door was opened a crack.

An omen. Before I could rethink it, I got out of the car and closed the door softly. Maybe I could just take a peek inside. I tiptoed so my black high heels would not announce me on the sidewalk. The door was set back into a tiny patio area.

I could hear my heart thumping. *Ba-run, Ba-run.* I ignored it. Besides, what could happen? At the door, I stopped breathing and tried to listen. Leaning a little closer, I almost fell in when the door swung wide open.

"Oh!"

I was staring at Detective Rossi. Behind him, on the floor, was a man.

The same man who attacked me. I could see part of his face and hair, and the black sling. The rest of him was hidden around the corner.

I wasn't breathing. Ohmigod! "Is he . . ." I leaned back against the beige stucco wall next to the doorbell. I felt like water was rushing past my ears, trying to sweep me away. The building was the only thing holding me up.

"Samantha Shaw." Detective Rossi stepped out of the apartment. "Now why would I find you at the scene of a murder?"

"He's dead?" Things were not quite sinking in. "You sure?" I looked up into Rossi's pale blue eyes.

His jaw tightened. "I'm sure."

I looked around. No cop cars or anything. "What are you doing here?"

"You tell me what you're doing here," Rossi demanded.

"I came to see if—that is, I thought that if the man who lived at this address was the same man who attacked me, then the police . . ." Dead? Murdered?

"Where'd you get the address?"

"Off the escrow papers from the sale of Heart Mates."

Rossi shook his head. "You took a stupid risk. What did you think you were going to do? Or were you supposed to meet him here?"

Staring at him, my mouth opened, but nothing came out. Good thing, too, cause my stomach was rolling over and I didn't think Rossi wanted used yogurt on his shoes.

"I've got to call this in." He walked away and went to the car parked right next to the Hyundai in the parking lot. It was a square, American-made deal with big antennas. I dropped my head into my hands. Some sleuth I was. I'd parked right next to an unmarked police car and hadn't even known it. TJ and Joel would be so disappointed in me.

I looked back at the partially closed apartment door. That was the man who attacked me, right? If he was dead . . . My stomach heaved. Dead. Murdered. But if he was dead, then this whole mess was over.

The door beckoned as Rossi's voice and radio crackled from the parking lot.

I had to know. Sucking in a breath of courage, I pushed the door open. There was a small entry hall. The man lay just beyond that, sprawled on his stomach with his head turned to the living room. His sling-encased arm was flung out toward me. I moved into the entry hall and edged closer to the body.

There was a small hole in the back of his Hawaiian shirt. Same shirt. But the dark stains were new. *Blood.* Squeezing my eyes shut, I willed myself to calm down. One look at his face. Just to be sure.

Opening my eyes, I leaned over him just far enough to see the entire half of his face.

The same man. I whirled around to run out of the apartment.

"Oooooff." I slammed into Rossi. Both of us did a dance for balance, until Rossi ended up supporting both of us. He put his hands on my shoulders and jerked me back. "What the fuck are you doing? This is a crime scene!" His blue eyes were hard on my face.

"I had to know if it was him."

"Crime scene." He said the words carefully, his fingers squeezing into my shoulders. "Did you touch anything? I swear to God, if you fucked up my crime scene, I'll have you arrested."

Was he nuts? "He's dead," I felt obligated to point out. "It's not like he can be murdered twice."

Rossi released one of my shoulders to rub his eyes. "A victim can only be murdered once, but a crime scene can be murdered a thousand times."

"Uh-huh." I was wondering if Detective Rossi had, maybe, been to one too many crime scenes. I was having trouble dealing with one dead body. Maybe he'd gone over his quota, bending his mind into a pretzel. "I just wanted to know if it was the same man that attacked me."

He scissored his jaw before getting control enough to ask in a lockjawed fashion, "Was it?" He let go of my other shoulder with an obvious effort.

Glad to be off the subject of his crime scene obsession, I answered, "Yes." Having a murdered man sprawled a few feet away was ruining my relief at having the threat to my kids and me gone.

Rossi turned and walked the few steps out of the apartment.

Since I didn't want to be accused of murdering a crime scene again, I followed him. "What were you doing here? Did someone call in reporting his death?"

He turned in a graceful, yet tired, gesture. "No. Perry Wilkes was under suspicion last year for drugs. After yesterday, I decided to see what he's been up to. I didn't expect to find him dead."

"And?" I had wondered that too. I mean, if it was him, then why wait a year before demanding the money from me?

"He's been in jail on a shoplifting charge. Just got out this week. He lives here with his brother. Or did."

A chill went down my back. The pasty-white complexion that I had thought made him an accountant! Jail explained that. "Where's his brother?"

"Not home. But I think he left a bullet behind in his brother's back."

Brothers usually don't kill their brothers without a reason. Was the money everyone seemed to think I had that reason? "This isn't good, is it?"

Rossi stared at me. "Murder is never good."

"No, I mean"—I leaned back against the stucco wall— "do you think his brother killed him for the money? The money they think I have?" I heard police sirens. Seconds later, two cars skidded into the parking lot with their lights flashing.

Rossi ignored them to focus on me. "Drugs, money, women, I've seen it done for all those reasons. So yeah, money could be motive enough for one brother to shoot another."

I read between the lines. Someone wanted that money real bad.

"Sam." Rossi's voice gentled slightly. "You want me to have one of the officers give you a ride home?"

I blinked, trying to follow his shift in topics. "No, uh . . ." The police officers came up carrying yellow crime scene tape. Looking back at Rossi, I said, "I'm going to work." I walked away toward Blaine's Hyundai. I'd go to work and then try to think what to do next. This puzzle had moving pieces. And dead pieces. How could I figure out who the bad guy was, if they kept dying and being replaced?

Driving back to the office, the picture of Wilkes on the floor with a bullet hole in the back of his Hawaiian shirt kept flashing in my head. It didn't get more serious than that.

Gabe was right. I had to get proactive about this. If Rossi's theory was correct, and Wilkes was killed by his brother for the money, then the money was the key. Drug money? How did it all fit? Heart Mates and drugs? Trent and drugs?

The logical place to start was looking through Heart Mates' old records.

* * *

I hurried through the door to my office. Blaine was back from his errands, eating a hamburger and reading a car magazine. He looked up at my entrance. "I heard about you finding Wilkes. What do you think it means?"

"I didn't actually find him. How'd you hear?" A stall tactic—I didn't know what it meant. That question scared me. If there was money, if Trent had some money, where would it be? My head spun. I had to face the fact that Trent, according to dead Perry, might have been involved in drugs. But if he'd had money, it sure wasn't in any of our accounts after he died.

Where do people hide drug money?

Blaine waved a hand at the telephone. "Your mom called."

"How'd she find out?" I nearly wailed. I'd already had my quota for disaster. It was a sure bet my mother would be here as soon as she could.

Blaine gazed at me. "Come on, boss, your mom knows everyone in this town. Apparently, her Avon lady lives in that apartment complex you found Wilkes at. She recognized you, and the cop who knocked on her door to ask if she'd seen anything confirmed who you were." He shrugged. "News travels."

"Great. Brought down by an Avon lady." Sighing, I brushed my frizzy hair back and tried to focus. "Did you get the old employee records out of the computer?" I'd asked him to do that when I had him help me find the escrow papers for Heart Mates.

He wiped his hands on his jeans and handed me a thin stack of papers that were sitting in his printer tray. "Here they are."

"Thanks." I started to walk to my office, then stopped. "Do you think we should do some advertising for Heart Mates?"

Blaine winked at me. "Keep finding dead bodies, and you won't need to do any advertising."

What did that mean? Since I had the feeling that I didn't want to know, I turned around and went into my office. Sitting down, I spread out the printer sheets and started reading.

Luke Wilkes was Perry's brother. He was listed as the emergency contact. The address was the same one I'd been to this morning. So that was a wash.

But there were four dating consultants—Maria, Debbie, Joan and Hazel—who had worked for Perry. None of their names stirred any memories from when I had used the dating service to meet Trent. There were phone numbers and addresses for all of them except Hazel. I put her on the bottom of the stack and decided to visit the ladies before TJ and Joel got home from school.

I drove the T-Bird to the address for Maria, the first on my list of the former dating consultants. It was in a run-down set of row houses across from the lake. There were lots of white undershirts, tattoos and shaved heads hanging out in the middle of the day.

Not a good sign.

The apartment I wanted had a freshly painted door in the middle of a five-unit building. The door looked out of place since the other four had a fading paint design.

Maybe I should go home and get Ali?

Maybe I should go home and get some courage? I wondered if Grandpa could buy that off the Internet. Or did I have to travel all the way to Oz?

It was hot in the car since I had left the hard top with the sexy little portholes at home in the garage. The sun was staring at me with the full brunt of summer. I got out, trying to tug my skirt down over my thighs. I could feel

eyes staring at me. The men hanging out all clustered together, gawking.

I ignored them. If I could handle a bunch of hormone-
driven seventh graders at a school dance, I could handle
this bunch. Let 'em look. I walked up to the door and
knocked.

No answer. I have to admit I was kind of relieved. The
atmosphere was hot and still, making me uneasy. Decaying
carp from the latest fish kill in the lake thickened the air
with a sulfur smell that made me think of dead people. I
turned around to leave.

The hoods were in my car! Two were in the seats, and
the rest were having eye-sex with my car, touching the fins
on the back, caressing the curve over the headlights . . .

They hadn't been lusting after me. They'd been after
my car. Like Trent. He had loved his classic cars more
than his family. Fresh anger surfaced just looking for a way
to make me stupid. "Hey!" I shouted, fast-walking toward
them as swiftly as my heels would let me. "Get out of
there!" I was breathing hard by the time I stopped ten feet
from the T-Bird.

Six pairs of eyes set in sullen, challenging expressions
turned on me. I glared right back. Almost tripping over a
murdered body this morning had put me in a kick-ass
mood. I was not afraid; I refused to be afraid. I had lived
my life afraid.

But I sort of wished I had a stun gun and Ali to back me
up here. Maybe a real big canister of that pepper spray, too.

And Gabe. Gabe knew how to take care of himself. I
knew how to make peanut butter and jelly sandwiches or
bake six dozen cupcakes on demand.

"Those the keys?" a man with chain links tattooed
around his impressive biceps asked, pointing to the keys
in my hand.

Gabe, where the hell are you now? "I need to leave. Can you please step away from my car?" Yeah, I mentally groaned, that oughta scare them away.

"We're gonna take it for a ride." Chain link was joined by two of his friends. They swaggered toward me.

Terror clawed up the back of my throat. My brain screamed, *Give them the keys! It's only a dumb car!* But some deep part of me, the part that had been entombed in a generic mini-van with thousands of other soccer moms while Trent was out playing capture-the-panties wouldn't let me.

It was my car! Mine. I had changed my life, quit the PTA and the perpetual team mom club to be a real person, a businesswoman, and these street thugs thought they were going to take it away from me. "No." I shook my head back and forth, my hair swinging wildly.

Then I heard the click.

I stopped swiveling my head and stared at the enormous knife. "Is that a switchblade?" I'd never really seen one before.

"Toss the keys, Blondie."

Okay, I had two choices here. I could be sliced up into long strips of human jerky, or I could give him my car keys. There were six men against one woman. My odds were something like negative eight million in my favor. I was mulling this over and trying not to pass out when squealing caught my attention.

Oh, God, a black Jeep. I knew, but did not believe— Grandpa! The odds just got scary. The passenger door sprang open and eighty pounds of snarling, snapping, growling German shepherd flew out.

The switchblade clattered to the sidewalk as the tough guys scattered, hitting the doors of the row houses to get inside.

Ali barked once, then came back to me and nosed the

switchblade lying at my feet. I was trembling and felt like my teeth were going to crack. I sank to my knees next to the dog and hugged her to me.

Ali looked up at me with her liquid brown eyes.

"One beer," I told the dog, my head buzzing with adrenaline. "One beer a night, that's the deal." Hell, I'd buy her a keg a night if I had the money. I *loved* this dog.

Grandpa leaned over and picked up the switchblade. He folded it up.

"How did you know?" I looked up at the man who had been a father to me since my bio-dad went missing with the news of his impending fatherhood.

"I called the office to tell you about a message that came to the house. Blaine told me where you were. Thought maybe Ali could add a little incentive to your interviews."

I focused on that one word. "Message? Grandpa, what happened? Are the boys okay?"

He reached into his pants pocket, a difficult task since his pants tended to slide down his thin body, and pulled out an embossed gold card. It was the same size as the folded cards that come with professionally wrapped gifts.

Ali went to sniff around the grass. I took the card and opened it. "Bring the money to Mulligan's by Friday night, or you'll be as dead as Trent and Perry" was printed in gold stick-on letters against a white background.

My body was getting a full workout from the adrenaline rushes. Lurching to my feet, I asked, "How did it come to the house?"

"It was attached to a black helium balloon and delivered from Frank's Flowers."

Who did I look for? I still didn't know what money. Who was doing this was getting more confusing by the dead body. Perry Wilkes had been the first one to threaten me, but he wasn't threatening me from the morgue. His brother Luke? But men who murder their brothers don't usually play with gold stick-on letters. I still needed to talk to the girls who had worked for Perry—they could tell me how Trent had been involved in whatever was happening at the dating service.

Things were getting worse faster than I could find any answers.

I went to Frank's Flowers across from the north end of the lakeside campground on Riverside Drive. It was a small shop with the same cloying, funeral smell of most flower shops. Frank was busy doing a birthday arrangement. I knew him because his kids had played soccer with mine. His wife and I had sat in our lawn chairs and chatted at many practices.

"Yeah, Molly had a delivery for you this morning, Sam," Frank said as he mixed balloons and flowers into a ceramic bowl that the lucky recipient could use over and over. Wiping his hands on the blue apron, he went to the receipts in the drawer below the cash register. "Here, it was ordered by a woman named Jane Smith at about eight-fifteen this morning." He looked up, over the edge of his bifocals. "I don't really remember her. She wore shorts and had nice-looking legs, but that's all I remember."

Jane Smith and she had nice legs. That'll help. I sighed. "Thanks, Frank."

"Is it true that you're a private investigator now?"

That stunned me. "What? No, where would you get an idea like that?"

He shrugged. "My kids mentioned it. I guess TJ and Joel might have said something to them. And I heard you found a body this morning, so I guessed it was true."

I had to smile. TJ and Joel were as determined as my mother was to change my career. "I'm just doing a little investigating on a few problems ... uh ... with my business."

Frank shook his head and went back to his arrangement. "I always thought it was strange that you would buy that place."

That stopped me cold. "Why is that?" But I knew.

Frank's eyes got huge behind his bifocals. "I only meant that dating services don't really seem your type of thing ... I mean, well, you're different now, but ..." A flush stained his neck and spread to his face.

"Frank"—I leaned on the counter—"please tell me. I have to know what Trent was up to those last months. It's part of my problem." A big part.

"Sam"—Frank didn't meet my eyes—"everyone knew Trent prowled around. We just thought you didn't care. You were the real domestic type, and Trent was a player."

"And he played at the dating service?" My tongue wanted to stick to the roof of my mouth. What a fool.

Shrugging, he just said, "Folks saw his car there a lot."

My automatic response floated up. "He had an account with them. It was part of their safe dating program to hand out samples of condoms." I heard myself and shut my mouth. How many years had I said the lines? "Thanks, Frank. You've been a big help."

He smiled in relief as I left to go join Ali waiting for me in the T-Bird. She liked the top down. We headed to the supermarket for beer and dog food before going home.

Half an hour later, I was standing in the grocery store parking lot and wondering where to put twenty-five pounds of dog food in a two-seater T-Bird. I managed to wedge it in next to Ali, begging her not to tear the bag open. I stored the beer in the trunk by the spare tire. No amount of begging on my part would keep Ali from that. Then Ali and I headed home, where I expected to find

Grandpa with the boys. Going through the usual home-work and dinner thing seemed refreshingly normal.

Ali whined and nudged the dog food as I paused at a stop sign by the elementary school on Machado Street. "Don't you dare," I told her, glancing in my rearview mirror.

My paranoia was in overdrive, but wasn't that the same car that had followed me out of the grocery store parking lot? A blue Datsun type? The driver wore dark sunglasses and some kind of baseball cap. Driving through the empty school intersection, I hung a right on Lincoln. The farther up the street I went, the more expensive the houses got. But I had only gone as far as the horse property-homes on the right side when I saw that the blue Datsun was still with me.

I turned into a small tract of homes with huge back-yards.

The Datsun turned too.

Hell. My sweaty hands slipped on the steering wheel. I swung the car around, got out of the tract and raced up to the next tract, taking a hard right on Terra Cotta. This old car was not meant for stunt driving. I had to make two more turns that landed me back on Terra Cotta Street, but now only one side of the street had homes. The other side was a weed-choked field dotted with walnut trees and who knew what else. Farther ahead the street would con-nect with a tract of homes that was fifteen or twenty years old.

I had to turn around. No way was I getting caught where I could be forced off into the field. I slowed down to do a U-turn.

The blue Datsun hurled around me and squealed to an impressive stop that blocked me up against a curb.

Shit. *Shit.* I wanted to bang my head against the steering wheel. Gripping the wheel tightly, I watched the man get out of the Datsun. An unbuttoned, short-sleeved, dingy white shirt fluttered around his bare chest. I guessed him to be about five foot nine or ten inches and to weigh a good forty pounds more than me.

I didn't know how much the gun in his hand weighed.

Ripping my gaze from the gun, I tried to gauge his expression. Maybe I could reason with him? Beneath the heavy black-framed sunglasses, the clench of his jaw had whitened his lips into thin fury. The thought struck me— he looked like a man who had nothing to lose.

I didn't know what to do. He'd almost reached us. With no top on the car, we were completely vulnerable. Ali began growling low in her throat. "No, Ali, he'll shoot us both." I didn't want to explain to Gabe how I got the dog he brought me shot.

"Get out."

I looked at the gun pointing at me. When the car door was wrenched open, I scooted out. "Is it money? I only have ten dollars, but you can have it." *Please, let him want money.*

His white lips twisted in a derisive sneer. "Ten dollars? No way, toots. I want the whole half a million."

"Half a million? Dollars?" My mouth fell open as the thought of that much money tried to make itself known to my brain.

"You're going to take me to the money. Let's go." He waved the gun toward his car. Using his other hand, he grabbed my arm and started dragging me past the hood of my car.

"I don't have the money!" Half a million dollars? "I don't know what you're talking about!" Something finally managed to penetrate my fear. "You're Perry's brother." Who else would be chasing me? "You can't kidnap me, the police are looking for you." We were almost to the driver's door of his car.

A low growl interrupted my protests. The man shoved me into the opened door of his car. I hit the jagged door frame hard, tearing my skirt straight through to my hipbone. The impact knocked me back onto the pavement at the same time that I heard a ferocious roar.

Rolling over, I struggled to get up. "Ali!" I tried to run, but my legs buckled and dropped me to my knees, ripping out both legs of my nylons. Jumping back up, I sped to where Ali had the man pinned on his back. He was frantically waving his gun in his right hand.

I couldn't let him shoot Ali, so I raced up and kicked his gun hand hard. The impact went straight to my hipbone, but the gun flew out of his hand.

"Get it off me!" he bellowed, thrashing beneath Ali.

Breathing hard and fighting dizziness, I looked around the street. Did I dare leave Ali to run to a house and call the police? "Watch him, Ali, he killed his own brother," I warned the dog. She was quickly becoming more than a dog to me.

"I didn't kill him! I thought you did!"

"What?" Now he had my full attention.

He was real talkative for a man who had a set of teeth backed up by eighty pounds of angry canine muscle at his throat. "I didn't even know Perry was dead until I saw all the cops at the apartment. One of the neighbors told me the police thought I did it and I took off. I figured you did it to keep the money Trent stole from us."

"Stole? What money did Trent steal?" I was starting to feel more in control. Until I saw the second gun slide out of Luke's belt. "Ali!" I screamed. "Come!"

He fired the gun and Ali yelped.

Oh, God! She was already running to me. Was she hit? I was moving on some kind of terror-induced automatic. "She's okay," I told myself over and over. I jumped into the driver's seat of my idling car as Luke rolled up off the ground. Ali leaped over the passenger door, landed on the dog food and whimpered. I whipped the car into reverse.

Luke caught up to me, sticking his smaller gun right in my face before I could get the car moving. I pictured my brains splattered all over the upholstery. But then they'd never find the money, my fright-fried brain reasoned. I spat out the information. "You can't shoot me if you want the money!"

Ali made threatening sounds in her throat and shifted on the torn bag of dog food, but she didn't attack.

Luke had lost his sunglasses. He looked a bit older than his dead brother. His brown eyes were alive and furious. "I can kill your kids. One at a time and maybe that old man you live with. Then we'll see how stubborn you are."

I stared at him. He knew about my kids. All the white noise of terror was instantly lost in a roar of fury. The faces of my boys, first as babies, then as they had slept in their beds last night, rolled through my head. And I knew, without a second's hesitation, that I would do anything to protect TJ and Joel. The love I felt for them was more powerful than my desire to live. I leaned my head back and stared up at him. "You touch my kids, I'll kill you." The words came out from someplace inside of me that I hadn't known about. Some place dark and deadly. I meant each and every word. There was no place he could hide from me if he hurt TJ or Joel.

His tight, nothing-to-lose expression didn't change. "You bring the money Friday night to the arcade. Or I'll kill them." He turned and limped back to his Datsun.

Panting like I was in labor, I turned to look at Ali. Her side was bleeding, a small, thin trickle of blood dripping over the pellets of dog food that had exploded out of the bag when she landed on top of it.

Not only had he threatened my kids, he'd shot my dog.

4

I finally stopped shaking at the veterinarian's office. That was an improvement, but I don't think the receptionist was impressed. "Phone." I pointed through the little window to the multi-lined unit sitting on the desk next to a computer.

"Excuse me?" She was a perky twenty-something with her hair pulled back except for the two long strands hanging in her face. I swallowed and tried again. "Phone. Police." I couldn't get my thoughts to slow down enough to make sense. I had to make sure my kids and Grandpa were safe. The police had to go there right now and . . . do something.

"Uh, is it local?"

"It's 911!" My frustration was at peak level.

"That's local?"

I turned and looked out the big picture window. In and out. If I breathed, maybe then I wouldn't, in a furious and oxygen-deprived state, euthanize the twit receptionist.

But I didn't need to call the police. They were already here. Or at least Detective Rossi was. I saw him walking into a sandwich shop across the strip mall from the vet's

office. I whirled around to the twit. I had to call home.
"Give me the phone."

She picked up the machine and set it on the window
ledge. "As long as it's local."

Ignoring her, I stabbed the phone number. "Joel?"
Relief made my knees weak. "Honey, is everything okay at
home?"

"Yeah, Mom. Where are you?"

"Ali scratched her side and I'm having a vet look at it." I
glanced out the window again. "Then I'm going to get
some sandwiches for dinner." Right after I yelled at a certain detective. "Let me talk to Grandpa."

"Sam?"

"Grandpa." Just hearing his voice calmed me down.
"Listen, make sure the security system is on and don't let
anyone in."

"Why?"

Thankful that he was staying calm and not scaring the
boys, I told him about being chased and almost kidnapped by Perry Wilkes's brother, Luke.

"Everything's fine here. Trent and Joel finished their
homework and I was teaching them a few card tricks."

I groaned. "Are you teaching them to cheat at poker?"

"Gotta go, Sam, it's my turn. I want pastrami." The
phone disconnected.

Setting the handset back into the cradle, I almost
smiled. Grandpa had taught me to cheat when I was eight.
Looking at the twit, I said, "I'll be right back," and headed
out the door.

Two people driving by stopped their cars and stared as I
strode across the lot. The rip in the leather skirt at my hipbone was flapping as I walked. My black hose were shredded, and drying blood was forming into scabs at my knees.
And I was pissed as hell. Detective Rossi was holding out

on me. Right now, I didn't care if he had a gun. I yanked open the door of the sandwich shop.

He was sitting on one of those curved orange plastic benches at a small rectangular beige table against a yellow half-wall. The colors fed my rage.

"Rossi!" I yelled, storming to his table and leaving the two teenaged girls huddled over a bag of chips and cokes opened-mouthed.

Looking up from a leaking sandwich, Rossi's blue eyes narrowed. "What the hell happened to you?"

I stopped at the bench across from him. My purse slid off my shoulder and hit the table, forcing Rossi to grab his cup of soda before it landed in his lap. I was disappointed. "You happened to me!" This was his fault. He was good-looking, dammit. "The whole town thinks I found a dead body, the dead man's brother came after me, tried to kid-nap me, shot my dog and accused me of murdering his brother. He demanded money I don't have, but he might as well take a number because he's the second one today. You hung me out to dry, Rossi, and I swear to God if one of these slime-balls hurts my kids, I will shoot you with your own gun."

I slung my purse back over my shoulder and spotted his drink. I reached for it, but Rossi's hand clamped around my wrist.

When I looked up into his blistering blue eyes, our gazes locked and should have set the fizzing soda into a roiling boil. "Let go."

He tugged me closer. "Why is it that I can't find Luke Wilkes anywhere and you just stumble onto him in a fit of greenhorn luck? How the hell do you stir up all this mur-der and treasure hunting, Ms. Shaw?"

"You think I have the money." He wasn't going to help me protect my kids. The loneliness slammed into me. I had to do this by myself. There weren't going to be any romance novel-like white knights in my life. I had to protect my kids, and myself. The sheer magnitude of that left me speechless. Weren't the police supposed to zoom in and protect the innocent?

And why would Rossi even think I had the money? What else did he know that he was holding out on me? I narrowed my eyes, trying to see Rossi, to understand him.

His gaze did that body-search thing again. "You don't add up. You used to be Holly Housewife and Patty PTA, and then you bought a business without so much as having a CPA look at the books. I don't think you're that dumb."

He'd investigated me! I tried to yank my wrist from his grasp, but he merely tightened his fingers just enough to make his point. "Police brutality," I hissed.

"Would you rather I cuff you?"

Shit. "I have to get my dog."

"Your dog that was shot?"

So he had been paying attention. I felt a frisson go down my spine. Fear? Sexual heat? Frustration? His touch sent crackles through me that quivered every already overworked nerve in my body. Had a day of dead bodies, car chases and guns roused my libido? I nodded in mute answer to his question.

"You're in over your head, Sam. Can't you see that? They're never going to let you walk away with their money."

He'd been holding out on me, just as Gabe had said. He suspected me. I felt hysterical laughter bubbling in my chest. I had bought Heart Mates because it was my dream. It had been a decent place when I met Trent there, and I had been blinded by my nostalgia and my head-in-the-sand approach to life.

But it was still my dream. I wanted to make Heart Mates into a place where grown men and women could meet together and find what they were looking for. If they wanted romance, Heart Mates would provide romantic dating packages. If they wanted companionship, then Heart Mates would be the place to find it. Heart Mates was about finding your heart's desire. I no longer believed in happily ever after, but I believed in other people's right to search for whatever they wanted. And Heart Mates would help them find it. I had plans, ideas. Maybe just not the business skills to do it.

Not yet, anyway.

It hurt like hell to bend over, but I put my face right into Rossi's. "What if you're wrong, Rossi? What if I don't know a thing about this money and my kids end up hurt. Can you live with that?"

He let go of my wrist. I left.

Dinner was pastrami sandwiches all around, except for Ali, who got roast beef. We sat out on the back patio. I had exchanged my torn nylons and skirt for a pair of running shorts and a tank top.

"If the dead guy was the one who threatened you yesterday, then who chased you in the car today?" Joel asked from his spot next to me on the redwood bench.

I smiled at him. At eleven he thought any adventure was cool. "His brother, I guess."

TJ looked up from his sandwich with his too-serious expression. "It's all for this money?"

"I think so, TJ."

"Like a treasure hunt?" Joel piped up, then dug into the bag for more potato chips.

"Dad did this to us, didn't he, Mom?" TJ set his sandwich down and leveled his intense blue eyes on me.

I glanced at Grandpa and caught him slipping Ali bits of his sandwich. Turning my gaze back to TJ, I wished I had the right answer. "I think it might have something to do with him, TJ. I hope not."

"Where would Dad have hidden money?" Joel looked straight at me. "I mean, you would know about something like that, wouldn't you?"

I took a drink of my iced tea and studied my youngest son. He was just crossing over the age of believing that his parents were the smartest creatures on the earth. It had been hard enough when Trent died and I discovered money was missing from our savings account. "I should have known something like that, Joel, but there were things I didn't pay enough attention to."

"But . . ."

"Shut up, butt-dart." TJ slammed his sandwich down. "You're upsetting Mom."

I reached over to touch his arm. "No, TJ, he's not. I'm upset at myself, not you or your brother. But I promise you both, I am paying attention now. I will take care of you two boys."

"Grandpa helps too," Joel said.

I smiled at that. "Grandpa helps."

"Oh, yeah, Mom, a bunch of stuff came for you today. It's in a box in your room." Joel changed the subject.

My throat closed up. "What stuff?"

Grandpa stopped feeding Ali. "I told you, Sam. I ordered you some spy stuff."

Ali dropped the bit of sandwich she was eating and growled deep in her throat. The hairs along her back stood up.

"Mom?" Joel scooted closer to me. I put my arm around him. "What is it, girl?" I said to Ali.

"I'm packin', Sam, not to worry." Grandpa pulled out a pen and heaved himself off the bench, just as Ali laid back her ears and barked viciously at the south side of the house. I held my breath, wondering what the hell Grandpa was packing. Before I could fully descend into panic, Rossi came around the corner of the house.

My heart fell back into place with a painful thump. "It's okay, Ali." I patted her head.

"Don't you people ever answer your door?" Rossi strode across the patio to us.

Grandpa did a slow turn to face Rossi and held up his pen. "You come any closer and I'll spray you!"

Rossi's blue eyes went over Grandpa, then settled on the pen. "With ink?"

"Grandpa, this is Detective Rossi." Standing up, I slid my arm off Joel to walk around the table.

Grandpa was staring at the pen in his hand. "Hey, this is my flower pen—where's the pepper spray!" He pulled the blue cap off and out popped a bouquet of tiny yellow daisies.

"Christ." Rossi stared at the flowers. "I've been shot at, attacked, cut with a knife, chased down in trucks and had some asshole use a stun gun to keep me from arresting him, but nobody's ever threatened me with flowers."

"It was supposed to be a spray of the hottest white pepper."

Suspicion bloomed bright in my chest. Whirling around, I looked at my two sons, who had a sudden and vivid interest in the remainder of their sandwiches. I held out my hand. "All right, give it to me."

"What?" Joel's big round blue eyes feigned innocence without even trying.

"The pen you swiped from Grandpa. If it isn't in my hand in two minutes, no Nintendo, no phone and no ice cream."

Both boys shot up off the bench and ran for the house. I kept my hand out and turned back to Rossi. "Why are you here?" 'Cause if he was going to arrest me for murder, he was going to be doing it with an eye full of pepper spray. There weren't enough cops in Lake Elsinore to separate me from my kids.

"Can we talk in private?" His pale eyes watched as the pen slid into my hand. His handsome face worked hard not to look impressed. "How did you know?"

Closing my hand over the pen, I answered, "Because I'm a mom. Believe me, Detective, when you have kids, a certain kind of rapid logic becomes mandatory. Do you have kids?" I was buying time. What did Rossi want?

He shook his head. "Two ex-wives, but no kids. What were your sons going to do with that defense-spray pen?"

Real curiosity mingled with natural police suspicion. Amused, I wasn't about to tell him. Let him try and figure it out.

Grandpa didn't have the same idea. He gave Rossi a challenging stare. "What would you do if you thought your mom was in danger, Detective? They know Sam doesn't approve of guns." He didn't wait for an answer, but waved them both off. "I'll stay out here while the boys finish their dinner, Sam. Why don't you take the detective in the kitchen? And while you're in there, do something about your knees."

I looked down. Blood was dripping from one of the cuts. I must have hit it on the table when I jumped up.

In the kitchen, I got Rossi a glass of tea, wet a paper towel and sat down at the table with him. Exhaustion spread through me at an alarming rate. My arms and legs were leaden and slow, but my mind kept whirling. I didn't think I'd sleep tonight, but instead my overactive mind would have me sitting up in my bed scared shitless. What a wimp. Sighing, I dabbed at the blood and tore the rest of the forming scab.

Rossi's hand closed over mine. I snapped my eyes up. He was kneeling in front of me. He'd taken his jacket off, leaving his black shoulder holster stark against the white shirt tucked into his Levis. No tie. There were thin, faint threads of silver highlighting his brown hair. "Got any antiseptic?"

My mouth was dry. Too much tension had yanked my hormones out of retirement and made me flush. "In the cupboard over the coffee maker, but I—" Was talking to his back. The view was interesting as he reached up for a tube of antibiotic ointment. Long muscles in his back rippled down to his tight butt.

God, what was I thinking? It had been so long since I'd felt these sparks. Somewhere along the way of my marriage, I had suppressed my sexual feelings. It was just easier. Trent had lost interest in me, and I got tired of the hurt. I immersed myself in being a mom and forgot about being a woman.

Rossi made me feel like a woman. All woman. Maybe even a capable woman.

He came back to the table holding the small tube. I needed something more than antibiotic ointment. Kneeling down, he spread a thin layer of the ointment over my scraped knees.

"I see you're still wearing the marker." His gaze climbed up the faded words and caught on my chest before finding my eyes.

"I can do that." I wrenched the tube from his fingers. I had to get myself under control. Now. "What do you want?"

Rolling up to his feet, he picked up his glass of tea and sat down. After drinking half the tea, he pulled his customary small notebook and pen from his pocket. "What did the man who attacked you look like?"

Business. All business. I sighed and told him the best I could remember.

"And his car?"

Finishing with the ointment, I said, "An old blue Datsun."

"License plate?"

"I was kind of busy."

"How about the gun? Didn't you say he had two?"

"I don't know anything about guns. One was smaller than the other was. Why are you asking me this now?" Was that what he had come over for?

He put down the notebook. "We had a murder in town this morning, in case you've forgotten. My superiors really like it when I arrest the murderer. Thing is, the murderer seems more interested in you than me. Wonder why that is?"

"Luke says he didn't kill his brother." But if he didn't, then who did? Someone who knew about the money and didn't want to share.

"The same guy who pulled two guns on you said that? And you believed him?"

Okay, so he had a point.

"Who else is after the money?"

Playing with the tube of ointment on the table, I arched a brow at him. "Besides Luke?"

"You said Luke was the second one today. Who was the first?"

I could see why he had made detective. He had heard every rambling word I had bellowed at him in the sandwich shop. "I don't know. I got a note with a balloon. When I went to Frank's Flowers to find out who sent it, the name was Jane Smith, and all Frank could remember about her was that she had nice legs." All men were dogs. If they weren't looking at legs or boobs, they were looking at cars. Predictable. I leaned back in my chair.

"Where's the note? I want to see it."

Standing up, I asked, "If I give it to you, will you go away?"

He rose, coming close enough for me to smell his tangy aftershave. "I don't think you want that, Sam. I'm the best hope you have of getting you out of this mess. Besides, I liked your thong."

I tried not to be flattered. I wasn't flattered. Tilting my nose up, I glared at him. "You almost got me killed, Rossi. You never told me that Heart Mates was being investigated, or that I could be in danger." I took an outraged breath. "You investigated me!"

"I'm still investigating you."

"Why? I don't know where the money is!" How many times, and to how many people, was I going to have to say that?

"Did you have a safe deposit box, or anything like that? Did your husband have a special place for important papers? What about his family? Did he have a girlfriend? Do you have a boyfriend?"

I blinked in the face of his onslaught. The last question rang the loudest. "I don't have a boyfriend!"

He grinned. "I know, but then there was that thong."

Dammit. I swore under my breath and stalked through the kitchen, hanging a left down the hallway to my bedroom. I went to my desk, moved the stack of books I needed to review this month and got ahold of the card.

When I turned, Rossi was standing in my room watching me. "Here." I held out the card.

He didn't take it. "How many people have touched it?"

"I don't know. Me, Grandpa, probably Frank and Molly. Molly is Frank's wife. She delivered the balloon and card."

"Where's the balloon?"

"In the trash." I was still standing there holding the card

out in front of me. It was the only thing between Rossi and me. We were alone in my bedroom.

"Christ, I'm not digging through the trash. Besides, he probably never touched the balloon."

"Frank said it was a woman, and men don't play with gold stick-on letters. It was a woman."

Rossi pulled a small bag out of his hip pocket, shook it open and nodded for me to slip the card inside. "Or it could be a woman doing it for a man."

I dumped the card in the bag and looked up at him. "I never thought of that."

He did his slow grin. "That's why I get paid the big bucks, Sam."

I brushed my hair off my face. "Who's doing this, Rossi? Why? Luke said Trent was skimming money, but skimming from what? I closed our safe deposit box and sold our house. I would have found the money."

"What about relatives?"

I shook my head. "Trent's parents are dead and his sister lives abroad."

Rossi's sexy grin dimmed. "Did Trent have a passport?"

I did a mental groan. "Passport! I never found it! Yes, he had one. He kept it in the lockbox we had. It wasn't there. I never realized . . ."

"Can you think of anything else that was missing?"

"No." Staring at Rossi, I formed the reluctant question. "What does it mean?"

"Maybe he was going to join his sister. Where does she live?"

"I don't know. She didn't even come for his funeral. They weren't all that close. She lives in one of the Bahama Islands." Which one? I couldn't think.

"I'll see what prints we might be able to get off the card," he said and turned to leave.

"Rossi, am I still under investigation? Do you still think I have the money?"

He stepped closer. "Everyone lies, Sam. That's the first thing a detective learns. What lies are yours? That's what I have to find out."

He was close. I could feel the body heat coming off him. Or was that me? This was not love-lust, the kind that's coated in dreams of romance and happily ever after. This—this was body lust, the get wet, naked and sweaty kind of lust. All about joining bodies and nothing about joining hearts. Holding my ground, I looked at him. "Even you, Detective? Do you lie?"

He touched my shoulder. "Absolutely. I'd lie to get you in bed." With that, he left.

I stood there until I heard the front door close. I glanced at the box on my bed, the one that Grandpa said contained spy stuff he'd ordered off the Internet. I went to the bed and ripped open the box. Looking inside, I knew the item on top wasn't an electric razor.

Gingerly, I picked up the black unit. I could see the prongs on the end where the electrical shock arced back and forth. I ignored the slight queasiness from the memory of being stunned by Perry Wilkes. Hmm, how much trouble would I get in if I tested this out on a detective?

Everyone lies. I turned over the stun gun, trying to get more comfortable with it. *Everyone lies.* I did know that. When I had been on the PTA and a soccer team mom, I had learned how to get around those little lies parents told to get out of helping at school or soccer functions. I had gotten so good at it that I had a Rolodex phone tree with notes on each family. Who worked where, what their weaknesses were—for instance, Frank and Molly at the flower shop could always be relied on to think of future business for any discount they gave the PTA.

I stopped playing with the stun gun and set it back inside the box with several other items I hadn't looked at yet. Getting up, I went to my desk and picked up my Rolodex. My phone tree. Information. I had all kinds of information right here. All I had to do was figure out how to use it.

What did I need to know? Who was behind searching for the money, where the money came from and what Trent had to do with it. Then there was the fourth question—where the hell do you hide half a million dollars? The dating consultants might be able to tell me how Heart Mates, the Wilkes brothers and Trent were involved. With my limited experience, it seemed better to start trying to track down one name instead of four. Maria was the one I went looking for today.

I'd start there. But instead of chasing down their last addresses, I'd start calling through my phone tree to find someone who could contact Maria and set up a meeting for me. In a safe place.

Where I didn't have to fight off a six-pack of thugs trying to steal my car.

"Mom?" TJ's voice called softly behind me.

Setting the Rolodex down, I turned to see both boys standing in the doorway. "What?"

Joel's eyes were fastened on the box of spy stuff. "Uh, can we have ice cream? We gave you the pepper-spray pen back."

TJ sighed. "That's not what Grandpa told us to say."

Joel dropped his gaze from the box to the floor. "We're sorry, Mom. We shouldn't have stolen Grandpa's pepper-spray pen."

Going to my sons, I hugged them both. "No, you shouldn't have. Promise you won't do that again?"

They agreed and I let them go.

"Mom, Grandpa said for you to come out and have ice cream with us." TJ's gaze slipped over to the box opened on the bed. "What are you doing in here? What did that detective want? You were, like, really cool in the backyard with him, Mom."

Cool, huh? Couldn't get a better compliment than that. "Detective Rossi wanted some information." And sex. God, I think I needed some ice cream. "Come on, guys, let's go get that ice cream."

Later tonight, after the boys were in bed, I'd start calling around.

The house was quiet. TJ and Joel were asleep with Ali in their room. Grandpa was reading in his room. Getting a beer out of the fridge, I remembered my promise to Ali, and got two bottles out. Opening the bottles, I wasn't surprised to see Ali pad quietly into the kitchen. I poured one beer into Ali's dish and took my bottle to the kitchen table.

My Rolodex and legal pad were there. Getting the phone, I sat down and dialed.

"Hello?"

"Sue, this is Sam." I pictured the heavyset mom with unusual cat-shaped gray eyes that I knew from PTA. She had twin girls and was a talented artist. We always used her to paint sets for plays and that kind of thing. "I'm sorry to call so late, but . . ."

"Sam! I heard about your trouble. Finding a body, that must have been awful."

"I didn't actually—" I shut my mouth and thought. Maybe she'd be more willing to help if I didn't clarify that Rossi found the body and I just showed up. "Yes, it was awful. And now I need to find a woman. She used to be an employee of Heart Mates, my dating service. It's important." I gave her Maria's name.

"Hmm . . . Sam, it doesn't ring a bell. Why don't you try Carla. Remember our kids played soccer together? She lives on the other side of the lake. Maybe she knows someone over there who knows Maria."

"Thanks, Sue." That was a good idea. I hadn't thought about that. I began thinking about geography. There was a better chance of finding Maria if I called women from different parts of town rather than from all one neighborhood.

Ali came over, sat down and leaned against me. She burped softly. I dialed the phone. "Hi, Carla—"

Forty-five minutes and two beers later, I had an appointment with Maria tomorrow at ten o'clock. I'd go to work first thing in the morning, then meet Maria for coffee at the Coco's Restaurant on Casino Drive.

Leaning back in my chair, I was thinking that detective work wasn't so hard after all.

Sound asleep when the phone rang, I made the mistake of answering it.

"Have you seen the paper?"

Falling back on my pillows, I managed to wake up at least eight separate aches and pains that were screaming at the same pitch as my mother's voice. "I was asleep, Mom."

"Romance Broker Finds Dead Body!"

I was awake now. Swinging my feet over the side of the bed, I stood up and stared at my desk filled with books I had to read. "Me? I'm in the paper? Is Heart Mates in there? They're calling me a romance broker?" I looked at my alarm clock. Five-thirty. Good God, I was up before Grandpa!

"They're saying you found a dead body! The whole article goes on about how you own a dating service and when you went to the house of the man you bought it from, you found him dead."

"Rossi found him first. Does he get any credit?" That's the trouble with five-thirty in the morning. I don't know what I'm saying.

"Samantha, you have to close that place down and sell it. Or give it to the IRS. I will be at your house at seven Saturday morning to pick you up for your real estate class." She hung up.

I stared at the phone. It was Wednesday. I had barely three days to find someplace else to be on Saturday morning. Heart Mates was my career.

After my shower, I noticed I was running low on skirts. Having people after me was hell on my clothes. Angel and I were going to have to make plans to go shopping.

This Saturday sounded good to me, if I just got through the supposed-to-be-at-the-arcade-with-half-a-million-dollars- on-Friday-night problem alive. I chose a blue sleeveless dress that almost covered the permanent marker on my thighs. Using an anti-frizz gel, I managed to tame my hair to my shoulders and covered my fatigue with make-up.

Following the scent of coffee, I found Grandpa in the kitchen, banging away on his computer. He was dressed in checked golf pants and a plaid shirt, complete with a white hat perched on his nearly bald head. "Morning." I kissed the side of his face and went to pour us both some coffee. "What are you doing on the computer so early this morning?"

"Meeting the boys this morning. Rosy Malone is in the hospital and I'm getting the scoop on what she's having done."

"You're breaking into hospital records?"

"Not exactly breaking. I have access. Sort of. Anyway,

she told Hank and them that she's having her gallbladder removed. Ha!"

There was a huge senior social scene that I had never known about until I moved in with Grandpa. Curious, I leaned over. "What's she really doing?"

"Face lift."

"You're gonna tell?"

"Might, might not."

The thing about magicians was that they were tight with their secrets. 'Course, Grandpa was a gossip too. One could never tell. He could, and would, keep certain secrets to his grave, like the secrets of magic. But gossip? I'd lay my money that the whole town would know about Rosy's face lift by noon.

Halfway through a sip of hot coffee, I thought of something. "Grandpa, can you get into prison records or find out things about a person if I give you a name?"

"Always good to have a Social Security number, Sam. But I can gain access to most any system given enough time to find the right . . . connection."

Grandpa was well known in the magic community and the Triple M magic association that he belonged to was worldwide. Over his lifetime, he had made thousands of friends. That was how he got access to things. "Can you try and find out about Perry Wilkes? I have his Social Security number on the escrow papers. Just look around and see what might help us? Now that he's been murdered, I don't know what we can learn. Damn, I wish I had his brother, Luke's, Social Security number."

Lifting his own coffee cup, Grandpa swiveled in his seat to look at me. "Know where he works?"

I shook my head. "I'm going to the office first thing, so I'll check around in case we happen to have Luke's Social Security number. Oh, and later this morning, I'm meeting with Maria, one of the dating consultants. I'll try to ask her what she knows about Luke."

His fading blue eyes twinkled. "Maybe it's in the police files. I could take a peek there to see what there is to know about Luke Wilkes."

"Just be careful." My grandpa—the James Bond of the Internet.

5

I got to the office intending to have some quiet time to think about how I wanted to approach Maria at Coco's later that morning.

But the office was not quiet. As soon as I stepped in the door, everyone started talking to me at once. I finally got through the five women and one man spread out on the folding chairs to Blaine's desk. I met his gaze as he fiddled with the forms and clipboards. "All these people are here to sign up for our service?" I whispered.

"All but one. I put her in your office. She said it was personal."

I had a vision of my mother in there armed with a real estate class that starts today. "It's not my mother, is it?"

He shook his head. "Linda Simpkins."

"I should see the clients first." I nodded my head and tried to snag a clipboard from Blaine.

"They have to fill these out, boss."

Narrowing my gaze, I whispered, "Linda is the PTA president. She might want me to chaperone the next dance."

"Sounds cool," Blaine said.

"Humph." I looked around the office. I was too busy to

chaperone a dance. Lifting my head, I went into my cubicle.

Linda had exchanged the soccer-mom uniform of stretch shorts and T-shirt for a dress. A loose-fitting dress that hid the fast-food stops. She had her blond hair curled rather than in a ponytail. "Linda, what can I do for you?" I sat down behind my desk, trying to appear very business-woman-like.

"Sam, you've got to help me." She leaned forward.

Oh, no, here it comes. "The thing is, Linda, I'm swamped. I've got all those clients out there and—"

"But there's no one else who can help me. I heard that you're doing private investigating, and this has to be very private. I can't go to just anyone, and especially not a man."

Okay, now she had my attention. I glanced at my watch. It was just after eight. I could hear her story, process those in the lobby with Blaine's help and still make my appointment with Maria, the dating consultant.

First I had to clear up the private investigator thing. "Linda, I'm not a private investigator. I think you have to be licensed to do that." Probably. Gabe had some kind of license. Maybe it was for fishing, I never really looked.

She waved her hand. "But you found that body, and you spent last night tracking down a woman on the phone."

The ability of small-town moms to process and pass on information would make the FBI jealous. "That had to do with business."

"Sam, I don't have anywhere else to go."

What about all her friends that she had spent hours on the phone with gossiping about me after Trent died? The whole town went on a buzz when I pulled out of the PTA, hung up my team mom stripes, got augmented, starting exercising and bought Heart Mates. By the time I joined the local Tae Kwon Do, I was big news. Mid-life crises?

Breakdown? Tramp? Husband Snatcher? They went through them all.

Not one of them ever told me my husband was screwing around on me when he was alive—they preferred talking about me behind my back. "I'm in a time crunch here, Linda."

Tears suddenly pooled in her eyes. "Please, Sam, I know you'll understand. I have to get those videos back."

"What videos?" I handed her a tissue.

She blew her nose. "Three videos out of my collection are missing. I have to get them back."

"Linda, maybe the kids loaned them out or something. I'm sure it's not serious."

She was shaking her head. "No! Not these videos!"

Hmmm. I was really getting interested. "How do you know?"

"They were in my bedroom closet. They were . . . uh . . . personal."

"Personal? Like having your babies?" As soon as I said it, I knew. Was it possible? "You mean that you and Archie videotaped yourselves when you were having sex?"

The tears spilled down her full cheeks. "And now they're missing!"

By the time I had promised Linda I'd look into her missing PTA-Prez-Does-Hubby videos and sorted out the new clients in my office, I was running late for my meeting with Maria.

Checking my watch, I rushed inside the restaurant. The first thing I saw was the bakery case.

Hunger pangs hit, and I did a quick mental calculation on how fast that humongous chocolate-chip muffin would spread over my thighs. Damn. Regretfully, I turned away to see a woman sitting on the dark-stained wood bench opposite the cash register.

I walked up to her. "Maria?" At her nod, I extended my hand. "I'm Sam Shaw."

She stood up to her petite height of about five foot two with heels. She was Heather Locklear in dark hair and eyes. Definitely no chocolate-chip muffins for me.

After we were shown to a table and ordered coffee, I began with, "Thanks for meeting me, Maria."

She stirred cream in her cup and fixed a hard-eyed stare on me. "I was curious about you. You're not what I expected."

"You know me?" I didn't like this. Too many people knew me and I didn't know them. Could this be the lady with nice legs who sent me the gold-lettered threat?

She shrugged. "I knew Trent."

Ignoring my coffee, I put my elbows on the table and leaned forward. "Knew him how?" He had been a cheating pig, but he'd been *my* cheating pig.

She leaned back. "I can't tell you anything. I already told the police that I haven't talked to Perry since he fired us, then sold the place."

I was going to kill Rossi. He'd never let on that he had talked to Perry's employees. Bet he knew if Maria had donated her panties to Trent's collection. Quickly realizing that I was getting nowhere, I sipped my coffee and debated how to make Maria talk to me.

Pepper spray on my key ring from my box of toys Grandpa had ordered? Nah, I'd probably just spray it on myself, then get arrested for pollution. *Think.* Sympathize with her, understand her plight . . . "Bet you were pissed off when Perry dumped you. What are you doing now?"

"I work at a bar."

I raised both eyebrows. "You probably make good tips." She was pretty, and working at the dating service must have given her experience at being friendly.

"I do okay. How come you bought that place?"

Her dark eyes watched me with genuine curiosity. She either didn't know about the money, or she was a fantastic actress. I did know a little bit about reading women from years of talking them into doing what they did not want to do for the PTA or soccer. I leaned back in my chair and tried to relax. "I didn't like the way 'Fast Food Technician' looked on a business card, so I opted for 'Business-woman'."

"You had no idea what you were doing, did you?"

"There were a lot of things I didn't know," I confided, trying to draw her in. "Perry ran the place into the ground. The IRS has an unhealthy interest in my business, and now the police are asking me what was my husband's connection to a murdered man. I am learning real fast." To lie. Yessir, I was a real quick study. Didn't Rossi say everyone lies?

We both were quiet while the waitress poured more coffee and asked, again, if we wanted to order something. I settled on a bagel, no cream cheese. When we were alone once more, I said, "What was Trent's connection to Perry Wilkes?"

Maria put more cream in her coffee. "Perry bought a supply of condoms from Trent to promote safe sex among his dating clientele."

I was ashamed I had ever believed that line. "Hogwash. Trent was up to no good, and I want to know what that SOB was doing while I was schlepping the kids around town, making posters for the spring dance and cleaning toilets." I hadn't exactly planned that outburst, but it felt pretty damn good. Going with it, I added, "I'm not the police, Maria."

She regarded me with a practiced look and said, "Trent figured out how to move more drugs. We were just doing a little dealing on the side, but Trent . . ." She looked around, stirring her coffee with an acquired caution.

The restaurant was nearly empty. Waiting until the waitress set my plain bagel down and left, I asked, "How?"

"There were four of us dating consultants. When I first hired on, it was all legitimate, but then Perry got the idea he could make more money dealing coke on the side. So, the way it worked was a client would come to see a dating consultant and put in his order. I would tell Perry, and he would try and score the coke. I'd call the customer and tell them that we had a match. They'd come in and pick up the coke."

"When did this start?" God, it was all so sleazy.

"About two years ago, maybe longer."

"How did Trent get involved?"

"Someone told him we moved coke, and he came in with an idea. He thought we could move more with his connection. He had the idea of sealing it up in the foil condom packets."

I choked on my dry bagel. Coughing, my eyes burned and tears began to run down my face. Finally, I took a drink of the coffee and was able to breathe. Using a paper napkin, I wiped the mascara tears off my face. Trent had a drug connection? "How? I mean the condoms are sealed and . . ." Safe sex, my ass. That bastard had preached to me about AIDS and other diseases when he was a drug-dealing disease himself.

"He would make a small slit, insert the coke, and use one of those seal-a-meal deals that are sold on infomercials to seal the condoms back up. If he was stopped on his way to his connection in San Diego, it looked like he was just a condom representative out hawking his product. It really was brilliant."

I thought of the house I'd sold, Trent's Beemer that had been repossessed, my minivan with its new owner, two classic cars, cell phones, pagers, computers, laptops—all the stuff we had been acquiring and I never really questioned. He always just said it was commission money.

And when he died, our savings account had been empty.

It was too much to take in. Trent had been a drug dealer. I had thought he had been a cheating husband who died of a stupid peanut allergy. But maybe he had been killed on purpose. Maybe he had been skimming money.

"Maria, what happened when Trent died?"

"The connection dried up. Perry was furious and fired us all."

This was delicate. How did I ask about money? I didn't want to let Maria know that there was a half a million dollars, at least according to Perry's brother Luke, floating around somewhere. Had Perry found out Trent was skimming money and killed him? Then how did Luke find out? "Maria, what was Perry furious about? Were there any problems between Trent and Perry?"

She lifted one dainty shoulder. "I don't know. The girls weren't in on their conversations. All I know is that Perry started acting weird just before Trent died, and he got worse right after."

I had to face this. "What about Trent? Maybe you spent some time with him?" Maybe you lost a pair of silk panties and he was keeping them for you?

She gave me a look edged with contempt, one that said, Surely you didn't think he was selling condoms all those nights away from home on "business" trips? "Any time I spent with him was not for conversation."

I pushed the bagel away. The thought of Trent out there doing anything with panties worked better than diet pills. I forced myself to think. "Do you know anything about Luke, Perry's brother?"

"No. Nothing. I mean, he came around once in a while, but that was it."

My mind was a whirling mass of raw, stinking sewage. But out of that, I did think of one thing. "How did Trent find out Perry was selling drugs?"

"His mechanic told him." She closed her eyes and said, "His name always reminded me of flying—airplane, plane, ah, Blaine. That's it—Blaine."

Blaine? My assistant?

I had to go home and get my stun gun. And Ali. Then go by Angel's house and borrow her very real, bullet-shooting gun.

Or maybe all I needed was a baseball bat.

But that would take too much time. I was in a hurry to commit bodily injury. I pulled into the parking lot of Heart Mates, shut off the Bird and stormed into the office. I stopped short.

My mother was sitting behind Blaine's desk talking on the phone. "Ms. Shaw is practically triple-booked, but I will sneak you in at one, provided you are here at precisely one."

My mouth fell open. "Mom?" I looked around, but no one else was here. Where was Blaine the Traitor? I looked at my watch; it was fifteen minutes to twelve.

Hanging up the phone, my mother ran her gaze over me. "Samantha, I can see your bra strap. You should wear a jacket with that dress to class it up, and you need fresh lipstick. I have a new diet for you to try."

Good thing I didn't have my stun gun. "Mom"—I tried for calm—"where's Blaine and who were you talking to on the phone?"

My mother patted her dyed blond hair. Her nails were a taupe today to match the silk jacket she wore over a matching shell. I knew her skirt beneath the desk was cut just above her knees. At almost fifty, my mom was nice-looking but a little pudgy, mostly in the middle. She fought that battle like a warrior queen, tirelessly hunting down every diet and diligently following it for at least as many hours as it took her to find the diet.

Then she would go to the next open house and gorge on junk food. Real estate agents were to party trays what cops were to donuts. Somehow, my mom believed that calories consumed during business were free. I tended to carry my weight in my hips and thighs. I know this because my mother has told me so—a gazillion times.

"Samantha, it wouldn't hurt you to lose a few pounds. The competition for a man is tough, and they like slender legs."

My left eye did not twitch. My whole face did. I would not have slender legs until that short-skirted lawyer on TV and I had surgery to switch legs. What I had were muscular legs with big calves and thighs. I tried to stay focused. *Blaine.* I had thought he was my friend as well as my assistant. But he'd known all along that Trent was involved in drugs and Heart Mates.

That betrayal stung. But I was not going to feel the pain alone. I was going to share my pain with my assistant. Just as soon as I found the back stabber. "Mother, where is Blaine?"

"He left."

"Why? Did he say where he was going?"

My mother sighed and folded her hands on the desk. "I stopped by to see you, and Blaine said he had to go. That was it. I think you should fire him."

That was a first. My mother and I agreed on something. Although I doubt she would approve of me using real flames when I fired him. "Mom, who were you talking to on the phone?"

"That was Molly. She and Frank just do the most beautiful thank-you baskets. I use them to send a basket to all my clients when I close a deal."

It was interesting. The twitch settled back into my left eye. If there was a God, my mother would not talk real estate to me. "What did Molly want?"

"I told her that you would see her at one o'clock. She said she needs a private investigator. One who can be discreet."

"I'm not a private investigator!" Why did that small fact elude everyone?

"Of course you're not. You're going to be a real estate agent, dear. But you must learn to make connections. I went to a great deal of trouble this morning to make sure that everyone believes that you are booked up. Being in great demand will help you get a better price for this"—her thin nose wrinkled as she looked around Heart Mates—"*place* when you sell. We're getting your name out into the buying and selling public for when you get your real estate license."

"I'm not selling Heart Mates." I had to force the words through an odd quiver I had developed in my top lip. "I have to go find Blaine. And I need to lock up."

My mother was already shaking her head. "You have a client at one, dear. That's only an hour from now." She reached down, presumably to her purse on the floor, and pulled out some kind of catalogue. "Why don't we go over a few things for your class on Saturday."

It had been like this my whole life. My mother rearranged things to suit her. Like my father, for instance. She changed stories about him as the mood struck her. I had no idea who he really was. Grandpa and Grandma had taught me not to care. They had always made me feel special enough not to need a dad.

They couldn't do anything about my mother. "I am not going to that class on Saturday. I have too much work."

Besides, I wasn't sure I was going to be alive, since so far I'd been stun-gunned, almost kidnapped, seen a real gun from the barrel end and now found out my friends were lying to me.

My mom's taupe nails dug into the page of the catalogue. "Samantha, I have gone to a lot of trouble and expense to get you into this class."

"I'll pay you back." That was the reason I had agreed to take on Linda's videotape mystery. Well, that and Linda was desperate. She needed *me*. After all the years of talking about me, now she *needed* me. I was becoming an important part of this town instead of just a source of endless gossip. This PI stuff was pretty cool.

But I did wonder how I was supposed to investigate missing sex tapes. Maybe I should have thought this out a little more.

Blaine lived in a trailer park off Machado Street, not far from an elementary school that had been there for more than thirty years. I didn't know how old the trailer park was. Pulling the T-Bird into the complex, I drove around the narrow streets to the single-wide trailer that he had in the back of the park.

His Hyundai wasn't here. I sat in the car staring at his mobile home painted a chipped green with rust patches. Strangely enough, Blaine had a little flower garden with a couple of green plastic chairs in the front where he liked to sit and drink beer with his mechanic buddies. Big, beer-bellied men among the flowers—it was quite a sight.

But he wasn't home now. I didn't have to go up to the door to know it. Either he went for a long lunch, or my assistant had just skipped out on me. He knew I was seeing Maria; in fact, Blaine was the one who had accessed the employee files for me.

Was he just holding out on me? Or was Blaine involved?

Maybe he'd figured out that Trent had owed Perry a lot of money and had killed Perry? Then what? He would meet me at the arcades, take the money and run?

Maybe, except that Blaine wasn't a killer. He was a nice guy. He was my friend.

He had also been Trent's mechanic. Maybe he knew where the money was? Maybe he was waiting for everyone to give up and killing those that wouldn't give up, so he'd get the money himself?

I smacked the steering wheel with the heel of my hand. "Damn you, Blaine." There had been something so satisfying about convincing him to come to work with me. See, Trent, I'd thought smugly, I could even take your friends.

What a dupe. I started the car and headed home. I needed to sort this mess out.

At home, I found my front door open. Again. Grandpa's Jeep wasn't in the driveway. There was no relentless squeal of a security alarm. All kinds of horrible thoughts roared through my head. Very real and vivid anger surfaced. I'd had enough. In fact, I hoped a bad guy was sitting on my couch right now, waiting for me to come in and kick his butt.

Pausing, I listened. I thought I heard faint movement in the kitchen. Why wasn't the alarm going off? I pushed the door open the rest of the way and walked in. Slipping off the blue shoes that matched my dress, I had a fleeting thought that today was the first time this week that I hadn't ruined my clothes. But the day was only half over, and I was beginning to think there was a prowler in my house.

The possibilities for ruining this dress were wide open. I just hoped it wasn't going to be my blood that did it.

I tiptoed quietly into the kitchen.

"Hey, Sam, how's it going."

I blinked. Gabe was leaning against my kitchen sink in a

pair of running shorts and Nikes, no shirt. He was drinking a beer, and since another empty bottle was sitting on the counter top, I suspected that the stuff Ali was slurping from her water bowl was beer.

"You gave me a drunk for a guard dog!" Less than a minute in his presence and my heart pounded fiercely against my chest and my mouth was bone dry. I watched Gabe take another drink of his beer, the long column of his throat working right down to his naked chest.

It was not lust I felt.

Just to prove it, I shouted, "What the hell are you doing in my house?"

"Having a beer."

Running shorts and shoes. Fading sheen of sweat, hair slicked back. "You've been out running." It came out as an accusation.

"I ran right into Barney."

"Grandpa? How did you run into Grandpa? He doesn't run."

"Okay, he almost ran me over with his Jeep."

"Cripes, did he hit you? Were the boys in the car with him?"

"Babe, you are seriously stressed. The boys were at school. Barney got wind that I was back in town, and found me."

Respect actually gleamed in his dark Italian eyes. "He almost ran you over," I reminded him. "Why was Grandpa looking for you?"

"He claimed it was a coincidence that he saw me running on the road, but then he mentioned the trouble you've managed to get yourself into."

I was hungry. For *food.* I had ended up leaving my bagel mostly uneaten. That accounted for the gnawing feeling inside my belly. Not Gabe—standing there with his beer bottle, looking like a picture of hot, sweaty, mindless, bad-boy sex. The kind of sex a woman fantasizes about but would never sample in real life.

Not if she didn't want to get burned.

Ali finished her beer and padded over to nose my hand. The cool, wet snout in my sweaty palm yanked me out of my dangerous thoughts. I scratched her ears; then she went to lie down by the table and sleep off the beer. Food—I was hungry for food. Going to the counter, I pulled down two plates. I got out two big Kaiser rolls, went to the refrigerator and found roast beef, sliced turkey, pro-volone cheese, lettuce, tomatoes and some bell pepper. Slicing up the tomato and bell pepper, I gave Gabe a quick rundown of my morning, from waking up to my mother's phone call about the newspaper article through the meeting with Maria and ending with my mother taking over my office. I had at last succeeded in shooing her out.

"So Blaine wasn't home?"

"No." I layered the meats and cheese, then added the lettuce, tomato and bell pepper.

"What about Rossi?"

The knife clattered on the Formica. I stared at the sand-wiches. How many calories were in those?

"Sam? Are you going to tell Rossi about Blaine?"

Putting both hands on the edge of the counter, I sucked in a lungful of air. "He didn't tell me that he'd interviewed the girls who used to work for Heart Mates. All he's told me is that he would lie to get me in bed." Ohmigod! I could not believe I'd just said that.

"Most men would, babe. You're a sexy woman."

He was behind me. I could feel the heat coming from him. Not the Detective Charming Pants heat of Rossi, but the unpredictable bad-boy street heat. Where exactly did Gabe come from? What about his family? Why had he never married? Or maybe he had—I didn't know. All I really knew was that Gabe took an early retirement from the police department after getting shot in the line of duty and then opened a security company.

"Flattered by Rossi's interest?"

Oh, yeah, I was flattered. "He has a job to do." I knew that Rossi was not going to cross over some invisible line and compromise his career. Unless *he* had killed Perry—then he probably wouldn't have any qualms about sleeping with a sort of suspect/witness to his murder case.

"Doesn't mean he can't want you. It just means he'll wait until you're in the clear to do you."

I turned around to find myself naked nose to naked chest. I looked up. "He's not going to do me!"

A grin softened his mouth. "No?"

Jeeze, he had an uncanny quality of giving me space to figure stuff out. It was the sexiest thing I'd ever seen in a man—the complete confidence that no matter how many stupid and naive things I did, I'd eventually get it right. But I had been too burned by a good-looking man to fall for any sexy tricks. Besides, I didn't want any man in my bed. Didn't trust them. "No. I have my boys and a career." I nodded my head to convince myself.

"Doesn't mean you don't have desires, babe. Needs. You didn't go from housewife to hot for the sheer thrill of pissing off the PTA."

Actually, I sort of did. I don't think a man can understand what a husband's cheating does to a wife's confidence. Then having everyone in the town know about it. I had to prove something—still did, I guess. But I knew bed-hopping wasn't the way to do it. I had always been choosy and always would be.

My mother hadn't been choosy, and my bio-dad made tracks at the first glimmer of a baby. I had never wanted to do that to my kids. No, instead I'd found them a skirt-chasing, panty-collecting, dope-dealing dad.

Okay, I wasn't a good judge of husband material. Nor did I want to rely on a man again.

Gabe lifted a hand to play with the edge of my bra strap peeking out from my dress. "Don't you think you oughta take these for a test drive?" He tugged on the bra strap.

Well, that was a little crass, but still, somehow, sexy. "What makes you think I haven't?"

He did that bad-boy grin. "Sweetie, you're wound so tight, even a monk could see it."

"I am not." I grabbed a plate behind me and handed it to him—hard into his naked stomach.

"Oooof." He dropped his hand from my bra strap and caught the plate before I let it go. A dangerous glint darkened his brown eyes to a black smoke.

"Sex is not a solution for everything!" An adrenaline rush hit my nervous system and revved up my mouth. "Trent left a mess that could get me killed or my boys hurt! People I don't know are chasing me down and threatening me, and my friends are betraying me. Excuse me if I don't feel like getting naked with the first stud that comes along!"

Gabe picked up his sandwich and took a bite while watching me with those dark eyes. "You think I'm a stud?"

I wanted to scream. Hell, I didn't know what I wanted more, to hit him over his head or drag him to my bed. I didn't think either one would help me find out where this money was, or who was trying to get it. And I still needed to figure out how to find Linda's missing videotapes so I could pay my mom back for the real estate classes.

"Shit!" I had forgotten! I had the appointment at one with Molly.

"You think I'm shit? Aw, babe, I'm hurting here." Gabe eyed me with a bit of wariness as he finished his sandwich.

"I have an appointment. I have to go." Grabbing my purse off the table, I slid my feet back into my pumps.

After telling Ali to sober up and protect my boys, I set the alarm and locked the door. When I turned around, I saw Gabe leaning against my car. He had his arms crossed over his chest, and his long legs spread wide.

"You want a ride?" I figured I could swing by and drop him off at home. It wasn't far out of my way.

I pulled out onto Grand and hooked a left up Lincoln to go into a tract of homes behind the middle school. "Do you have a license?" I wondered if the investigating thing was going to get me in more trouble. What could Molly want?

"For driving?"

I looked over at him. He was squirming on the seat; then he pulled out a few stray chunks of dog food from beneath his butt. He gave me a quizzical look.

"Don't ask," I said. "A private investigator's license."

"Yes, from the Bureau of Security and Investigative Services. And no, you can't get one. You have to have three years of investigative work and a host of other requirements before you can apply."

I huffed. "I run a dating service. I have no intention of becoming a private eye."

"We don't call ourselves that. Now tell me what's really going on."

I ran down the missing video thing.

He whistled softly. "What a small-town scandal. Now if you can just tie in the city council or school board. . . ."

I couldn't help but laugh. Small-town politics were serious business, and every election year produced new shenanigans that would probably overshadow a PTA president sharing her love life on video. "What do I do?"

"CYA first."

"Huh?" I was weaving into a tract that had a lot of curves and traveled up a hill.

"If anyone asks, Sam, say you are affiliated with my com-

pany. That way you're covered by my license, although"—
his look turned to a dark street warning—"you're putting
my butt on the line. So don't do anything stupid."

"Me?"

He snorted. "Then start by finding out who had access
to her house, particularly her closet. Who might know she
had tapes like that? If they were in some kind of club—"

"Club? Like a sex tape club? Oh, I don't think . . ." I
trailed off. The idea was ludicrous.

"Everyone lies, Sam. It's the first thing you learn on the
streets. She's probably only telling you what she thinks you
have to know. If no one but her and her husband knew
about those tapes, they'd still be in her closet. Check out
maids, window cleaners. Has she gotten new carpet?
Things like that."

I turned into the one-story house with a front porch and
three-car garage. Gabe lived here alone. I got the impression he bought the house after he retired from the police
department. He ran his business from the bedroom-
turned-office that opened off the living room. I hadn't
been to the other bedrooms.

Yet.

Idling the car, I turned to him. "What do I do about
Blaine? And everything else?" I just stopped short of
telling him the truth. I was scared. When Trent died,
everything in my life changed, but I thought it was a real
life. Then I learned that many of the things I had believed
were false. Like Trent's faithfulness. I had struggled for
eight months to recover from that and make myself
strong.

Now it was happening again.

Gabe touched my shoulder. "Tonight, come over, bring
your stun gun and all the stuff Barney got you off the computer."

"But the boys . . ."

"They'll be fine. Leave Ali and use the system."

"Okay, but it has to be after dinner. I always have dinner with TJ and Joel." It sounded silly, but it was something they could count on. That seemed important to two boys whose dad had died on them.

Gabe grinned. "And?"

I brushed my shoulder-length hair out of my face. "No sex."

He opened the car door, got out and closed it. Then he leaned down and looked at me. His gaze was hot. "I must be getting to you, Sam." He left and I sat there like a sex-starved female, watching his long-legged stride into the house.

Damn, he was getting to me.

6

I didn't have an assistant, my phone was ringing and I had three new customers, plus Molly, standing outside Heart Mates watching me struggle with the key to open the door. I hadn't had this much business in a month, let alone a single day.

Going into the lobby, I tried desperately to figure out how to handle everything. Standing on the front side of Blaine's desk, I wondered where he kept the clipboards with the information and security sheets attached.

The phone kept ringing.

"Sam." Molly was standing at my elbow. "I need to be back at the flower shop by two."

I glanced at Molly. She had pixie-cut brown hair that hung limply, brown eyes and a pretty smile. Right now the smile was strained.

"Go on into my office"—I waved my hand toward the cubicle—"I'll be there in a minute."

There were two thirtyish women who whispered back and forth nervously. Clearly they had used each other to get up the courage to come here. And a lone man, standing quietly by the door. He was late forties, just a tad taller than me and built like a teddy bear.

"Please have a seat and I'll be right with you." I gave them my best professional smile and snatched up the ringing phone. "Heart Mates."

"Sam? Where's Blaine?"

"Angel? What are you doing right now? Do you have a job?"

"I'm getting a pedicure. I'm calling from my cell phone. Your mom was just in here."

"She's not coming here!" It came out as a screech. The very idea panicked me. My mother would sweep in and sell these nice people homes before they remembered they had come here to find dates.

"She had a customer. She's on her way to Temecula. She said Blaine was missing and that you're going to fire him."

Where were those clipboards? Blaine always had them ready to go. I went around his desk and started opening drawers. "I can't explain right now." I opened the bottom right drawer and nearly shouted "Hallelujah!" He had almost a dozen boards slid in like file folders, already with forms attached. I pulled out three. They even had pencils tied on a little rope.

Where was my assistant? Had he really betrayed me? "Sam?"

"Angel? Can you come over here and fill in? Please? I have customers and . . . well, can you?"

"Be right there! Sounds like fun."

The phone clicked off. I set it down in the cradle and wondered if I'd done something dumb. Angel was . . . fearless. I snapped out of my thoughts, handed the clipboards to the potential clients with swift instructions on filling in the blanks, made a quick pot of coffee in case any of them were not hot enough in the hundred-plus-degree heat wave and rushed into my office.

As I dropped behind my desk, my stomach growled. My

sandwich—I'd left it on the counter at home. Why did I think my beer-drinkin' dog was eating better than I was? I would trade my augmented breasts for that sandwich right now. "Molly, what can I do for you?" I flashed a quick smile at her and began opening my drawers, looking for food.

I found one of those diet bars that are supposed to replace meals. It was chocolate fudge. I figured that would slim my thighs down.

"Uhmmmm . . ." Molly crossed her legs. She had taken her Frank's Flowers apron off and was wearing a Storm T-shirt for the town's minor league baseball team and a pair of loose-fit denim shorts. Delivering flowers kept her trim, if not toned.

"Molly, you have to be back at the shop at two," I reminded her gently. Swallowing, along with the diet bar, the need to scream that I was under a little stress here and would appreciate her using full sentences like an adult.

"Right. Frank said you're a private investigator now, and I have this little problem."

Her pause was my cue to encourage her. "I'm not a private investigator. That is, I don't have a license, but . . ." What had Gabe said? "I do a little investigating with Gabe's Security now and again." Hey, sounded good. Professional. I was going to add it to my business cards.

"Oh, well, if you take on a case, you don't have to tell anyone else, do you?"

I set the rest of my starvation bar down. "Why don't you tell me what this is all about?" I had a weird feeling as I watched her look down at the green-stained hands in her lap. I think it's from the clay stuff they use to anchor flowers into arrangements.

Then she sucked in a deep breath, pushed her bangs off her face and said, "I'm missing some videotapes."

I needed a Diet Coke. Laced with rum. No, I need rum, laced with Diet Coke. Leaning forward, I barely felt my elbow sink into what was left of the chocolate fudge diet bar. "Videotapes? Would these be tapes that you and Frank took of yourselves in, uh, marital relations?" Did everyone in the PTA do this and no one told me? Ugh, who would want to see pictures of themselves doing it? It would ruin my fantasy of being a threat to Cindy Crawford or any of those other supermodels who worried I would one day film myself and leave them looking for a new career.

"How did you know?"

Molly stared at me with round brown eyes. I wondered if private investigators had a client confidentiality thing going. "Well," I stalled, "what other kind of tape would have you this distraught if it turned up missing?" My head was buzzing with ideas. And questions. I reached into my side drawer and pulled out a yellow tablet. I had stacks of them for writing down new words and phrases to use when writing my critiques of romance novels.

That was when I used to be bored at work.

"Okay." I forced my mind to slam a lid on thoughts of Frank and Molly, or Linda and Archie, doing the wild thing on video. Wiping the diet bar off my elbow, I began, "How many tapes do you have and how many of those are missing?"

"You'll take the case? How much will it cost?"

How much? Do I charge by the case? The day? The hour? The clue? "Uh, yeah, I'll look into this. My fee is . . ."

Well, I knew how much I charged for the dating service packages. A two hundred dollar basic package got the client three matches, male or female, who might be compatible. Then there were extras, like the one-year membership and a wine dating package that ran upwards of one thousand dollars.

That fee scale didn't seem to apply here. "Twenty-five

dollars a day, plus expenses." I'd heard that *plus expenses* on all those TV shows dating as far back as *Magnum PI.*

Molly nodded in agreement. "There are three videos, and all of them are missing."

Same as Linda. I tried not to jump to conclusions. It didn't seem professional. "Who else knows about these videos—besides you and Frank, of course?" I was making the assumption that they were not stealing their own videos. "Oh"—I thought of a new question—"and when did you notice them missing?" Damn, I was getting good at this.

"They were gone when I was putting laundry away yesterday. I don't know how long. They were in my bedroom closet." Her gaze slid to my chocolate-smeared elbow. "No one else knows about them. They were private."

Everyone lies. "Molly, someone knew about them or they wouldn't be missing. I want to help you find your videos, but you have to level with me. What about people who do work around your house? A maid? Someone washing windows for you? Have you gotten new carpet? Or do you and Frank belong to any clubs that could be connected with this?" I pulled out a second yellow tablet and said, "I need you to write down everyone you can think of who might have found out about those videos." And why would two married couples' sex videos be missing?

"Will anyone else see this?"

I heard Angel out in the lobby and stood up. "No, only me. I keep my clients' confidentiality. I have to check into a few things while you work on that list." I left my office.

"Sam."

Angel was sitting behind Blaine's desk. Her long red hair was in one of those ponytails where the hair is pulled back through itself to look chic and elegant. It made the bones in her face stand out. The green silk shirt was a perfect contrast. I assumed she was wearing her long, slim black skirt with the killer slit up to her thigh. She had great thighs. She was also holding the phone. I gave the three waiting for my attention an apologetic look. "What?"

"There's someone named Debbie on the phone. She says that her cousin got a call from a gal she did a booth with at the last Harvest Festival at one of the schools and that she's getting in touch with you like her cousin asked. Do you know what she's talking about?"

I blinked before the name registered. "Debbie? Oh, that's my phone tree at work. I'll take it." Debbie was the second dating consultant who had been fired before dead Perry sold the business to me. "Hello, Debbie? Thanks for calling me. When would be a convenient time to meet with you?"

I grabbed Blaine's car magazine and wrote down the Storm stadium parking lot at four o'clock. The stadium was officially named The Diamond. The phone disconnected before I voiced any protest.

Couldn't an empty parking lot, pretty much out in the middle of nowhere, be dangerous?

I sighed and handed the phone back to Angel.

"What's a phone tree?"

Startled, I said, "I kept a Rolodex of phone numbers for all the soccer teams that I did the soccer mom thing for, and the PTA. I kept it updated, listing on the back things like what kind of work the parents did and how it might be useful. Or if the mom went back to work and that was her excuse for not doing something, I found out what kind of job she got in case we could use that somehow."

Angel's green eyes widened. "Boy, you were ruthless."

"Had to be," I said, then turned around when I heard my office door open.

Molly stood there. "Sam? I finished." She walked out holding the yellow tablet. "I have to run to get back to the shop. Here's the . . ." She held out the legal pad in her green-stained fingers. "Uhh, the list you asked for."

My other potential clients were shifting on the hard folding chairs. Flashing a quick smile at Molly, I said, "Thanks, Molly. I'll call you as soon as I look this over and do some . . ." What? Guessing? ". . . Preliminary work." It was the best I could do with the pressure of a roomful of clients, an AWOL assistant and two individual cases of missing video-sex tapes, not to mention thugs after a half million dollars I didn't have. But not helping Molly never entered my mind. She needed my new skills as a PI. Okay, maybe an amateur PI in training.

As Molly left, I set the legal pad with her list aside on Blaine's desk and started to turn back to my restless clients.

Then I thought better of it. Grabbing up the list, I said, "Angel, I need one more minute!" I took the list into my office and closed the door. Grabbing the phone, I called Linda Simpkins. "Please be home," I whispered.

"Hello?"

Relief flowed over me. "Linda, it's Sam. About that matter we discussed in my office?" I didn't know who was at her house or might hear this conversation, and I was pretty sure she wasn't going to forget asking me to help her find her sex tapes. That kind of thing stuck in a woman's mind. Especially when that woman was the president of the PTA.

"Yes?" Her voice was slow and cautious.

"Could you make a list of anyone who might have been in your house? Things like cleaning people, plumbers . . ." I was in such a rush my mind was blank. I looked down at Molly's list in my hand. "Uh, clubs that you might have meet in your house, babysitters, that kind of thing?" I planned to compare the lists to see who might have been in both houses. Maybe they both had their closets reorganized by one of those companies that advertise to double your space. That might narrow down the scope of this investigation real fast. Other than that, I didn't have any ideas.

"I could do that. Only you would see it, right?"

Grateful that I'd had the wisdom to grab Molly's list and not leave it out on Blaine's desk for anyone to see, I said, "Yes, only me. I'm in a hurry here, but if you could do that and drop it off to me as soon as possible, it would be a big help."

"Okay," Linda agreed.

I made quick work of getting off the phone, stuck Molly's list in the drawer by my purse and hurried back out to deal with the waiting clients.

Breathing hard, my last thought before I plunged into information sheets and my sales pitch was that I hoped Angel knew how to operate all that media equipment in the interview room.

It took Angel and me the next hour to get through the three new clients. I shuddered at the thought of trying to put all the info in the computer and do the cross matches. Blaine did that for me with his two-fingered wizardry. The program matched interests, appearance and temperaments of clients and spat out candidates; then Blaine and I would take it from there.

With the clients gone, I sat behind my desk and took a minute to recover and catch my breath. Angel came into my office, carrying two diet sodas she'd gotten from the liquor store. She sat down in the chair across from my desk. "How'd I do, boss?"

"Beats me why you can't keep a job, Angel."

She leaned back and put her sandled feet on my desk. Her calf-length black skirt split, revealing a pair of slender, well-shaped legs. "I just haven't found my niche. The thing I love."

"That's not true. If you got paid for stalking your ex-husband, you'd have a career." I opened my soda and enjoyed the fizzy taste of chemically treated water. The truth was that Angel didn't need money. She'd had the wisdom to marry a man with family money. She'd come out of the divorce with a nice chunk of change that she invested well. Then his family cut him off for being a sleaze, so all her ex ended up with was a teenaged bimbo for a wife and an ex-wife who wasn't through wreaking revenge. Hugh Crimson likely rued the day he'd ever decided to boink Angel's manicurist. Hugh's family owned a law firm in Temecula. Hugh himself held a law degree but had never managed to pass the bar. The family liked their ex-daughter-in-law better than the son who had cheated on her.

"Stalking is a crime, Sam. I merely keep track of Hugh in a discreet, and mostly legal, way."

I gazed at her. "You have night-vision goggles and once put a tracking device on his car."

She grinned. "That was the time I called the police and gave them his license number and the make of the car he was driving as a possible drunk."

I tried to look stern. "He was taking what's-her-name to Vegas to get married. Is nothing sacred to you?"

She wrinkled her nose and drank her soda. "So now what? Where did Blaine get off to?"

Glancing at my watch, I saw that I had over an hour until I had to meet Debbie at the stadium. "I don't know. I found out from Maria, one of the dating consultants who worked for Perry, that Blaine was the one who told Trent they were dealing drugs here at Heart Mates." I filled her in on the story and that Trent was likely skimming drug money.

"Where's that money? What was he going to do with it?"

I resented being forced to keep facing reality. "His passport was missing. I think he was going to leave the country."

Angel set her can down. "And leave you?"

"And me." I hated putting it into words. It's one thing to be widowed, but for Trent to have been planning to dump me while I lived in the land of the clueless—that just pissed me off. "Trent must have hidden that money somewhere and was planning to leave all of us—TJ, Joel and me."

"Was he going alone?"

Sometimes, facing reality sucked. I took a little detour. "He'd be so pissed if he knew I sold his Mustang and was using the T-Bird for myself. He never let me drive his classic cars."

"You let him tell you not to drive them," Angel corrected me.

I lifted my soda to her. "Right. I let that cheating prick tell me I couldn't drive the classics. But guess what? I got the last laugh—he's dead."

Angel brushed a speck off her thigh. "But he's still screwing you, Sam."

It had been so long since I'd had any screwing that I doubt I could remember what it felt like. Taking my cue from Angel, I slipped off my shoes and put my feet up on the desk. "No, he's not. I've already figured out that pantyboy found a favorite out of his collection and was going to whisk her off to the Bahamas. I don't care about that." Much.

"You have to find that money, Sam."

"Yes, Rossi mentioned that," I said dryly.

"Really?" Angel dropped her legs and leaned forward. "What else did he say?"

"He thinks I have the money."

Freezing the can halfway to her mouth, Angel responded, "It must be your lifestyle that gave you away. So, where would Trent hide that kind of money?"

I had been over this. "Not the house—I went through everything when I sold it. Obviously not here at Heart Mates, or Perry would have found it. He could have some kind of safe deposit box that I didn't know about. That's one of the reasons I'm tracking down the dating consultants. They saw Trent in those last days, so maybe they can give me some clue."

"Or maybe Blaine knows where the money is?"

That wound was still raw. "If he's still in Elsinore, I'll find him. I'm going to go by the garage he used to work at after I see Debbie."

"How many people are after the money?"

"Two that I'm sure of. Luke, Perry's brother, and the woman who left the note with the balloon. Whoever she is."

"And who are you not sure of?"

I finished my soda, half afraid to voice it. "Detective Rossi and Blaine."

"Rossi?" Angel's green eyes widened like a mascara commercial. "Tell me!"

I shrugged, thinking out loud. Probably because I didn't want it to be Blaine. "Rossi just happened to be at the site of Perry's murder, and Luke seemed to think that I'd killed his brother. I didn't do it, so who did? Also, it's bugged me why Detective Rossi responded to the stun-gun incident. Something like that usually doesn't get a detective's attention."

"Maybe your mystery woman killed Perry. What are you going to do?"

I'd already had the same thought. Fighting the feeling of water closing over my head, I took a deep breath. "I'm going to find the answers and nail the bastards who are threatening me and my kids. That's what I'm going to do. And while I'm doing that I'm going to check into another little matter, getting the money to pay off my mom. In the meantime, all the publicity is growing my dating service." That was the bright side.

Angel gave me a look. "You're turning into an amateur private eye, Sam."

I smiled. "Yeah, I'm going to put that on my business card."

I guided the T-Bird down Diamond Drive, past the tire shop. The green and red-brick stadium rose up on my right in what was essentially a flood plain on the east end of the lake. The stadium seated just over six thousand people and another twenty-one hundred fans on its grassy area. There was a full-service restaurant on the third-base line, assorted concession stands and even an arcade area and souvenir shop. The mascot was a sea serpent named Hamlet who was known to dance and ride all-terrain vehicles. The stadium shot off fireworks that could be heard and seen across town for every home run.

A sign informed me that there were three parking lots, one for season ticket holders, one for general parking. I was past the sign before I could read what the last lot was for.

The Storm stadium was a pretentious piece of work for Lake Elsinore. The cost overruns and other assorted details still had the city divided. The battles were vocal and amusing to watch on our local cable channel. Better than Jerry Springer. But the stadium itself was majestic. Even more so for the fact that it sits on a flood plain, sort of like a mirage in the desert.

Of course, one serious rainy season and baseball could take a back seat to fishing. But for now, the stadium is a community jewel where concerts, high school football games, graduations and occasional weddings are held, and even commercials have been filmed there.

I ran out of road. I turned right, since left would take me away from the stadium and back toward my office. That brought me alongside the ticket booths and front entrance. But the parking lots were all gated off since the stadium was closed. There was a lone man out in the afternoon heat walking one of those small dogs that run all over TV looking for tacos.

Looked like an Ali-snack to me.

There didn't seem to be anyone else around. The street ended in the flood plain that ran alongside the outflow channel and, in the distance, the lake. I grew uneasy.

I should have gone home and gotten my stun gun. At least I had the pepper spray on my key ring. I sat there idling the Bird, thinking about that. If I turn off the car, that limited my escape, but if I left the keys in the ignition, then I couldn't get to the little canister of spray next to the huge gold bear with the fake diamond in its belly that Joel had given me for Mother's Day.

I could try and force the key off the ring while it was in the ignition. The sound of another car approaching snapped me out of my dilemma. I put the car into gear and did a three-point turn. Wrestling with the steering wheel, I thought of modern cars and power steering, but I got the Bird facing the right way to make an escape.

A blonde was driving a small, beat-up orange truck. The first thing that popped into my mind was—had her panties been in Trent's collection?

She pulled the truck up alongside me so that our driver's-side doors were next to each other. "Samantha Shaw?"

According to Gabe, one of the things a good investigator does is take control of the interview. "Yes, you must be Debbie. Thank you for meeting me." Her blond hair had a curling frizz thing going that added to that hard street look she wore. Behind the door of the truck, I got the impression that she was taller than I was and had a body kept thin by non-FDA-approved products.

I bet she had cellulite on her skinny butt.

"How much?"

Huh? I was pretty certain she wasn't asking me how much cellulite I had. "How much what?"

"How much you gonna pay? I didn't tell the cops nothing, and I ain't telling you anything for free."

"Rossi," I muttered under my breath. The suave detective was always one step ahead of me. 'Course, he was a cop and did know what he was doing. I was just trying to stay alive. Mentally, I went over the money I had in my wallet. Counting my emergency stash for gas, I had twenty bucks. "Twenty bucks now and another twenty if the information you give me checks out."

"Fifty now and what do you wanna know?"

She didn't look real bright to me. "Do you know who I am?"

"I read the papers. You found Perry's body. I didn't have nothing to do with that. He wasn't worth a bullet anyhow."

No love lost there. I reminded myself that I could be dealing with a murderer and/or an extortionist. I was pretty sure she'd look good in a pair of shorts and could spell Jane Smith. I bet she knew how to play with gold stick-on letters too. Was she the lucky panty-wearer Trent had picked for a one-way trip to the Bahamas? "I need some information about my husband, Trent." I wanted to see her reaction.

"Yeah?" She blew a strand of bleached-to-straw hair out of her mouth.

"Was he more friendly with one of you girls than the others?" That was the best I could do and not throw up.

"He was friendly with all the girls."

I closed my eyes. What do I ask now? What do I need to know? Where could Trent have hidden the money he skimmed?

"But he had a special fondness for one."

I snapped opened my eyes to find her gaze trained on my face. Female cunning was stamped there.

"Give me the money and I'll tell you who it was."

I pulled my last twenty out of my wallet. "What's the name?"

She snatched the money. "Hazel. And Perry didn't like it none."

"Did Perry like Hazel?"

Her blue eyes narrowed. "Hazel always thought she was better than us. She was doing the same as us, selling the same shit as us, but she thought she was better."

"So what didn't Perry like?"

"Didn't like her being so chummy with Trent."

I ignored the sly contempt in her voice. "What does Hazel look like? Where does she live and work? How can I find her?"

Debbie shook her head. "Hazel took off right after Trent died. She didn't wait around to be fired by Perry. She knew Trent was the one with the brains to keep our little operation going. When he died, she jumped ship and left the rest of us to sink."

Having a name put to the girlfriend did nothing to improve my mood. "That last day, the day Trent died, was he at Heart Mates?" Maybe she could give me a clue to where he stashed the money.

A full sneer thinned her nose. "I bet you were a smug bitch, waltzing around town thinking you were better than everyone else and all the while your husband was out screwing every woman he could find."

I thought about the pepper spray. I could visualize the thick eyeliner and clumsy mascara running black rivers down her face. Searing pain would reduce her to a black puddle of sorry slut. I was a little tired of having my folly thrown up in my face. It took a real effort to keep my voice level. "Just tell me if you saw him that day he died." Or I'll zap your eyes and watch twelve dollars worth of cosmetics end up on your lap.

"It'll cost you."

"How about I write you a check?" Okay, I was pissed off. "And then I'll drive over to the police station and tell those nice folks in them snazzy blue uniforms everything I know. They may not be able to arrest you, but I think they'll find a way to make your miserable life just a smidgen more wretched than it already is."

Her face hardened. "He came to Heart Mates that morning. That's all I know." She shifted her truck into reverse.

"One more thing."

She gunned the engine. "What?"

"Did anyone give Trent a box of candy that day?"

"How the hell would I know?" Her truck leaped into reverse and hauled backwards all the way through the stop sign; then she squealed into first and out of my sight.

After my little chat with Debbie-dating-consultant-number-two, I ended up at the grocery store. No matter how many disasters befall me in a single day, I was still a mom. No way was I going home to the empty refrigerator and two hungry boys. I tossed enough in my cart to keep TJ and Joel from starving, but not zero out my already strangled checking account.

Although I could have used the twenty bucks, it had been well worth handing it over to Debbie. I now knew that Trent had been at Heart Mates the day he died. It was possible he got the chocolates that killed him from someone there.

So someone at Heart Mates very likely killed Trent. Someone who knew about his peanut allergy. Why had they killed him? The money? Or something else? And just how clever was that to kill someone with their own allergy?

I had more questions than answers. Guiding my cart to the front of the store, I quickly checked out and drove home.

Once there, Ali met me at the door. She pushed her nose at the heavy grocery bag I was lugging to the kitchen, trying her damnedest to trip me. That way the six bottles of beer in the bottom of the bag would break and she could lap it up.

"Lush," I accused her and made my way into the kitchen. "Hey," I greeted TJ and Joel. They had books and papers spread out on the table. "How was school?"

"My science teacher took away my fake thumb," Joel complained with a full mouth.

"You know better than to play with that stuff in class." The fake thumb was a magic trick.

"Make her give it back, Mom."

"Sorry." Unpacking the bread, milk, crackers and various other items, I added, "Her class, her rules. How about you, TJ?"

"Fine," he grunted.

Glancing over, I saw him with his light-colored head bent over graph paper, writing algebraic equations in his tight, precise scrawl. I pitied the teacher who had to read that. He reached over and grabbed a piece of candy out of a square plastic box covered in a winter scene. My hand froze on the beer. "TJ, what's that?"

"Algebra."

"No, the candy." My voice was rising. "Where'd you get it?"

He looked up. "This? It was on the porch when Grandpa brought us home."

"Who left it?" I let go of the beer and went to the table. My heart was pounding in painful thumps. A prickly sensation broke out under my arms and across my back.

Trent had died from eating candy. *Homemade candy.*

The box was one of the generic plastic types of candy or cookie holders that stores sell around Christmas to pack homemade treats in. Resting on wax paper were chocolate squares.

The whole room tilted as panic shot up my spine and roared into my head.

"Mom? What's wrong? Grandma always drops off the stuff her clients give her for us. See, it says on the top . . ." He turned the lid over to reveal a snow scene with a blue snowman wearing a bright red hat and muffler. Covering the picture were press-on gold letters that read: "See how easy it is, Samantha? Be there Friday night, nine sharp."

Ohmigod.

"Grandma always calls you Samantha. Everyone else calls you Sam." TJ's voice had turned pleading. "Did I do something wrong?"

"Mom?" Joel said.

There was no time to explain. I grabbed his arm. "We have to get you to the hospital."

7

I recovered my wits before I actually dragged the boys to the emergency room, screaming that they'd been poisoned. Neither TJ nor Joel had any food allergies, nor did they show any signs of a reaction to the candy. Instead, I ran to the phone and dialed the police.

Grandpa came out of his room to see what was going on. TJ and Joel watched with white, frozen faces. Hanging up the phone, I turned to look at them. My sons. The two halves of my heart. With a supreme effort, I used the calmest voice I had. "Why don't you two put your books away and play video games for a while?"

Then I raced for the bathroom while hearing Grandpa's voice talking to the boys. Once I was finished dry-heaving, I splashed water on my face and composed myself. I had to be strong, to protect my boys. Opening the door, I nearly tripped over Ali sitting there waiting for me. She looked up at me with her liquid brown eyes and slim nose. Reaching down to pet her, I asked, "You wouldn't let anything happen to them, would you, girl?"

Ali and I went out to the kitchen. Rossi had arrived while I was busy vomiting in the bathroom. So much for my dignity. Taking a seat at the kitchen table across from him, I saw the container of chocolates sitting in front of him.

Shoving my damp hair back, I angled my head toward the container. "What are you doing? Aren't you going to have those tested?"

"Sure." He looked up at me, his blue eyes intent. "But there's nothing in those but caramels covered in chocolate with a little peanut butter stirred in."

I glanced into the living room to see TJ and Joel sprawled on the floor, playing a video game. The fact that they weren't tormenting each other clued me in that they were listening. But they had to know the dangers so they wouldn't eat candy that appeared on the porch again. Turning a glare on Rossi, I demanded, "How do you know that's what's in the candy?"

"Taste test."

"You ate one!" Why was I worrying? My kids had eaten several. Unable to stop myself, I looked back at the boys. They were fine. No one was trying to kill my sons. But I was not fine. I was scared. The candy thing scared the hell out of me. It was too easy to get to my kids.

"Eating one"—Rossi leaned his elbows on the table— "seemed the fastest way to determine what was in them."

His very reasonableness irritated me. I was way more worried than he was about thugs trying to get money I didn't have and threatening to kill my sons if I didn't come up with it. "What's going to happen when I don't show up with that money?" I demanded of him.

"Maybe you'd better get the money," Rossi suggested as he pulled out an evidence bag and slid the container of candy inside.

"Here, Sam, drink this." Grandpa set a glass of Coke in front of me. "It'll help settle your stomach."

"Thanks." Grandpa materializing out of nowhere didn't surprise me. He had the magician's ability to melt into the background, or command attention. But my face burned from my overreaction. I had to control myself. Falling apart would only endanger those I loved more. I sipped the soda, then turned back to Rossi. "Go away, Detective. If you're not going to help me, then just go away." Dammit, I was dangerously close to tears.

I'd never felt this helpless. That message had hit its mark. *See how easy it is?* Too damn easy to get to one of my kids or Grandpa. This was not Luke-with-the-two-guns work. No, this had a more delicate, sinister touch. A woman. I'd rather face the gun. Ali put her head in my lap and sighed. I petted her head and felt a kinship with the dog. She'd been fretting and whining ever since my bout with hysteria.

She also wanted a beer.

"Where do you suppose your husband put the money?"

I looked at Rossi. He was drinking iced tea and appeared tired. His blue eyes had slight dark circles beneath them. His mouth was tight, but his voice was smooth and soothing.

"I don't know." I dropped my head into my hands. "Have you checked out the condom company? Uhmmm . . ." I was so rattled, I couldn't think of the name. "Gladiators? Yeah, that's the name."

Rossi's mouth twitched in a slow smile. "Yeah, I ran a check. They said they boxed up all his stuff and sent it to you."

"It was just Trent's notebook computer, a couple coffee cups, briefcase, stuff like that. I'm sure I would have noticed a half-million dollars."

He got out his notebook. "What were Trent's hobbies?"

My stomach was feeling better. "Bimbos."

He gave me a pitying look. "Anything else?"

"Classic cars, wine and cigars." Coming down off another adrenaline high was leaving me hungover and exhausted. I wondered if I needed a twelve-step program. Maybe I was addicted to the high. "Collecting panties, but I burned all those."

Rossi stopped writing. "You're tired."

I held up a hand. "Don't you dare be nice to me. Do you hear me, Rossi? Not now." The tears formed a big soppy lump in my throat. "I'll find a way. I'll deal with this. I . . ." I forced my sluggish mind to focus. Friday night. Half a million dollars or bad things would happen. There was no running. I had to go to the arcade Friday night and find out who was doing this. "That's it!"

"What?" Rossi narrowed his eyes.

"Friday night. I have to go to the arcade—you can be there and see who it is that's trying to get this money from me. Then you can arrest them."

"I've been working on that. I don't think you understand what it takes to set up that kind of stakeout. This is a small town, Sam. We don't have a lot of police, and something like that has to be cleared through my sergeant, who has to clear it with his boss. Unlike certain civilians, we cops have to adhere to procedures."

"But it's your chance to find out who killed Perry."

"Probably his brother, Luke, killed him."

"Maybe, or maybe he didn't. I've talked to two of the girls who used to work for Perry, and Luke wasn't around much. I don't think he was involved when Heart Mates was selling drugs."

His blue eyes hardened. "You've been busy. What else did you find out?"

"Trent was scoring drugs in San Diego for Perry, transporting them in the condoms right past the border patrol and to Heart Mates. They passed them out, supposedly, as part of the safe dating campaign, but they were really selling the drugs concealed inside the condom packets. It was all Trent's idea. I was married to a drug pusher who likely got himself murdered for skimming money." I stopped and saw the expression on Rossi's face. The same expression that he'd worn when I discovered that TJ and Joel had stolen the pepper spray pen from Grandpa. He was impressed.

"Not bad. I could never figure out where they were getting the drugs from."

Bells went off in my brain. Was Rossi involved? "How did you get involved, Rossi? Why were you investigating Heart Mates?"

He sighed. "A nineteen-year-old girl died of a heart attack. From coke. The best we could determine, she'd gotten the drugs from that dating service, but we could never prove anything. It went down as an overdose, but . . ." He brought his thumb and forefinger up to rub the bridge of his nose. "Every once in a while, we all get a case that just sticks in our nightmares. This girl came from a good family, didn't have a record or any indication of prior drug use. Beautiful girl that didn't look more than fourteen—"

He trailed off and I got it. I sat there, my fatigue forgotten. He'd told me once that he'd had two wives and no kids. I'd bet I knew why—those cases. They were his cause, the reason he'd work twenty-four-hour shifts. The young girl who had messed with drugs once and died. Someone had to give her those drugs. I still didn't trust Rossi, not one bit, but I think I got him. He hated pointless, stupid death.

Had Trent been the one to give that girl the drugs? The shock was not the heart-pumping horror of fearing someone was trying to kill my kids. No, this was a slow, sick horror that slumped me in my chair. Had I slept in the same bed with a man who dealt death to nineteen-year-old girls? If I had yanked my head out of the sand sooner—could I have saved that poor girl? If I'd known what Trent was doing, would I have had the guts to confront him or go to the police? It weighed me down—shame, guilt and intense sadness.

Rossi got up. "I'll talk to you in the morning, Sam."

I forced the despair back. "Wait, what about Friday night?"

He was quiet for a minute, his blue gaze intense on me. "Who are you, Samantha Shaw? What makes a woman change so drastically? What drives you?"

The interrogation was couched as male interest, but I wasn't fooled. "I lived my whole marriage afraid, Rossi. Afraid because my mom could never hang on to a man and afraid because my own bio-dad wanted nothing to do with me. But when Trent died and I realized our marriage had been a lie, I woke up. There's only one person who can make me strong and that's me. I won't be afraid anymore. I will do whatever it takes to take care of my two boys. Does that clear it up for you?"

He moved in close. "And who takes care of you, Sam?"

He smelled of something leathery and solid. He had a good half foot on me in height. He looked so safe. I tilted my head back. "I do, Detective. Good night."

That slow, handsome smile rolled over his face, probably hoping to disarm me. "Night, Sam." Then he left.

Grandpa appeared and sat down at his computer. "Got some information for you, Sam."

I wanted to stand beneath a hot shower, hug my boys, then go to bed and sleep through until Sunday. Instead, I pulled a chair up next to Grandpa. "What?" I asked, trying to look interested.

"Perry was in jail on a shop-lifting charge, but you knew that. His brother, Luke, has been in and out of jail for stuff like public drunkenness and non-payment of child support."

"Luke has a kid?"

"Yep, and he owes a lot of money on that kid. He is divorced and his wife lives in Temecula. She has a lawyer who's riding his behind. Luke does some small-time dealing. Otherwise, he supports himself by hiring out as a day laborer."

I blinked. There were a few spots on Main Street where the day laborers hung out in the hopes of someone coming by to pick them up for a job. I had passed the clusters of tired-looking men many times. "How did you find all this out?"

"Just checking around," Grandpa said vaguely. "Perry and Luke's father is unknown and their mother is dead. Perry bought Heart Mates with the small inheritance from his mother's life insurance when she died of heart disease. She had worked for the County of Riverside for fifteen years when she died. Before that she worked odd jobs for short periods of time. It appears that she had pulled her life together."

"Any other brothers or sisters? Seems like Luke and Perry must have been a disappointment."

"No other siblings that I can find. Sam—" Grandpa turned his face up to me. "Luke doesn't look very smart. Not smart enough to deliver the candy laced with peanut butter as a threat to you. Don't misunderstand me, I think this Luke is dangerous and feeling cornered. But there's someone else after the money too."

Nodding my head, I tried to think. "Have you checked on Trent in there?" I waved to the computer screen. "Maybe we can figure out where he hid the money."

He shook his head. "Honey, I can try, but a computer is a tool. It can't do your thinking for you."

Why not? I could really use someone to think for me.

"Grandpa." Joel wandered in. "Did you show Mom the new business cards that TJ and me made for her?"

I hooked my arm around Joel's waist as he stood next to me. From my sitting position, my youngest son looked so big. "You made me new business cards? I still have plenty of the old ones."

TJ came in with Ali at his side. "But you're a PI now, Mom." He leaned across me to open one of the small drawers in the rolltop desk and took out a stack of light blue cards. "See?" He handed them to me.

Samantha Shaw
Owner/Operator of HEART MATES
Serving your needs for
Romance & Confidential Investigations

I stared at the card. They had included the phone number and address of Heart Mates, along with a line saying that the Investigation Service was affiliated with Pulizzi Security and Investigation Services. Gabe's company. I wondered how he was going to take that.

"I decided to keep Gabe's PI license number off the card," Grandpa said.

"How did you get his . . . never mind." I waved at the stack of cards. "These are beautiful, boys, but I don't think Gabe would want me passing myself off as a private investigator affiliated with his company." To say the least. He had only given me permission to claim that affiliation to the people I talked to about the missing videos. He was helping me out. This was definitely going over the line.

"Mom?" TJ planted his slim hip on the edge of the rolltop desk. "I'm sorry about the candy. I mean, I really thought Grandma left it for us—but I should have been more careful. I never meant to scare you."

"Oh, honey." Unhooking my arm from around Joel, I stood up and hugged TJ. He had always been a serious child, but he'd gotten more so since his dad died. "It's not your fault. You had every reason to believe that candy came from Grandma." Letting him go I looked into his blue eyes. "I am proud of you two boys. You've been a big help to me since this whole mess started." Kissing his face, I thought, *Forgive me, Gabe.* "You made me these really awesome business cards." I'd find a way later to get them to change the card to something more acceptable. For right now, I made a big show of taking my old business cards out of the holder I used and putting the new ones in.

We had cereal and chocolate milk for dinner. Not up to Martha Stewart's standards, but we were all together—me, TJ, Joel, Grandpa and Ali, who had a special fondness for salted shredded wheat.

Once dinner was over, as much as I wanted to go to bed and dream myself a new life without treasure-hunting goons, I had to keep my appointment with Gabe. He'd told me to come over tonight when I'd dropped him off at his house earlier today.

I needed Gabe's help.

With the boys settled for the night under the guard of the alarm system, Ali and Grandpa, I drove to Gabe's house.

He opened the door and stared at me in the amber pool of his porch light. Gabe had this uncanny ability to make one arched black brow shoot up into a hard curve over his hot, sexy eyes. It wasn't a question, but a statement that went something like, *What the hell have you done now?*

"Don't start." I tossed my head back, straightened my shoulders and walked into his house.

The door shut. "You putting on weight, babe, or are you packing that vest with soup cans?"

"Not soup cans, equipment." The carpet in his living room was a beige Berber with a warm brown couch that matched a big square chair and ottoman across the brass-and-glass coffee table. There were some Western prints on the walls, lots of open land with buffalo roaming. Not bad for a bachelor.

Glancing down the hallway that led past the kitchen and family room to the bedrooms, I thought about how I'd ever only been as far as the guest bathroom. I had the urge to run in there right now and see if I had turned back into the woman who used to wear this vest. Sighing, I turned around to face Gabe. His expression was carefully blank, just like a cop. "What equipment?"

I unzipped the black fleece vest. It had two zippered pockets on the outside, and four more on the inside. "I used to wear this in my soccer mom days. I was always carrying Kleenex, Band-Aids, granola bars, paperback books, all kinds of stuff. Joel pulled it out of my closet and . . ." I shrugged and pulled the vest open.

His dark gaze slid over my white T-shirt, then traveled to the inside pockets. Coming closer, he looked down into the pockets. "Flashlight, defense spray, stun gun and cell phone."

He was so close that his breath disturbed my hair. A small tremor scuttled down my back. I tightened my fingers, gripping the edges of the vest, and swallowed a lump of instant lust.

"You are one equipped dating expert, Sam." His eyes traveled over my jeans and back up my T-shirt to linger on some of my other equipment.

Damn. Here two minutes and my libido was humming. Yanking the vest closed, I said, "Grandpa and the boys got all this stuff. They feel like they're helping me." Wait until he sees the business cards. "They wouldn't let me leave until I wore all this. I told Grandpa we couldn't afford a cell phone, but he and the boys bought the dang thing anyway." I knew I was babbling. "They even put the number on my new business cards."

His gaze sharpened. "Business cards?"

"Never mind." I needed Gabe's help and the business cards might put him in the wrong frame of mind. "I have to look for Blaine. Wanna come?" I needed answers and I needed them now. Blaine seemed a good place to start.

Folding his arms over his chest, he said, "Tell me what happened."

Time was running out. Quickly, I detailed the candy thing and what I had learned from Debbie.

"Slow down, babe. You're going in circles. What you need is a plan."

"I have a plan! I'm going to find Blaine. He knew Perry and Trent and all these girls who worked for Heart Mates."

Gabe rocked back on his heels, his dark gaze steady on me. Then he dropped his arms. "Come on." He went into his study that was across the entrance hall from the living room.

For lack of a better idea, I followed him. He flipped on an overhead light that revealed a big leather chair behind a heavy desk with a computer, printer, scanner, copier and a phone system that had a couple of boxes hooked up to it.

He sat behind the desk and rummaged in a drawer. I drew in a breath of impatience and looked at the pictures lining the walls. There were photos of Gabe as a cop, including a picture with the mayor of L.A. for some kind of commendation he'd received after the bank robbery that had ended Gabe's career. The wall by the desk held a slew of official-looking stuff. Licenses, certificates, all the stuff I didn't have.

Gabe pulled out a tablet of paper and a couple of pens.

"You think a woman was behind the candy threat tonight. And that she was the one who killed Trent. Tell me why."

Sitting down, I ticked the reasons off on my fingers. "First, it was a woman who ordered the balloon at Frank's Flowers. Second, gold stick-on letters looks female to me. Third, Trent knew how severe his allergy was and would only take something homemade from someone he trusted completely, not likely a man, and finally, this is how a female thinks. Men do the shoot-'em-up thing. Women are more devious."

He nodded. "Anything else?"

"Grandpa says Luke owes back child support, has been in and out of jail on petty stuff and is likely feeling cornered and desperate for money. When Luke confronted me, he used a gun and intimidation. Totally different style."

Shaking his head, he said, "Barney's been in some confidential files. But you're right. Let's assume for now we got two people after the money. We know one is Luke. Now, who's the other?"

"That's what I want to ask Blaine!"

"Sam, you have to know what questions to ask."

I fought down the panic that was closing my throat and giving me that feeling like I had to keep looking over my shoulder. "It would have to be someone who knew Trent was skimming money from Perry's drug profits." I forced myself to focus. "But that gives Perry the motive for killing Trent, not the woman." It was just one big jumble in my brain. I couldn't reason it out. I dropped my head into my hands. "Nothing makes sense. This is all a nightmare."

"It's real, Sam." Gabe tore a sheet of paper off his tablet and set it down between us. In the center, he wrote Trent, and below that Perry. "Okay, these guys are dead," he said, then began listing names of those who knew them. He wrote Luke, then looked up at me. "What's the names of the dating consultants?"

"Maria, Debbie, Joan and Hazel. Don't forget Blaine." I watched him list the names around them.

"Okay, and how are they all connected?"

"Trent ran drugs for them, slept with the girls, and according to Debbie, he favored Hazel. Maybe he was going to run away with her."

"Okay." He drew a line from Hazel to Trent and wrote *girlfriend* on it. Then he drew another line from Hazel to Perry and wrote *employee*. Then between Perry and Trent he wrote *business partners*. He had a triangle. "Now we know that Perry might have wanted to kill Trent because he was skimming money. What about Hazel? What reason could she have to want to kill the man who had the money and was going to take her away?"

Triangle. I looked at the triangle. And I knew. "Another woman. That bastard was cheating on me. Why wouldn't he cheat on Hazel?" I picked up a pencil and drew another line linking Trent, Hazel and the other girl I hadn't talked to, Joan. Now I had two triangles back-to-back like a kite. "I don't know if it's these particular women, but you get the idea."

Gabe studied the diagram. "That's possible, especially given what we know about the players. Hazel could have found out about Joan and decided to kill Trent for betraying her and keep the money for herself. Except it turned out that she didn't know where the money was." He looked up at me. "Now we know what to ask Blaine. Let's go."

We took Gabe's truck, since he thought the T-Bird was a little conspicuous. He also made me leave my toy-stocked vest at home. I glanced over at him. He wore tight jeans and a dark-colored T-shirt. And a gun.

I had my pepper-spray key ring and flashlight. I sort of got the feeling Gabe didn't trust me with any kind of weapons. But I did have a little thrill—we were doing some serious tracking. I was with a real private investigator. We were hot on the trail of . . . "Uh, Gabe?"

"Yeah?"

"Where exactly are we going?"

He turned onto Lake Street. "Targets usually stay in an area they know. Mother and girlfriend are the first place to look."

Filing that bit of info away, I asked, "How do you know about Blaine's mother or girlfriends?"

"First we're going by his house. Then you're going to tell me where his mom and girlfriend are. Buddies too."

Arriving at the mobile home park, Gabe followed my directions to Blaine's mobile home in the back of the park. His trailer was still dark. "Not home." I was disappointed.

Gabe shut off the truck and opened the door.

"Hey, where are you going? He's not home." I shoved open the door and almost fell onto the narrow road. "Wait." I followed Gabe. He was walking around the mobile home, looking in the windows, toeing pots of gardenia and vincas that Blaine had sitting around. Then he went up the steps to the back door. He tried the knob. "What are you doing?"

"We're going to take a look."

I shut up and my hands grew cold and damp. Fear stirred in the pit of my belly. But that was stupid. I wiped my hands on my jeans and grit my teeth.

"Do you have your flashlight? I need you to hold it on the door."

"Uh, just a second." I ran back to the truck, yanked open the door and fished around until I found the big black flashlight. Hurrying back, I aimed the beam on the door handle. "What's that?" Gabe had a large wallet thing that opened to show a set of tools.

"Quiet."

He was down on one knee working the lock. Picking the lock! "You were a cop," I hissed, "you can't do that." Could he? He still carried a weapon, and in fact I knew he had a license to carry it concealed. Was he allowed to break and enter? But cops had to have search warrants to do that door-kicking shit, didn't they? I was giving myself a headache.

The door slid open. Gabe took my flashlight from my cold hands and started in. It was dark and—I wrinkled my nose. "What's that smell?" God, it smelled like day-old puke. Lifting my T-shirt, I held it over my nose. Blaine was a lousy housekeeper.

Gabe was moving along the edges of the walls. We entered the kitchen. I could hear the refrigerator humming and barely made out its hulking shape to my left. Turning, I followed the beam of light from Gabe until my foot hit something slick and wet. "Oh!" I slipped, both feet went out from under me and I landed flat on my back.

The air was knocked from my lungs. My ears rang and I heard a horrible groan. I was thrashing on the floor, trying to get my breath. It felt like a huge boulder was pressing on my chest. I got my breath back, just when a hand touched my cheek.

I screamed.

The flashlight beam landed in my face. "Ohmigod!" I rolled over in some kind of stinky mess and lunged to my feet. "A hand!" I screamed.

"Sam."

Gabe said my name with a quiet fierceness. I couldn't see him behind the flashlight, so I looked in the beam. On a beige kitchen floor, Blaine lay in a pool of blood. His long, feathered hair was caked with it—and something else.

Vomit and blood.

The whole trailer swayed. "Is he—"

Overhead lights flashed on. "He's alive. Find a phone and call 911." I stumbled through the mess that I had fallen in and looked around. A phone. Where was the phone? Please let Blaine be okay, I prayed when my eyes landed on the phone sitting on the counter. It was a cordless one and I yanked it off the base, punching in the numbers 911.

Gabe grabbed some dish towels and was applying pressure to Blaine's head, while skillfully avoiding the vomit-and-blood mess. Tears filled my eyes.

"Please, don't let Blaine die!" I yelled at the 911 operator.

8

"Boss, you smell like dog puke."

Like I needed to be reminded of that. But Blaine was alive, and according to the doctors, he was going to stay that way. They were keeping him overnight for the nasty concussion. They only let us in to talk to him because that way they could get me out of the hospital faster and have the place fumigated and repainted with Lysol.

"It's your puke. Did you drink that whole bottle of Southern Comfort?" I asked. He had a bandage around his head, but they didn't have to cut too much of his hair to stitch him up. Blaine was happy about that. Both his eyes were sunken and had black rings around them. His skin was pasty, although he had more color than when we found him.

"I drank enough to not realize someone was in my house." His gaze skittered away from me to look at the TV lodged high on the wall.

"Why did you lie to me, Blaine? You could have told me Trent was running drugs. You could have told me a lot." The hurt was worse than my smell.

"I couldn't tell you." Blaine stared at a rerun on Nick at Night. "I didn't want you to know."

"About my husband? You were covering for Trent?"

"Sam." Gabe was standing by an open window.

"No, it's all right." Blaine looked at me. "I didn't want you to know that I did drugs, all right? I had a problem and I quit, but people like you don't understand that."

Speechless, I didn't know how he could believe that about me. But the shame was stamped clearly on his battered face. Embarrassment. "Oh, Blaine, I don't know what to say." What did I say? He hadn't thought me a good enough friend to stick by him if I found out that he'd had a drug problem in the past. "Don't you see, Blaine? That's what hurt the most—I thought you had betrayed me." My nose clogged up with tears, but I considered that a blessing since it meant I couldn't smell myself. "It doesn't matter. I swear it doesn't!" I refused to cry.

"I didn't betray you, Sam. I never thought it would get this serious. And I didn't recognize Perry when he came in that day. I dealt with the girls, not Perry."

"Forget it, Blaine. But who did this to you?"

"Luke. He thinks that you and I are in this together and have the money hidden somewhere."

I frowned. "Why would he think that?"

"Because I knew Trent, and after he died, I left my mechanic job to come work with you at Heart Mates."

"And when you didn't know where the money was, he started hitting you with his gun." I was sick. It was my fault. Well, Trent's fault, but I inherited the blame. "Blaine, I'm so sorry." I stepped up to the bed and took his hand.

He grinned at me. "Hey, I was so drunk, I never even felt him beating on me. But Sam, there is something you can do for me."

"What?"

"Take a shower."

Gabe pushed off the wall he'd been leaning against,

laughing. "Come on, Sam. You can take a shower at my house."

I looked up across Blaine's bed and shook my head. "I need to go home."

"I don't think so, babe. You show up at home like that, and you'll scare the boys. Besides, your car is at my house."

I opened my mouth to argue, but one look at his shadowed black eyes told me it was futile. Whatever his reasons were, I wasn't going to make him drive me to my house. In fact, I didn't think many people, given my current state of smell, were going to line up to drive me anywhere.

"Hey, Gabe." Blaine's voice interrupted our silent battle. "If I were you, I'd make her ride in the bed of your truck. You'll never get that smell out of the cab."

I stood under the shower at Gabe's house and let the hot water pelt me. Finally, I got the energy to douse my hair in a second dose of shampoo and go through the whole soap-up, rinse-off process again.

At least Gabe hadn't made me ride in the bed of the truck. Instead, he'd used his bad-boy charm to talk a nurse into giving him a blanket to wrap around my wet, ruined clothes and smelly hair. We drove home with the windows rolled down and the air conditioner on full blast.

Getting out of the shower, I wrapped my dripping hair in one towel and folded a second towel around my body. Gabe's guest bathroom had the standard sink and mirror as you walk in, toilet, then bath/shower combo. He had a dark blue shower curtain and dark blue towels. God, I was tired.

A knock on the door startled me. "What?"

"I brought you a shirt to wear."

Clutching the towel around me, I inched the door open. A masculine hand thrust a black T-shirt inside. "Don't you have a robe or something?"

"No."

Narrowing my eyes, I considered challenging him on it. But what was I going to do? March down the hall to his bedroom in a towel? I snatched the shirt and shut the door. Unwrapping my hair, I dropped both towels on the floor and yanked the T-shirt over my head. It was a standard black one with a pocket over my right breast. It fell to mid-thigh. The only good news was that the permanent marker on my legs was gone.

Getting a brush out of my purse, I swept it through my hair, but knew it was hopeless. It was going to dry to an interesting pattern of blonde-streaked frizz.

Maybe the doings of my hair would divert Gabe's attention from the fact that I didn't have any panties on.

Yeah, sure. Sighing, I opened the door and turned right down the hall, following the sounds coming from the kitchen. Gabe was pouring wine into two glasses at the white-tiled bar. There were two stools at the bar overlooking the kitchen, but I chose the couch facing the fireplace and TV set in a recessed wall unit.

"I called Barney, Sam. The alarm system is set and Ali's on duty. He said you should just sleep here and he'd get the boys off to school tomorrow."

My head throbbed, but I shook it anyway. "When my clothes are finished drying, I have to go home." TJ and Joel deserved a mom who was there when they went to school in the morning and who slept at home. "I gave them cereal for dinner." Tears welled up in my eyes. There was a time when I had cooked meals. I pulled my legs up on the couch and tried to stretch the shirt over them. Then I rubbed my tear-stained face with the backs of my hands. What a mess.

Gabe was behind me. His warm hands started massaging my shoulders. "You smell a lot better."

I couldn't help it, I laughed. He kept massaging, his

thumbs finding the two tension points on either side of my neck. "Uh, maybe you shouldn't do that." My knot of tears was turning into dangerous warmth. The tension in my neck was draining into another kind of tension in my lower belly. I had to stay focused.

His hands lifted from my shoulders and I had only myself to blame. He came around the couch and held out a glass of white wine for me.

"I'm driving."

That one eyebrow arched. "No, you're not."

Swinging my legs down, I straightened my back and glared at him. "What does that mean? I am going to leave when my clothes are done."

Taking a drink of his wine, he moved his gaze over me. "In my T-shirt?"

Standing up, I was still forced to tilt my head back. My heart began hammering. I wasn't afraid, but . . . "You said you were putting my clothes in the wash!"

"I did. Doesn't mean I'll let you have them until morning."

I could probably drive home in his T-shirt. With no panties. Or shoes. I wrinkled my nose. I wasn't going to wear those shoes again anyway. But who did he think he was telling me what to do? "You can't keep me here. That's uh . . . kidnapping or illegal imprisoning or something. You're a cop, you know what it is!"

"You would rather I let you drive home? Sure, babe." He lifted his wine glass in agreement. "I'll do that. Maybe crazy Luke will be lurking around, following you. Then he breaks into your house, sets off the alarm, panics and shoots. Maybe he'll hit you, maybe he'll hit Ali, or maybe . . ." He let the sentence hang.

I closed my eyes. "Damn you! What if he goes there when I'm not there?"

"I got someone watching your house, all right?"

"Who?" Why were things happening that I didn't know about?

"Someone who owes me a favor." He brushed it off. "Besides that, I promised Rossi I would bring you down to the station in the morning for an interview. He's a little suspicious of you being at every crime scene lately."

"Rossi has a thing about crime scenes," I muttered, remembering his obsession when I had stumbled upon him at the scene of Perry's murder. Or he wanted the same half a mil that had got Blaine beaten up.

"Cops are funny that way, babe."

Frowning, something just occurred to me. "How did you know that Blaine was in his house? His car wasn't there. It's at the garage where he used to work. He told us he purposely left it there and had someone drive him home."

"He did that so you wouldn't know he was home," Gabe added with a wry grin. "You do bring out the best in your friends."

Ignoring that jab, my mind was whirling. "Weren't all the doors locked? Isn't that why you picked the lock on the back door? How did you know, Gabe?"

Draining the remainig wine in his glass, he said, "The front door had blood on it. That's why I picked the lock on the back door, to preserve any prints or trace evidence on the front door."

"Wouldn't want to murder the crime scene," I said under my breath, the pounding in my head growing. "I have to go home." Our gazes locked. Fear and danger had scraped back all my defenses, making me feel a full year's worth of repressed sexual desire. But more powerful than that was the need to check on my children. It thrummed through me, mixing with sexual tension until I wanted to jump out of my skin. A shiver rolled over me, but I held his stare.

"All right. I'll get you a pair of sweats and take you home. You can pick up your car here tomorrow."

Narrowing my eyes, I wondered if he knew how dangerous I was right now. "If you had sweats I could wear, why did you just give me this T-shirt?"

The glint in his eyes practically threw black sparks. His mouth bent into a bad-boy grin. "'Cause you look so damn good like that." His gaze rolled down, heating on my breasts and gaining fervor by the time he inspected my legs.

"Uh-huh. Or maybe you wanted to prevent me from just leaving?" A man of many depths, Gabe was. He wanted me. I could see that from the front of his jeans. If he tried hard enough, took me in his arms—he could coax me into it. Maybe take the decision out of my hands. But Gabe didn't operate that way. His deviousness ran in directions that I didn't fully comprehend.

"That too." He set his wineglass down. "Come on, I'll get you a pair of sweats."

"No way. I'm not going back there with you." I had to go home to my kids. If I went into his bedroom . . .

He looked back over his shoulder. "Don't trust yourself in my bedroom?"

I gave him a look. "You were a cop. You probably have handcuffs back there."

He winked. "Sure, babe, if that's what you want." He disappeared into the hall, but his chuckles lingered.

At home in my own bed, I couldn't sleep. The fall into the vomit-blood mess and finding Blaine beaten to a bloody pulp left me overtired and restless. And I was trying not to think of Gabe sleeping out in the living room.

I should have known that Gabe had conceded to taking me home too easily. He'd simply decided to stay here and do his security thing. Did he still have someone watching the house like he'd said when I'd told him I was worried about the boys? I hadn't seen anyone when we drove up the dirt road, but that didn't mean anything.

Still wearing Gabe's T-shirt that I had put on after my shower at his house, I got up and quietly padded to the kitchen. Tylenol PM would do the trick. Peeking into the boys' room, I saw that they were sleeping peacefully.

In the living room, I barely made out Gabe's still form on the couch beneath a thin sheet. Ali was on the floor, curled up on top of his neatly folded jeans and shirt. Her amber eyes glowed in the dark when she looked up at me. Then she laid her head back down and closed her eyes. Good girl, I thought, hoping the boys hadn't brushed her today and she'd shed a week's worth of long German shepherd hair all over Gabe's clothes. I went into the kitchen, found the Tylenol and poured out two. Getting a glass, I ran some water into it.

"Can't sleep?"

I jumped, hanging onto the glass, but dropping the blue pills down the sink. "Damn!" That was the last straw. Tears welled up and spilled down my face. I set the glass down and hung on to the edge of the sink. All my emotions poured over me, shaking my whole body, but I refused to make a sound. The last part of my mind that was not soggy from bawling prayed that Gabe would just go away. Leave me to my breakdown.

But he didn't. He pried my fingers off the counter edge and pulled me into his arms. No words. One hand rubbed my back, the other slid into my hair. The storm raged over me, then receded, leaving me exhausted. And embarrassed. I wanted to be tough.

"I don't want to be scared."

His hand nudged my head back. I could make out his face, see the somberness of his features. The intensity of his eyes. "Scared's okay."

"You ever get scared, Gabe? You know"—I hiccuped, but was too curious to care—"when you did the cop thing?"

Something shifted in him. A deep shadow stirred about his face. "Yes."

"Bet you didn't turn into a sobbing mess."

His face softened. "We all do it different, Sam. The trick is to not let fear make you stupid. You have to learn to think around it, push it aside and think."

"Thinking seems to get me into trouble." Like, say, thinking about the fact that he looked damn good clad only in a pair of boxers.

He grinned, brought both his hands up to cup my face and kissed me. Soft, gentle and brief. Then he fished out the bottle of Tylenol PM, poured out two tablets and handed them to me along with my abandoned water. "Go to bed, Sam."

I did. Before I thought too much. Before I forgot about my two sons who were in the house and needed a mom to protect them. Not to sleep with the hunk playing bodyguard and nursemaid.

I woke up in a strange state of panic. The kind that comes after having a vivid dream, then once awake, you can't remember if the dream was real or just a dream.

But it was real.

I was up earlier than usual. I heard Grandpa stirring in his room, so it must have been around six in the morning.

What did I have to do today? Oh, yeah, find out who killed Trent, and who was after the half million dollars. Also, where the hell the half million was hidden.

Hearing Grandpa's bedroom door open, I remembered that Gabe wanted to take me to the police station to talk to Rossi. But I needed to talk to Blaine. First thing, I needed to find out what Blaine knew. That meant I was going to have to sneak out of the house without Gabe and figure out a way to get into the hospital to talk to Blaine before visiting hours.

Getting out of bed, I headed for a quick shower. Maybe that would clear out the cobwebs in my head and help me come up with a plan.

After my record-time fast shower, I had a plan for getting into Blaine's hospital room and dressed for the part. Getting away from Gabe was going to be a little trickier. I headed out to the living room while frantically trying to come up with an excuse. As it turned out, fate gave me the exact opening I needed to lose Gabe for an hour or so.

Was it my fault that Gabe, the slick private eye, was careless enough to leave his keys on the coffee table while he took a shower?

"Hey, Mom, why did Gabe stay the night?" Joel asked as he trudged out of his bedroom.

I looked up from the keys on the coffee table to see TJ and Grandpa coming out of the kitchen to stand behind Joel. "Uhh, I left my car at his house while Gabe and I did some work. After that was done"—I was making this up as I went along—"he brought me here, then spent the night because . . ." Before I could change my mind, I snatched Gabe's keys off the coffee table. "He knew I'd need to borrow his truck. Tell Gabe I'll be back real soon!" I made my escape before the holes in that story swallowed me whole.

Gabe's truck was big. Sliding behind the wheel, I saw three suspicious faces and a dog snout peering out the front window at me. I ignored them. What choice did I have? Gabe would force me to go to the station this morning, and I wanted to talk to Blaine first. My car was still at Gabe's house, and Grandpa needed his Jeep to get the boys to school and go for his morning coffee-and-gossip session. I think Grandpa had a magic show today, too.

I swung out on Grand and headed for the Fifteen Freeway. It was a smooth ride. The truck was really comfortable. Power steering. I sighed; that was one of the sacrifices I'd made to drive a retro-awesome T-Bird. Thumbing through the tapes was a disappointment. He went for the hard stuff with names like Nine Inch Nails, Limp Bizkit, Korn and Slipknot. Ugh. I'd have to remember to check out the music next time I stole a car.

Inland Valley Regional Medical Center was quiet at this time of the morning. Visiting hours didn't start until eleven, but this was an emergency, so I figured it would be all right to sneak in. I'd given this some thought while I was in the shower and had discarded the idea of posing as a doctor or nurse seeing as how I could get arrested for that. Going up to the second-floor unit, I marched down the hallway, my shoes silent on the floor. My wardrobe had taken a recent beating, but I'd managed to put together a pretty good outfit. I had threaded a black belt through my white jeans and fitted my cell phone on one side and a fake pager that was really defense spray on the other. I had the cell phone turned off. It had rung five or six times in the truck. I was pretty sure that if I answered it, I was going to be linked to one hot Italian ex-cop. Not exactly the kind of hot I wanted to arouse in Gabe either. Hot, sweaty sex was good. Hot, pissed-off bad boy was another thing altogether.

The final touch was the black blazer. I carried a slim black briefcase with file folders neatly arranged inside. To finish the look, I had coiled my hair up into a French twist.

I was a private detective here to see my client. Damn, I was good. I was thinking I would mention my black belt in Tae Kwon Do. Maybe not. Even I couldn't think how to make that yellow belt hanging in my closet black. It'd taken me four months to move up to yellow.

No one stopped me. I sailed into Blaine's room to find him eating a breakfast of oatmeal, a boiled egg and fruit cup. He glanced up at me. "Sam?"

I blinked at the colors bleeding into one another on his face. "Jeez, Blaine," I muttered, sinking into one of those square metal chairs with cushions that expelled air when sat on.

"What are you doing here?"

The other bed in the room was empty. I was getting all the breaks today. "I got a few questions. How are you feeling?"

"Hell of a headache. But the Tylenol's helping. They don't want to give me narcotics 'cause of the concussion." He finished off his oatmeal.

Knowing that Blaine distrusted anything that grew on trees, I snagged the fruit cup for myself. "I need to know about Trent. Everything. Like where the money is, who his girlfriend was . . ." I stopped talking and speared a piece of cantaloupe to get rid of the sour taste in my mouth.

"I knew he screwed around. I didn't know he was skimming money, though." Blaine shrugged as he peeled the egg. "Sam, Trent did lots of women."

Gabe had said to know what questions to ask. "I have a theory." I eyed his cup of coffee but figured that was pushing too far. Should I trust Blaine? Running my gaze over his face, I had to admit that I didn't think he'd hit himself with the butt of a gun over and over. "What if Trent was seeing one of the dating consultants, like Hazel, and promised her that he'd take the money he had skimmed from the drug thing and run away with her. Then he'd dumped her for another girl? Would Hazel maybe kill Trent?"

Brushing his hands through the feathered front of his hair, Blaine winced. "Hazel? I don't know, Sam."

"Come on, Blaine. What was Hazel like?"

"Pretty, not real tall, but leggy. And she had an air about her, sort of aloof. All the men wanted to break through that shell. She had dark brown hair. I don't remember her eyes or anything."

Of course not. That would require looking at her face.

"Sam, we have pictures of them in the computer files. Open the employee files and you can pull up their pictures."

"What about Joan? I haven't found her yet either."

"She was younger than the rest, and newer. I only saw her once before I quit doing that shit. Blonde, big breasts."

Naturally. I didn't bother asking what color her eyes were. "What about the money, Blaine? Where would Trent have hidden money like that?"

"In a bank somewhere?"

Shaking my head, I said, "No, I had Grandpa search around for any accounts under his name. . . ." I was cut off before I could finish.

"Visiting hours do not start until eleven."

I looked back over my shoulder at a woman who was my mother's age. She was standing in the doorway, both her hands on her white-clad hips, and she had a serious look on her face beneath her dark, short-cropped hair. I stood up, pulled my business card out of the pocket of my briefcase and handed it to her. "I am a private detective. I needed to see my client before he is released from the hospital."

"I don't care—"

I held up a hand to stop her and noticed that I needed a manicure. "He was attacked last night. His life is in danger. I am in charge of his security. Now I am very sorry if that does not fit into your schedule, nurse, but my client's physical safety is at stake here."

She looked down at the card, then back up at me. Her

brown eyes were unwavering, but I thought I saw a soften-
ing around her mouth.

"Get out, before I call security."

Damn, that hurt.

Juggling my large coffee with my briefcase while trying
to get the key into the door of Heart Mates, I made a mental note to stop at the store before returning Gabe's truck
to him. I was sure there was a cleaner or something that
would get that first cup of coffee out of the rug on the passenger side.

At least I didn't spill it on my white jeans.

I locked the door behind me and went to Blaine's desk.
I had a computer in my office, but Blaine's computer always seemed to work for him, so maybe it would work for
me. Sitting in his chair, I pushed all the switches and but-
tons to fire up them rams or whatever they were. While
the screen blinked and beeped, I sipped the coffee.

I wanted pictures of the two remaining dating consultants. There wasn't any reason I could name, more like an
instinct. Something lurking around in my brain sending
out signals. A picture of those two women would maybe
fish that something out and clear up the signal. All the little icons appeared on the screen. I used the mouse to
guide the cursor to *Employee Records*. From there, I typed in
Joan's name and waited.

There she was. Blonde, salon tan, big teeth, pug nose
and brown eyes. All the little details that Blaine missed. I
studied her. Youthful sexiness almost fried the wires of the
computer.

Bet I'd found a pair of her panties.

Disgust made me open the drawers of Blaine's desk
until I found that special paper he used to print photos.
Then I stared at the printer. I slid the paper in the top.
There was only one way to do it, limiting the ways I could

screw it up. Taking a chance, I hit the print icon and held my breath.

Miraculously, the printer grumbled, then started printing.

Flush with success, I typed in Hazel's name. While watching the screen shiver and quake, I gulped the rest of my coffee. But a picture did not appear. All that came up was the name and date of her hiring and termination.

Everything else was gone.

"Shit." I leaned forward and stared at the screen. I remembered now that I had noticed the lack of information when Blaine gave me the employee files, and that had been why I'd put Hazel on the bottom of the stack. At the time, I had been more interested in learning about Perry and his gun-totin' brother, Luke.

Okay, I was going to have to do this the old-fashioned way. Behind the interview room was a small storage area next to the bathroom. There were several gray metal file cabinets in there. Determined to find a picture of Hazel, I left the picture of Joan on Blaine's desk, along with my empty coffee cup, and headed through the interview room to the door that led to the storage area. A poster depicting a couple holding hands in snorkeling gear on a white sand beach in the Caribbean stared at me. I paused with my hand on the doorknob.

My imagination had no trouble putting Trent and big-breasted blondie, Joan, in the place of the couple on the poster. Trent had always been running after the dream on the travel poster, the best car, the newest cell phone, the oldest wine. . . .

None of it had been real. He'd had two great sons and hardly spent time with them. He'd rather spend time with his classic cars because they were a part of the dream.

Blinking, I pushed open the door. I might be living in a run-down house with my grandpa, but it was real and I loved it. Just like I loved Heart Mates. I wasn't going to abandon my dream the second a better or newer one came along.

The room was dark. I reached to the right inside wall to flip the switch of the florescent light.

A warm, hard hand closed over my wrist, yanked me into the darkness and swung me around. I screamed as I flew into a hard metal surface. When my forehead slammed into a metal protrusion, I recognized the filing cabinet just as my legs folded beneath me and I slumped to the ground.

9

A huge buzzing noise in my ears made me dizzy. Blinking, I took stock and discovered that my forehead hurt like hell. I was lying on the thin carpet of my storeroom.

And someone was in there with me.

The buzzing cleared as I struggled to my feet. Fear made me need to get moving. *Run.* Standing, I could see light coming in from the office through the opened door.

I heard someone out there. My eyes filled with a warm liquid. Moving toward the door, I ran the back of my fingers over my eyes to clear them. My hand came away with smears of blood. Must have cut my forehead on the filing cabinet.

Man, I was going to have a colorful knot and would probably end up looking like Blaine. Reaching the doorway, I put my bloody hand on the door jamb and looked down. Shit. There was blood on my white pants, mixed with streaks of gray dust. Anger roared up in my breastbone. Did these treasure hunters think I had an endless supply of clothes for them to ruin? These jeans were expensive!

My belt! I had my pepper spray stuff in the fake pager

clipped to my belt. Unsnapping the unit, I held my breath and listened. Stuff was being flung onto a surface—stuff from my purse! Wiping more blood out of my eyes, I looked down at the pager unit and located the button to release the spray. Walking as softly as possible, I spotted a hulking figure hunched over my purse, throwing lipsticks, a stack of my new business cards, my empty wallet—he took my money!

"Hey!" I bellowed, rushing out with my pager spray.

Grabbing my keys, he ran around the desk to fumble at the door for a second before unlocking it and fleeing outside. I went after him. No way was he stealing my—"Ohmigod! Gabe's truck!"

Going through the door to the almost-empty parking lot I remembered the keys I'd snatched off the coffee table while Gabe was in the shower. I heard the squeal of tires pulling into the parking lot, but ignored that.

I focused on Luke. It was definitely Luke trying to fit the keys I'd filched into the door of Gabe's truck. It was just my enduring luck that Luke had pulled that key ring out of my purse. My heart pounded. "Stop!" I bellowed as I hurried around the front of the truck.

Blaine's Hyundai shrieked to a stop and spilled out a big man. I couldn't make out who the man was with all the blood in my eyes. Not Blaine—he was in the hospital.

The lock in the truck door clicked open, recapturing my attention. I had to stop Luke from stealing Gabe's truck! I threw myself against the door just as he got it open. Ignoring the sickening pain in my head, I aimed the pager full of pepper spray.

That was when I saw the second man approaching. With a gun. That was all I could make out from my blood-filled eyes. "No!" I yelled and depressed the spray.

"Son of a bitch!"

Before I could figure out who was yelling, I was pulled

from the car and thrown to the ground. Rolling over, I climbed back to my feet and stood up in time to see Gabe's black truck back up into the tail end of the Hyundai, shoving it out of the way like it was no more than a bicycle, and then speed off.

I stood there, afraid to wipe my eyes and get some of that spray in them. Who was the other man? I must have missed Luke with the spray.

Uh-oh.

Turning, I saw Gabe doubled over. His muscular back gleamed in the bright morning sun. He'd ripped his T-shirt right off and was furiously rubbing at his eyes.

Running was pretty much the only solution I could think of to this latest disaster.

"Don't move." He managed to stand up.

I couldn't see well enough to know if he was blinking or staring at me. "Umm, maybe you should go inside and wash out your eyes," I suggested, hoping like hell that he'd left the keys in the Hyundai. I'd drive blind before I'd face that Italian temper.

He grabbed my elbow and dragged me into Heart Mates with him. So much for that plan.

Inside the tiny bathroom, I was thrust onto the toilet seat. Good thing it was down or I'd be soaking my butt in the toilet bowl. Gabe turned on the water and splashed his face and eyes. "Why don't I go call the police while you do that?"

"Mmph!"

Eyeing his naked chest, I decided not to make a run for it. He could body-slam me into the bathroom wall with no more than a single step backwards. Biting my lip, I tried to gauge how mad he was. "This wasn't my fault." My head was starting to seriously throb. I grabbed the towel off the small counter and wiped the blood out of my eyes, then used it to apply pressure to the bleeding gash on my forehead. I did not want to look in the mirror. "Luke attacked me in the storage room. I didn't even know he was in there!" My voice was rising.

The water shut off. I peeked from behind the towel. Gabe was drying his face and neck with a towel while staring at . . . Wait, if he had the towel, what did I have? I pulled the cloth off my forehead.

Gabe's black shirt. Slowly, I forced my eyes up to him. Even that movement was starting to hurt. "Sorry?" I offered lamely.

He did that eyebrow dance. "For stealing my truck? Or for letting Luke steal it after you? Wait, maybe you're sorry for getting in my line of sight and preventing me from stopping Luke from stealing my truck."

Gabe paused to breathe. His voice was getting louder, deeper, and he was kinda scaring me. "Gabe, I . . ."

"Once he was in the truck, I could have still shot him and stopped him, but you had to go and spray rat poison in my eyes." He closed his red-rimmed and puffy eyes, his mouth looking pained. "I heard a crash. What did Luke hit with my truck?"

Lie! My mind screamed, but my throbbing head couldn't think of a suitable fabrication. "Blaine's Hyundai. This probably isn't the time to ask what you're doing with Blaine's car?" I pushed Gabe's shirt back into my forehead. It was already ruined.

"My truck was gone, your grandpa needed his car to get the kids to school, so I had him drop me at the garage where Blaine left his car. You remember, he hid his car at the garage he used to work at so you wouldn't know he was at home."

"You didn't have the keys." I pointed out, ignoring his sarcasm.

He just looked at me.

"Oh." If he could pick the lock on Blaine's house, why couldn't he hot-wire his car? "You stole it."

The long column of his throat convulsed. "Actually, I called him on my cell phone and asked his permission, right after I gave up trying to call you."

This was going nowhere. "I only borrowed your truck. I was going to return it." I tried to calm myself down. Luke had been in my storeroom. I had the distinct impression that he'd been staying in there.

No wonder Rossi hadn't been able to find him. I shuddered, then winced at the pain in my head. "I'm sorry about your truck. I'll—I don't know, I'll do something about it. But right now, I have to . . ." What did I have to do? God, it was so hard to think. Probably I should go over to the hospital and get stitches in my head. I saw on one of those hospital shows once that, after something like six hours, they can't put stitches in because of infection. So I had about five and a half hours before my stitches window closed.

Windows . . . Frowning, I remembered. The picture! Hazel's picture. Slipping by Gabe, I left the tiny bathroom and went to the metal filing cabinet. I went to E for Employee Records. From there, I pulled out a file of pictures. Slamming the filing cabinet shut, I headed out of the storage room.

Gabe followed me. He stopped right behind me as I set the file on Blaine's desk. "You know, I can have you arrested for stealing my truck. And for assault with that defense spray."

He wasn't going to let this go. I dropped his T-shirt on the floor and sat in the chair. Before I could open the file, Linda Simpkins rushed into the office. "Sam, I brought that list . . . oh, what happened to your head?"

"An accident." While I had been the one to call Linda

and ask her to drop by her list of anyone who had been in her house ASAP, I couldn't deal with this right now. "Is that the list I asked for? Why don't you leave it with me and I'll get back to you later."

Linda went seamlessly into mother mode. "You might need stitches. Let me take a look."

"It's fine," I insisted, wanting to get back to the pictures. I held out my hand for the list she had brought me. "I'll call you today with any information I come up with from your list."

Linda started to hand over the computer-printed list, but her hand faltered halfway. "Sam, why do you have a picture of Joan?" She dropped the list on the desk and picked up the picture I had printed out of Joan.

Stunned, I said, "You know her?"

"Of course, she's in our Couples Bunko. We play every Thursday night."

"Wait right here." I got up and had to fight off a wave of dizziness. Then I rushed into my office. I got Molly's list out of the desk. The words were a little fuzzy, but if I twisted up my face, I could make them out. There it was—Couples Bunko. Setting the list down, I went back out to the lobby. "Linda, how long have you been playing Couples Bunko?"

"Oh, a year or so now."

"And how long has Joan been there? Is she married?"

"Joan's been there for about four months and yeah, she's married. They're both real friendly."

I couldn't make sense of it. Except that she had said they played on Thursday night. Today was Thursday. "Linda, do you think I could go to Bunko with you to-night? Maybe fill in for your husband?"

"It's Couples Bunko, Sam."

"Oh, right." It was an effort to not scream at her. I'd

been uncoupled when Trent died. That and the fact that I'd dropped a few pounds, made a surgical enhancement and forsaken the housewife wardrobe of dumpy comfort made me undesirable. "What about substitutes? Is anyone going to be missing tonight?"

"Well, yeah, but we were going to play with ghosts. You would have to have a boyfriend or something."

I smiled. It hurt the swelling on my forehead. "I do have a boyfriend."

Linda's eyes traveled up to pause on my forehead, then over me to crawl around Gabe's naked chest. Her thin lips disappeared as she pursed her mouth in disapproval. "I see. Well, I suppose you could fill in tonight. But how do you think that will help my case?"

Linda thought Gabe and I had been doing the wild thing and I got hurt. She was giving me the female disgust, but she was still willing to use me to find her missing sex tapes. God, was everyone a hypocrite? "It'll help," I assured her. Maybe not her, but me. Maybe Joan could tell me if she'd taken my husband away from his mistress and if that mistress was Hazel.

Two police cruisers pulled into the parking lot, drawing my attention away from Linda. I hadn't called them. What were they doing here? Unless Gabe called them. Hadn't he said he could have me arrested?

"Sam, why are the police here?" Linda asked.

To arrest me seemed like the wrong answer. Would Gabe really have me arrested? My heart pounded furiously. Dammit, he'd had me in his T-shirt last night, stranded at his house with no panties. I tried talking through clenched teeth. "It has nothing to do with your case. They are here on another matter."

"Oh."

I could hear her brain clicking. "A private matter,

Linda." I gave her a meaningful look, although with a swelling gash in the middle of my forehead, I'm not sure I pulled it off.

"I have to go. Call me later about tonight, Sam." She cast one last stare at Gabe, then left.

The police were at the door, but I swiveled my chair around to Gabe. "You called them."

"Yep, when I pulled into the parking lot and spotted Luke trying to steal my truck. Thought if I was going to do a takedown, I ought to have some backup."

"A takedown? You mean they aren't here to arrest me?"

His mouth twitched, but he didn't answer. He walked past me to greet the police at the door.

The pain was starting to wear me out. Fatigue was seeping in at the edges of my muscles and making me feel sluggish. I heard all the cop voices throwing around official-sounding terms, but I blocked it all out.

Setting Joan's computer-printed photo aside, I opened the file of employee records, thumbed through, and found Hazel's records. Her application was on top. There was a photo clipped behind it.

"Sam?"

I ignored the voices. The need to see the picture was too strong. Lifting the employment application, I looked at the picture of Hazel. "Ohmigod." Now I knew why the name Hazel had been trying to send signals to my over-loaded brain.

"Sam." This time it was Gabe's voice. He was leaning on the other side of the desk, his dark Italian eyes fixed on me. "What is it?"

I turned the picture for him to see. "This is Hazel. She's the one I sold Trent's classic Mustang to."

Standing in front of the hospital entrance waiting for Rossi, I caught the looks folks gave me. I had blood on my white pants and two stitches in my forehead covered by a tidy white bandage. Well, what'd they expect in a hospital? I had called Detective Rossi's cell phone number from my cell phone while the gash in my head was getting stitched. I had the picture of Hazel in my briefcase. A female police officer had driven me to the hospital.

I didn't know where Gabe went. He did most of the talking to the cops, insisted I go to the hospital, got into Blaine's banged-up primer-paint Hyundai and left. But that was Gabe. I wondered if he would play boyfriend for me tonight at Couples Bunko. No telling. Maybe I would arrange something with one of Heart Mates' male customers.

Rossi pulled up in a white Toyota Camry. The leather interior was cool and slick. "Nice car." I leaned my head back and closed my eyes.

"I went to Heart Mates straight from home this morning when I got the call." The car slid smoothly out of the hospital onto the road that led to the Fifteen Freeway. "You going to have a scar?"

Opening my eyes, I turned to him. He had a nice profile, firm but not sharp. There was a shadow of crow's feet that deepened when he smiled. Right now his expression appeared concerned. "A thin one. Guess it's better than dead. Have you guys found Gabe's truck yet?" Rossi had gotten to Heart Mates right after I left for the hospital, or at least that's what he told me on the phone. I assumed they had police out looking for Gabe's truck with Luke inside it. Maybe they put out one of those BOLO—Be On the Look Out—things. I was too tired to ask.

He shook his head. "No, but it's pretty clear from what we found in the storage room that Luke's been sleeping there nights."

A shiver raced up my spine. Three Tylenol had pretty much killed my headache, but my fear was growing.

"Why did you go see Blaine this morning before coming to give your statement to me, Sam?" Rossi asked.

He was expertly weaving through the light morning traffic. There were vast spaces of open land in Wildomar, where the hospital is located. The sun had dried out the foliage to a crisp brown. "It seemed more important to find out what Blaine knew first. In case you hadn't noticed, I'm in a little trouble these days."

"You attract trouble, Sam. You had no idea Luke was in your storeroom? Didn't you change the locks when you bought this place?"

I flushed and focused on the road. "No, it never occurred to me."

"It looks like Luke must have a key. Probably took it off his brother after he killed him."

"He said he didn't kill his brother," I reminded Rossi.

"He beat the hell out of Blaine with the same kind of gun that his brother was killed with and left a gash in your forehead this morning. Do you think he would tell you the truth?"

"Because he thought I killed his brother. It wasn't like he just denied doing it, he actually looked surprised when I said he killed his brother." I stopped talking. Rossi was right, damn his handsome face. Handsome men were grief. I think handsome men run the hell for women. Sighing, I tried to gather my thoughts, "I'm running out of time. I'm supposed to show up with that money tomorrow night. I don't have the money. And even if I did, two people that I know of are after it." I hadn't had breakfast, and my stomach growled loudly. "Hey," I finally noticed, "you passed the turnoff for the police station."

His gaze slid off the road and centered on me. "We'll pick up something to eat and I'll take you home so that you can change clothes. We'll eat there and talk."

Hell. Handsome men were in charge of hell for women

and what was I going to do? "You hoping to get another glimpse of my thong, Rossi?"

His chuckle was sexy.

Both of the boys were in school, Grandpa was doing a magic show for a children's hospital in Orange County and I was alone in my house with Rossi. Except for Ali. She opened one eye from her place by her water bowl on the cool linoleum floor, then yawned and went back to sleep.

"Yeah, you're a real guard dog," I muttered, getting a can of coffee out of the refrigerator and dumping some of the crystals into the coffeemaker. Out of the corner of my eye, I got a glimpse of Ali's head coming up, and her long nose sniffing the air.

Putting the coffee away, I turned around just in time to see Ali snatch a glazed donut out of the opened box on the table and run to the back of the house.

"Thief!" I called after her without any real passion. I had a soft spot for a female who goes after what she wants.

Rossi was standing there looking into the box of eleven donuts. "She did that without touching the others. She was so fast, I didn't even . . ."

I cracked my first smile. "She's on the most-wanted list of the Animal Control."

His gaze lifted to me. I turned away and got two coffee cups down and filled them before the coffeemaker was done brewing. Taking the cups to the table, I pulled my briefcase off the chair and took out the picture I had stuffed in it. Placing the photo on the table, I said, "This is Hazel. She used to work for—"

"I know who she is."

I looked up at Rossi. His face was neutral as he stared at the picture. "Oh, have you found her? Talked to her?"

"No. Not yet. We're still searching for her. I think she may have left the area."

"No, she hasn't! Or at least, she was here when I sold her Trent's Mustang!"

Rossi pulled a chair over and sat down. We were knee to knee. "You think you sold her Trent's Mustang?"

"I know I did. I remember her. She's hard to forget." I pointed with my chin toward the picture. Tall, slender, long chestnut hair, Hazel had things working for her. She screamed class. In the picture, she didn't actually smile, but did more of a bored lip curve. She was the kind of woman that very rich men buy.

"You think this links her to Trent?"

"What do you think, Rossi? Someone killed Trent, that much was obvious from the candy left for my kids. It was likely a woman." I took a breath and ran down the same reasons that I gave Gabe. Then mentioned the idea I had of a kind of lovers' triangle between Trent, Hazel and another woman, possibly Joan. "And then she bought his car. Why?"

He leaned forward. "Why do you think, Sam? What would she get from that car?"

I remembered what I had gotten from that car. A sour taste washed up the back of my throat. "Trent had hidden about a dozen pairs of panties in the trunk. They weren't mine," I added.

"And you found them after he died?"

"Yes. I sold his car and spent the money on . . . uh, me and the boys." Our knees were touching. His blue gaze dropped to my breasts. Tension curled in my belly. "Do you think he had the money in the car?" I blurted out.

He found my eyes again. "If he did, and Hazel found it, then she wouldn't be threatening you now to get the money."

"We have to find Hazel."

He nodded. "Did you file a Notice of Release of Liability with the DMV?"

I blinked. "What's that?"

Rossi shook his head in frustration. "It's a form that you fill out to make sure that no parking tickets or whatever go on your record in case the buyer of the car doesn't do a change of ownership."

A distant memory surfaced. "I think maybe Grandpa had me fill out something like that . . . I really don't remember. What would that tell you?"

"Well, it would give us a trail. But you must have the license number of the car. I can run that through the DMV and see where it leads. I'll do that as soon as I get to the station."

"What about Luke?" Okay, I was scared. Dammit, I was tired of being scared.

And where the hell did Gabe go? What was he doing? Why did he leave? I suspected it had something to do with borrowing his truck, then getting it stolen. Men—so emotional over a hunk of metal. Sheesh.

"Hey." Rossi cupped his hand around my cheek, staying clear of my bandaged forehead. "Take it easy, Sam. I'm here to help you."

I looked into those blue eyes and melted. "Thank you, Rossi. I appreciate you bringing me home."

"No problem. Let's take it one thing at a time. I'll look for Hazel, and you think about the money. Where could it be? And stay out of Luke's hiding places."

"If Hazel thought the Mustang had something to do with the money, what would it be?" I summoned Trent up from the worm-infested grave I'd assigned him to in my head. Trent always insisted on only the best for himself. The best car, best briefcase . . . where would he hide money? His sister? No, I mentally shook my head. Trent craved possessions and he didn't share—case in point, he'd never wanted me to drive the two classics. "He had the money in his possession somewhere. Where he could take it out and look at it."

"Good. So any ideas?"

Rossi's hand on my face was distracting me. Dropping my gaze, I thought while staring at his elbow resting on the table next to my coffee cup. "I suppose it's possible he stashed the money in the Mustang, but like you said, Hazel would have found it. I don't know." Frustration clawed at me. Then a horrible thought hit me headlong, and I raised my gaze to Rossi's eyes. "His Beemer! It was repossessed. What if it was in there?"

Rossi shook his head. "Too dangerous. First, someone could easily steal his car. Second, he was meeting with drug dealers, and he wouldn't carry that kind of cash around them, unless he was a special kind of stupid."

"Trent was not stupid. Greedy, egotistical and horny, yes. But not stupid. He could sell you the wallpaper off the wall in your office. He was good-looking and charming to a fault. But not stupid." It was all rushing back in uncomfortable gushes. I bought his lines of bullshit for too many years. No, the title of stupid belonged solely to me back then, but no longer.

Rossi dropped his hand from my face, hit my coffee cup and dumped the hot liquid smack onto my lap.

"Shit!" I leaped up, then launched into a frantic dance. "Hot. Ouch. Hot."

Rossi grabbed hold of my arm. "Get the pants off. Hurry." His voice was calm, steady and soothing.

I unbuttoned the jeans and peeled them down my legs. The air hit my wet skin and cooled my legs. Toeing off my shoes, I stepped out of the pants and looked down at my legs. They were slightly pink.

"You don't look burned."

Rossi knelt down on one leg. I could feel his breath on my thighs.

"Would you look at that?"

"What?" There was a distinct catch at the back of my throat. Rossi's thick brown hair was swept back off his face. He lifted his gaze up, then reached out a hand and ran his finger across my thigh. "No permanent marker."

Danger signals went off like a fire alarm. Trouble was, I'd been having a lot of danger lately, and no sex. I opened my mouth, almost believing I was going to tell Rossi I was fine and to please get his face away from my . . .

"But you do have on a thong." His finger slid up my thigh and beneath the edge of lace lining my white thong.

10

Ali shot out of the hallway and cut through the kitchen, barking and growling as she ran to the sliding glass door that led to the backyard.

I blinked, stuck on the sight of Rossi's finger beneath the rim of my panties. Then he withdrew the finger and rolled up to his feet, pulling his gun out of his shoulder holster.

Slowly, I turned to see what Ali was growling at.

"Do you know that woman staring through your sliding glass door?" Rossi asked.

Could this day get any worse? "It's my mother."

"Your mother?" Amusement danced beneath his words. "Has she always had this timing?"

I was dressed in a black shirt and white thong. "Oh, yeah, always. Why don't you go let her in and I'll be right back." I escaped through the kitchen and down the hall to my bedroom, slamming the door behind me. Leaning against the door, I eyed the window across the room. I thought about running away.

But I didn't have my car. It was still at Gabe's house. Going to my closet, I pulled out a pewter skirt and drew it up over my thong. Exchanging the black shirt for a rose one, I slipped my feet into a pair of sling-backs and headed for the bathroom.

I damn near screamed when I saw myself in the mirror. My hair was a wild mass of blond-streaked tangles. The bruise on my forehead captured all the blues and greens of the rainbow. Most of my make-up had been worn off and I had bags under my eyes.

No way was I facing my mother like this.

A little foundation, some powder, smidgen of mascara, dab of concealer, blush, lipstick, hairbrush . . .

An improvement, but not by much. Sighing, I put down the hairspray and decided I'd stalled long enough. Truth was, I had expected my mother to storm right over Rossi and barge into my room. Wonder if Rossi handcuffed her? Going out into the hallway, I almost tripped over a lump of fur.

Looking down, I saw Ali lying across my doorway. "Hey, what's the matter? Mom scare you? Aren't you the same dog who chased after the six goons with a switchblade?"

Ali opened one amber eye, rolled over on her side and went back to sleep.

Or she was pretending to be unconscious? Clever girl. I stepped over her and went back into the kitchen.

Rossi was sitting at the table with my mom, drinking coffee and eating donuts. I stopped in surprise. My mom's wedge haircut seemed a little softer this morning. Her pale blue skirt and jacket were wrinkle-free and attractive. She had a smile on her perfectly glossed mouth.

"Samantha's father was in the war, you know. It's a sad story really. A love story. We were just kids, so in love, and well . . ." Mom turned away, her face awash in bittersweet sadness. "We couldn't wait, you know? But he'd be home on leave soon, and we planned to get married." Lifting her mug of coffee, Mom let the moment play out. "Then I got the telegram. Samantha's father was killed in action, leaving me pregnant with his baby."

I swallowed a groan and glanced around the kitchen. My white jeans were soaking in the sink. Which Samantha's Father story was that one? I tried to remember—number fourteen or twenty-two? There were so many of them. Squaring my shoulders, I said, "Mom, what brings you over here?"

"Samantha, why, there you are! What do you mean what brings me here? Heart Mates wasn't open, and rumors are flying that police were all over there this morning." She paused, then added, "You look dreadful. Will you have a scar?" Turning to lift her tote-sized leather bag off the ground, she said, "Where's that card for my plastic surgeon?"

"Mom, I don't need . . ."

"Detective Rossi told me all about your little incident. The sooner we get that place sold, the better. And the coffee on your jeans"—she was still rifling in her bag—"I don't know if we can get that stain out. Really, Samantha, you have to be more careful than to trip with hot coffee. What if you had scarred your legs?"

Indeed, what if I had? Then what? Oh, that's right, I wouldn't be able to get a man. "Mom, not now."

She stopped rifling. To my surprise, my mom got up and walked over to me. "Samantha, are you all right? Honey, you look tired." She reached out and took my hands. "Let's get the boys out of school and go away. Just until the police get this mess cleaned up."

She was worried. Really worried. My mother avoided reality as long as she could. But a moment of clarity had struck, and she was facing the fact that we could be in danger. Touched, I could see the very real and solid concern in her expertly lined eyes. I swallowed. It didn't matter that I was in my thirties with two sons of my own, the little girl inside of me basked in my mom's love and caring. I squeezed her hand. "It's okay, Mom. Running won't solve this anyway. But the pieces are starting to fit." Sort of.

"What about your grandpa, Samantha? He's an old man."

I had to grin. "Don't let him hear you say that!" I did understand her worry for Grandpa. I worried too.

She smiled back. "You'll let me know if you need me?"

My mom and me, we weren't the touchy-huggy type, but I hugged her anyway. In spite of her flaws, she truly loved us and, while her rearranging of reality to suit her needs drove me crazy, I knew she thought she was helping. Maybe even protecting me. I suspected that the deepest truth inside my mom was that—whatever had really happened with my bio-dad—she didn't want that disaster or heartbreak to happen to me. That was why she fought so hard to keep Trent pure and good in her memories. Because at least then he had died loving me, not abandoning me. Releasing her from the hug, I assured her, "Of course, Mom."

Recovering her composure quickly, she said, "Okay, well then, I need to go meet some clients." She went back to the table and began gathering up her large purse. "Oh, and Samantha, don't eat any of those donuts. I had quite a view of your backside from the window." She lowered her voice. "Cellulite." Then she was gone.

I stood for one second in the kitchen, then snapped out of my trance and went to the table. I pulled out a huge chocolate donut and sat down to seriously devour it.

"Your mother?"

Glancing up, I nodded at Rossi. "My mother," I said, then took another bite of donut.

"She's, uh . . . Was that true about your father?"

Getting up, I found a clean cup and filled it with coffee.

"Doubt it, but can't say for sure. Mom changes the story of my dad like other women change purses."

"That might account for . . ."

Sipping the coffee, I studied the eight donuts left in the box. Glaze, jelly, sugar, buttermilk—that'd do. I'd sunk my teeth into the rich pastry when I realized Rossi had left the sentence hanging. He was sitting in the chair watching me. "Account for what?"

That slow, sexy grin appeared. "You."

Swallowing my bite, I glared at him. "You've had your last peek at my thongs, Rossi." God, when exactly had I turned into such a lusty gal?

"Next time you won't be wearing underwear?"

"Get out, Rossi." I couldn't do this. "Go run the license plate on the Mustang I sold to Hazel." I went to the tablet of paper by the phone and wrote down the license plate number from memory. Tearing it off, I stomped back to Rossi and handed it to him. "Find Hazel and maybe we can end this nightmare."

He stood up. "You got chocolate frosting on your mouth."

I backed up a step. "Go." Hadn't Gabe taken off on me? Rossi had every intention of doing that too. Of course, he just thought maybe he'd get a little sex first.

He closed the distance between us, but didn't touch me. "It's just sex, Sam. Why so skittish? You were getting hot before your mother arrived."

"Are all you cops the same?"

His expression shifted. "Thought you didn't have a boyfriend? You and Gabe got a thing? He sure was running interference last night when I got to the hospital to interview you two and Blaine."

"You didn't want to interview me at the hospital last night, Rossi. I stank, remember?"

"I never said that, Sam."

His voice had softened and gone quiet. I blinked. "Gabe said . . ."

"Everyone lies, Sam. Even Gabe. He's an ex-cop whose career ended on a bullet. Things like that can make a man bitter. Can make him think the world owes him something. Can make a half mil look mighty good. You see where I'm going with this?"

The donuts turned to rubber in my belly. "You think Gabe might be after the money? But . . ." I shook my head. "You don't understand Gabe. He's not like that."

"Hey, I'm not saying he is after the money, Sam. I'm just telling you to be careful. All we really know about Gabe is what he's told you."

Angel had a blood-red Trans Am that screamed down the street as she drove me to Gabe's house to pick up my car. Inside, her CD player was belting out a ballad by the latest Latin sensation. Was it Marc Anthony or Ricky Martin?

I couldn't concentrate on the music thumping out of the stereo enough to determine the singer. So many things stirred in my brain. Where was Hazel? Why had she bought Trent's Mustang from me? I tried to make some order of this. Hazel had worked for Perry at Heart Mates, I knew that. She must have met Trent there. She had obviously known Trent was dead and wanted his Mustang for something. What? It didn't seem possible that Trent could have hidden a half million in there, and I didn't find it.

But how would Hazel know that? Had Trent told her he didn't let me drive the Mustang? Had she thought that, even after his death, I had obeyed Trent?

I didn't even want to think about what that said about me. I had been that person. I couldn't even blame that on Trent. I made my own choices.

Hearing the song on the CD player change, I let my thoughts slide away from my own failings and back to Hazel. Had she sent me the gold-lettered threats and candy warning?

Then where did Joan fit in? How did she end up on both Molly's and Linda's lists of people in their homes? There was no connection between the missing sex tapes and Trent's skimming money, was there? It didn't make sense. But at least I should get a chance to talk to Joan tonight at Couples Bunko. Somehow, I'd talk Gabe into playing the part of my boyfriend.

And what about Gabe? Rossi was right. All I did know about him was what he had told me. That twisted inside of me. I thought of Gabe as my friend. My hot and sexy friend. He couldn't be involved in this mess, could he?

"Sam." Angel's throaty voice cut into my merry-go-round thoughts set to a Latin music background. "Didn't you say Gabe's truck was stolen?"

We were already on Gabe's street. There, parked in the sloping driveway of his one-story house sat his black truck, right next to my white T-Bird. The left rear fender had a dent that marred the line of the truck. I wondered what Blaine's poor Hyundai looked like.

"Quick, Angel, drop me here." I fished in my purse for my keys. I wanted to get the car and get out of here.

I wasn't ready for Gabe. I had to talk to him about going to Couples Bunko, but I couldn't bring myself to do it now. Not with Rossi's warning ringing in my ear.

I was learning to be more careful.

Closing my hand around the keys, I opened the door of the Trans Am and got out on the sidewalk. It idled louder than a Lear jet. Shutting the door, I leaned in the opened window. "Thanks, Angel."

"Where are you going, Sam? Maybe I can help you."

"I'm going to see our . . ." I closed my eyes, surprised at

how easily I had slid back into the married *our.* "That is, my old travel agent. I have the pictures of Joan and Hazel. I want to see if she recognizes them."

"Want me to come?"

My head throbbed. In four days, my body had taken more abuse than the births of both my children put together. I was sore. "No, I'll be fine." I had to be. "I'm going to be back in time to pick the boys up from school. Don't worry."

"I worry, Sam. You want me to get the boys?"

I shook my head. The need to see them myself was unexplainable, but very real. "I'll call you."

It finally dawned on me that Angel wasn't meeting my eyes. She was leaning down so that her long red hair swept her thighs and her green eyes kept wandering over my shoulder as I leaned into the car window.

The hairs on the back of my neck snapped to attention. "He's behind me, isn't he?" I whispered.

She shifted the car into gear. "Gotta run, Sam. Call me." She gunned the engine and peeled out. I watched until the car disappeared around a curve. Sighing, I said, "I'm getting my car." Without looking at him, I straightened my shoulders and turned toward my car parked next to his truck. Keys in my hand, I marched between the two vehicles and got to the driver's-side door. The hard top was on, and the car was locked. I slid the key into the door.

Gabe's hand closed around my wrist. "We need to talk. And to plan."

He didn't sound mad. Looking back over my shoulder, I said, "Rossi said they didn't find your truck."

"The police didn't, I did. Luke abandoned it at his old apartment parking lot. He probably borrowed a friend's car from there."

So he'd been looking for his truck. Staring at him, I

said, "Now that we have your priorities straightened out, let go of my hand!"

"No."

"I have more defense spray on my key chain. I have a stun gun in my purse."

His black eyes drifted up to my forehead. "Got stitches, huh?"

Why did he do this? He didn't care. That's why I didn't want a man; they encouraged a fantasy life. I read books for fantasy. Romance novels were a great escape. But in real life, I didn't need the heartache. "Let go, Gabe. You got your truck back, what more do you want from me?"

"Hey, babe, you set the rules. I'm just living by them. You asked for my help, I'm helping."

On second thought, I needed a fight. Jerking the keys from the door lock did not loosen his hold on my wrist. "All right, fine. Talk."

"In the house."

He tugged me behind him, leading me between the two cars, up the front sidewalk and into his house. He didn't let go of my wrist. Probably he thought I'd douse him with the defense spray on my key ring.

Once in his study, he let me go. I crossed my arms over my chest and glared at him. He wasn't Rossi good-looking. Rossi had the blue-eyed suave looks that encouraged trust.

Gabe had the dark, hot looks that screamed, Come on, babe, try and tame me. Dammit, he'd held me last night when I'd lost it in my own kitchen. He'd had me in his house dressed in a T-shirt and no panties. Wasn't he supposed to seduce me?

"You could have been killed today, Sam. You gotta learn to defend yourself."

"Huh?" I'd sort of been thinking of seeing Gabe naked.

He sat his tight butt down on his desk. "Defend yourself? Keep yourself from being thrown into filing cabinets, maybe try to actually hit your assailant with defense spray instead of me."

I don't take criticism real well. Tightening my arms under my breasts, I said, "I'm a yellow belt. I know self-defense." As long as it didn't require standing on one foot. That kicking stuff was hard. I didn't know how those little kids in my Tae Kwon Do class did it.

"Honey, you're a danger to yourself and anyone foolish enough to get within a hundred yards of you."

I felt like kicking the back of the chair I was standing behind. But I'd probably fall down. "I don't need self-defense, anyway. Rossi's helping me. I showed him the picture of Hazel, and he's looking into it."

Gabe thrust up to his full six-foot-plus height. His mouth tightened into something feral. "Not smart, babe. I thought you were learning to trust your instincts."

I backed up a step. Suddenly, I couldn't catch my breath. Staring at Gabe, I . . . He was so still, just watching me. He oozed danger, while I tripped over it and fell into pools of vomit and blood. I closed my eyes. "Not you. I swear to God, if it is you, I'll —" I jerked my purse in front of me and started rooting through my wallet, powder, lipstick, looking for my stun gun.

"What are you talking about?"

His voice was calm. Looking up, I stopped digging through my purse. "Rossi said that your career ended on a bullet and that you might be bitter. That I should be careful."

One eyebrow shot up.

I took my hand out of my purse. "Where did you go, Gabe? You just left." *Me.*

"I went after Luke."

"You mean your truck."

"Stop pouting. Pay attention, Sam. Think about this,

Luke is supposed to have shot his brother, right? Then he tried to kidnap you, and the only time he fired his gun, he just grazed Ali and didn't even come close to you. Then he went after Blaine to get information on where the money is, but he never shot him. You caught him in the storeroom and he didn't shoot you. Sam"—he paused to get my full attention—"I had my gun pulled on him this morning, and he didn't try to shoot me. And yes, he had his gun tucked into his belt."

Smarting over that pouting comment made me slow. But then I got it. "You don't think Luke shot his brother, Perry." Now I was thinking. "I believed him when he told me that, but Rossi said—"

"Go on."

"Rossi said everyone lies, and Luke's lying."

"Could be. Or it could be that Rossi has an easy suspect, Luke, and he doesn't want to complicate his case."

That made sense. "But if Luke didn't shoot Perry, then who did?"

"Rossi could be lying."

No! I mean, yeah, I'd kinda thought that once. But I was being paranoid. Rossi had helped me today, picked me up from the emergency room, and he was checking with the DMV to track the license plate of the Mustang.

Rossi'd had a pretty close look at my thong.

"Shit."

"That about sums it up. By the way"—Gabe reached into the front pocket of his jeans and pulled out a small card—"I found this next to the coffee stain in my truck."

My face flushed at the reminder of that stain. "Luke probably spilled coffee in there," I said, reaching for the card. Then I looked at the card. A business card. One of the new ones that the kids made for me. Uh-oh. "I can explain."

A bad-boy grin slid over his face.

"Really, you see, TJ and Joel were trying to help and—"

Gabe held up a hand. "Forget it, Sam. For now, we're working together. That is, under one condition."

That I sleep with him? "What?"

"You're going to learn some self-defense."

My knowledge was growing. Now I knew what one of the three bedrooms in the back of Gabe's house looked like. It was a gym with a wood floor, blue workout mats, free weights and a bench in one corner.

That accounted for Gabe's hard body. Right now that hard body was wearing only a pair of shorts. I dropped my gaze to his scarred knee. Even that looked good. Backing up a step, I almost tripped on the sweatpants pooling around my ankles.

"These sweats are too long," I complained. "I can't work out in these." He had loaned me a pair of gray sweats with a drawstring to tighten around my waist, and a white muscle shirt that hung dangerously low beneath my arms. As soon as I lifted my arms, Gabe was going to get a good side view of my breasts. Maybe I should wear a bra more often.

Gabe shrugged. "Take 'em off then."

I bent over and rolled them up. When I stood up, I tried for sympathy. "I just got stitches in my head. The doctor told me to rest."

"Too bad."

Slamming my hands down on my hips, I changed tactics. "Didn't your mother tell you not to hit a girl?"

"She told me not to diddle a girl without a condom. Any more questions?"

"Uh, no." This was going to hurt. He was going to get his revenge for that little pepper-spray mistake.

"Let's see your form."

"What form? Oh! You mean my yellow-belt form? I'm a

little rusty." Probably because I hadn't been to class in a couple of weeks. Or months. Who can remember?

"Block and punch, Sam."

All the playfulness was gone. Gabe stood with his legs spread and his arms loose at his sides. His eyes were sharp. Focused. "Okay." I figured I might as well get this over with. I got into the position. Feet apart, both hands fisted, arms down in front of me. Then I bent my left arm, using a windmill type block that would ideally push an assailant's incoming punch from my body, then remembered to draw my right arm back and snap a punch.

That was pretty good. I dropped my arms and looked up at Gabe.

"Yellow belt, huh?"

Pride filled out my grin. "Yep. You should see me in my gi."

"Babe, I could of had you on your back and naked before you ever threw that punch."

That was bad? Trying to clear my head of lust, I conceded that could be bad if it was, say, Luke tossing me on my back and relieving me of my clothes. "I have a stun gun and pepper spray. And Ali. Oh yeah, my flashlight is real heavy. I could hit someone with it." When I was little, my mother desperately wanted me to be a ballet dancer.

Today reminded me of my first and only ballet lesson. Except that, so far, I hadn't gotten my leg stuck on that bar. Quickly, I looked around the bedroom converted to a gym—no leg bar or whatever that thing was called.

"Sam, self-defense is about being smarter and faster than your attacker. You have to have the confidence to size up the situation, make a decision and act. Even if it means getting hurt."

"I've got the getting-hurt part down. I still have scabs on

my knees from my first fight with Luke when he tried to kidnap me, and a couple stitches from this morning."

His stare didn't change. "Cowardice is not a problem for you."

That got my attention. "Gabe, I hate to reduce myself any further in your estimation, but I'm a huge coward. Really big coward. I'm like the head chicken of cowards."

His thin mouth quirked. "Cowards run, babe. If you were a coward, you'd have run on Monday, right after you discovered what a stun gun could do to you. But you've hung in there and fought the best you knew how. I'm going to teach you how to fight better."

Boy, did he know how to turn a gal's head or what? "All right, what do I do?"

"What's the first thing you do if attacked?"

Just my luck, a pop quiz. Hiking up the sagging sweat pants, I answered, "Think. Assess what's happening, make a decision and act on it. Sort of like when Joel hit a rock while skateboarding and came home missing a good deal of skin and blood."

His eyes narrowed. "Did you panic?"

Shaking my head, I said, "Didn't have time to panic. I had to get him to the hospital and keep him calm."

"Exactly. If you're attacked, you have to do the same thing. Put the fear and panic away and deal with the situation. Let's assume your attacker is a man. He will not expect you to fight back, so that's in your favor. The goal is to strike and run. Got it?"

I nodded while retying the sweatpants tighter. "Strike and run."

"Your block was okay, but your punch was wild and had no purpose. I want you to aim . . . Sam, look at me."

Sighing, I hoped the sweatpants stayed up and gave Gabe my full attention.

"With the heel of your hand"—he demonstrated by thrusting his hand out—"use a stiff arm and slam your palm into his nose." He pushed his hand into my nose. "Aim all the way through, Sam, picturing your hand hitting the back of his head. Got it?"

Looking through his fingers, since the heel of his hand was at my nose, I nodded. "Through the nose and brain matter to the back of the skull. Uh-huh, I got it." Ugh.

"Block, heel to nose, fast. Then while your assailant is staggering, you're going to elbow him right in the solar plexus."

"Where's that?" It sounded sort of galactic.

Gabe put his hand on his six-pack stomach between his belly button and breastbone. "Aim slightly to the right. And aim through. Your goal is to hit a bunch of nerves that are in the back of the stomach. It's disabling."

His stomach looked good to me. It would be a damn shame to mar his belly with my elbow. Turning so that my right side was facing him, I bent my arm and said, "Like this?" I swung my elbow toward his stomach, but didn't make contact.

"No. Lock your hands, or grasp your wrists, and use a rock-the-baby motion, then slam your elbow into the solar plexus."

I winced, but practiced the motion.

"Good, now let's try it. I'll grab for you, you block my grab by pushing my arm away from your body, slam the heel of your hand into my nose, then do the solar plexus punch."

I blinked. "I don't want to hurt you." I felt the need to drop my gaze over his naked chest and belly—just to make sure he was okay.

"I'll take my chances."

He didn't think I could do it. Hiking up the sweatpants, I said, "Let's go."

Gabe came at me with one arm extended. I used the windmill block with my left arm, shoved the heel of my right hand up toward his nose—and tripped on the pooling sweats. Gabe got his arm around my waist before I hit the mat. I kept my head down, trying desperately to think of a funny remark. To laugh before he did. The heat in my face was awful.

Just like ballet lessons.

On the other hand, self-pity was not going to help me. Gritting my teeth, I raised my head and said, "I'll try it again."

"Take off the sweats before you fall and open the cut on your head."

His arm was still around me. I steered my gaze over his shoulder at the weight rack. "I'll roll them up."

"Off." He let me go and stepped away. "They're too big for you, babe. Take them off."

"But . . ." What the hell? It wasn't like he was dying to ravish me. In those shorts, I'd see the bulging sign. My pride was not going to swell today. I untied the strings and let the sweats fall to the mat, then kicked them aside. The muscle shirt fell to the very tops of my thighs, mostly covering the white thong with lace edging. I was getting pissed. "Come on." I got into my fight stance.

Gabe blinked once. "Right." He cleared his throat and shook his head a single time—sort of like Ali did when she got water in her nose from her drinking bowl—then seemed to refocus. He reached for me.

I used the outside edge of my left arm to throw his arm away from my body, aimed hard for his nose with the heel of my hand, and while he was ducking that, got a good rock-the-baby motion with my clasped hands and tried hard to send my elbow right through his solar plexus.

Gabe leaped out of the way, then reached out and caught my arm to keep me from falling with the motion of my attempt to elbow him. "That's it, babe." He drew me toward him.

I sucked in a breath at the same time that I realized he was proud of me.

And horny. No hiding that in his brief cotton shorts.

11

I looked up into his hot ebony eyes. This was worse than missing two meals and walking by Pizza Hut with no money in my purse. My pulse double-timed. "I . . ." Looked down. And back up.

"Uhmmm, I, that is . . ." I swallowed. "I should see my travel agent, ask around, gotta pick up the boys." Oh, yeah, and have sex with you. Hot, sweaty, die-the-little-death sex. Things were happening in my body.

"Sort of missing the point, aren't you, Sam?"

"Can't really miss it." I dropped my gaze again. "It's a really big point." Oh, God. Okay, I remember now. I'm a big girl. Sophisticated. Hadn't I had my boobs done? Bought short skirts? Looked at a town that had laughed at me straight in the eye? Sorta like Harper Valley PTA?

I couldn't help taking the slow road over his naked belly and chest before I let my eyes reconnect with his. "I'm older than you." Yeah, that was real sophisticated. And, while I was trying to look stupid, "I have kids."

His smile was wicked. "Seen your driver's license and met your kids. Anything else?"

"Yeah, one thing—are you always such an adult?" He did this kind of thing, I didn't. He was going to be the keep-the-sex-separate-from-business kind of guy, and I was going to write a romance novel in my head.

Still holding on to my arm, he tugged me forward until I caught the scent of his Irish Spring soap and smooth aftershave. "Hell, no." His gaze narrowed and I felt the tension coiled in his fingers, but he did not tighten his grip on my arm. "I catch Rossi sniffing around you again, I'll kill him. That adult enough for you?" He pulled me into his arms and kissed me. Not the gentle kiss of last night, but a deep, seeking kiss that made everything suddenly clear and simple.

Sex. *Now.* I wrapped my arms around his neck, meeting him for a game of tongues until I thought I'd pass out. One of his big, capable hands slid inside the arm of the muscle shirt and closed over my breast. My peeled nerves danced beneath his touch.

Backing me up to the weight area in the corner of the room, he was breathing hard and fast when he stopped kissing me. Slipping the shirt off me, he tossed it aside. Clad only in the scrap of thong, I stood in my lust-filled haze and—

"Christ, what the hell happened here?" Gabe reached out to touch my hip bone. I looked down, seeing his finger slide over the ripe bruise that surrounded a scabbed gash. "Luke's Datsun. He shoved me and I hit the door. It's fine."

His jaw went as rigid as his penis. For a flicker of time, I saw the street in his gaze. Fast and deadly in a way that was born in those who survived in a world I did not understand. Then his mouth softened and his finger rode the edge of my panties, sliding low across my belly, then dipping down. "You won't need this." He slipped to his knees and pulled off the thong.

Stepping out of the material, I looked down at his straight dark hair brushed back from his forehead. It should have bothered me that he was a well-built, sexy man, and I was a woman who'd borne two kids and was modeling nothing but cuts and bruises.

It didn't.

"You might want to sit down, babe."

"Sit down?" My mind had melted into a pool of lust. Words were not registering.

Gabe was in an interesting position, left knee on the mat, scarred right knee bent, and his head at my hips. My naked hips. He looked up with a grin and grabbed my waist to plunk me down on a plastic-covered weight-lifting bench. He wanted to do weights?

But then he was kissing me again, his hands roaming and finding—oh yes, finding. I ran my hands down his back and tugged at his shorts. Giving up, I cupped him through the cotton material and got a powerful groan in response.

He grabbed my hands, locking them down beside me on the bench, then moved his mouth to my breasts. Any protest about wanting to touch him locked in my throat. I leaned back against the cool metal weights, feeling them dig into my back, but not caring. When he slid his mouth lower, he let go of my hands to reposition my hips and spread me wide to his mouth.

"I—" Oh hell, I loved it. His hands wrapped gently around my butt, holding me to him until I came against him. It was so hot and sudden, I felt tears prick my eyes and a moan escape from my mouth. This wasn't what sex was like; this was something else. Something more powerful and . . . Where was he?

I opened my eyes. Gabe had stood up and peeled off his shorts. His penis was at my eye level, hard, visibly dancing with excitement. Without any thought but simple need, I wrapped my hand around him, feeling the throb that radiated to a full shudder in his body. It took no effort to draw him closer, pressing small, wet kisses to him, then take him all.

"God. Sam, enough." His words were tight and thick. I stopped, flush with power. I blinked, seeing that one hand hung at his hip. A green foil-packaged condom rested in his fingers. I stared at it, almost laughing out loud with my first thought.

Thank God it wasn't a Gladiator condom, the kind that panty-boy sold. But when Gabe tore open the package and slid it on, I lost all memory. "Here?" The bench seemed a bit awkward to me.

He gave me a rare, soft smile, then reached down to lift me up in his arms. He straddled the weight bench and pulled me down on top of him.

It was a hard workout.

The shower spray was warm on my sore muscles. Luke really had to stop throwing me around. Or I had to stop him from throwing me around. I kept my eyes closed, enjoying the feel of Gabe's hands soaping up my breasts and belly. "You had that condom in your pocket the whole time."

"Uh-huh."   .

I didn't have the strength to work up to any real indignation. "Thought you wanted to teach me self-defense."

He didn't answer, just kept spreading the soap. The water was running over the front of my body, and Gabe was standing behind me. He had me leaning back against him to keep my stitches out of the spray.

Bad idea. Leaning on him in any way was a bad idea. I pulled off him and started rinsing in the spray, all business now. "I have to leave. I have to go to the travel agent, then pick up the kids. Do you want to meet me for Couples Bunko tonight at Linda's house, or should I get someone else? Are you free?" I slid alongside him, ready to get out and let him shower.

He closed both hands around my waist, trapping me with my breasts pressed up to his chest. "Pouting again?"

This man was living dangerously. I knew self-defense and Tae Kwon Do. "Listen, the sex was nice, but this is business." I didn't feel the need to add my professional smile.

He snorted. Actually snorted. "I did not go after my truck, Sam."

"Then you left this morning because you were mad, or bored, or who the hell knows! I'm leaving now." Just as soon as I get his hands off my waist.

"I didn't go after my truck, I went after the prick that did this to you." He took one hand off my waist and ran his finger lightly over the bandage on my head. "And this." His entire hand folded over my bruised hipbone. "I needed to find and destroy the man who did this to you. That give you a better example of my priorities?"

Something really scary stuck in my throat. "What stopped you?" I might be a little naive, but one thing I knew was that if Gabe wanted to find Luke bad enough, he'd still be out there looking.

"Rational thought. Luke didn't kill his brother, and someone is fucking with us."

"Rossi?" Then I shook my head. "No, it's not Rossi. He wants to solve the murder, and help me, because of a young girl who died of a drug overdose. She'd gotten the drugs from Heart Mates. He wants to close that case too." I'd seen the sincerity in Rossi's face.

"Just because he spilled coffee on you and got you out of your pants doesn't make him the good guy."

The water was pelting our arms and sides. The room was filled with steam. The bandage on my forehead was slipping. None of it mattered. "How did you know that?" Ohmigod! Had he been watching? Could he have been at my house spying? Was Rossi right about Gabe?

"Let me go." I was not shaking. I was rock steady. Probably I was scared numb. Gabe dropped his hands. Without looking back, I stepped out of the shower, grabbed a towel and barely swiped it over my body.

I had to get out of there. I had to think.

Had I just slept with a man who was trying to terrorize me? I yanked on my panties and skirt and was working my rose shirt over my dripping hair when I heard the shower turn off.

Repressing the urge to look behind me at Gabe, I left the bathroom, hooked a fast right down the hallway and another right into the living room. I detoured into Gabe's office to snag my shoes and purse.

Coming out of the office to escape the house, I found a naked Gabe standing at the front door. He had his arms crossed over his chest, his wet hair plastered to his head, and he looked like some kind of dangerous warrior. What if he didn't let me leave? "Your hair's wet," he pointed out calmly.

My hair? I was worried about all the people I trusted betraying me. I was fighting the feeling that both Gabe and Rossi were somehow playing me, and he pointed out that my hair was wet? Remembering the shoes in my hand, I slipped them on my damp feet. Then I stood up straight and met his gaze. "My hair will dry. Now get out of my way, Gabe. I'm leaving." I had to. I didn't know who was the enemy. All I knew for sure was that I was going to damn well find out.

He stepped aside and watched as I pulled open the door and headed for my car in his driveway. The one I had left there last night. Good thing too, or I'd be hoofing it in high heels. One way or another, I was heading for the travel agency, and I was going to start getting some answers.

Starting up the T-Bird, I backed out of the driveway, barely missing Gabe's truck. I finally looked over at the house. Gabe stood in the doorway. Naked and watching me.

Just who exactly was Gabe Pulizzi?

My head was pounding when I got to the travel agency. It was in a strip mall with one of those big all-your-home-needs-including-the-kitchen-sink stores on one side and a pet store on the other. The big picture window in the front tortured me with my reflection. Steam-frizzed hair framing a drooping bandage falling off the vivid bruises on my forehead. My own brown eyes stared at me accusingly.

I'd hauled my butt out of that shower and raced out of Gabe's house. The look on his face stayed with me—the one that seemed to believe if he was patient enough, I might be able to find my sanity.

Gabe scared me. Worse than Rossi. I knew what Rossi was—good-looking man after a good time. Nothing more, nothing less. I'd even bet Rossi prided himself on pleasuring a woman. He'd be good, fun, maybe a little detached.

Gabe had been all there. Every inch of his body, every fiber of his being.

What did Gabe want? The money? Me? Fun and sex? I was five years older than he was, had two kids and didn't want any future with a man.

Didn't Gabe want a family of his own someday?

"Sam?"

I almost fell off my high heels. Turning from the picture window, I forced a smile onto my face and tried to recover my wandering mind. I held my hand out to Carrie McMillen. We'd gone to high school together. She'd been a cheerleader and dated the football star. Now she was a travel agent who had been on most of the exotic trips that she sold. "Carrie, hi, I was just coming in to see you."

She juggled some brochures and took my hand. "It's nice to see you, Sam. I was just getting these"—she angled her chin down to the pamphlets in her hand—"out of my car. Oh, I'm so sorry about your husband. You're looking well." Her gaze ran over me, then zeroed in on my bust.

Recovering my hand, I said, "Thank you, Carrie. Actually, what I came to talk to you about has to do with Trent."

"Oh? Well, come on inside."

I followed her into the small office with plush rose carpet and pale pink walls trimmed in glossy white wood. I sat down in one of the deep striped chairs and reached into my briefcase.

"What can I help you with, Sam?"

I really had to start thinking this stuff out ahead of time. "I believe that Trent was looking into a trip before his, uh, accident. What I need you to tell me is which of these two women"—I pulled the pictures of Joan and Hazel out of my briefcase and set them down on the desk in front of Carrie—"Trent was with when he was in here."

I watched her eyes skim the photos, then come back to me. "They were both in here at different times."

She had kept her voice neutral. "Yes, I knew that. What I meant to ask is which one was in here last with him?"

"I see. Well, let me think." She went back to studying the photos.

Her cheerleader cheekbones were flushing a charming pink and I would bet her hand was twitching to get on the phone as soon as I left. "It's part of an investigation that I'm working on," I said, reaching into my briefcase and latching on to one of my new business cards. Handing the card to her, I added, "I appreciate your confidentiality."

Carrie studied the card. "Well, I heard you had become a private detective, but I didn't think—" She stopped and looked up at me. "That is, I thought you were doing that dating service thing."

"I still am." I froze my smile. "Now if you could recall which of these two women was in here last with Trent?"

Carrie leaned across the desk. "Is it a divorce? A husband wants proof of his wife's sleeping around?"

Once a cheerleader . . . "I'm not at liberty to say."

Her face fell. "The last one in here with Trent was this one." She pointed to Joan.

Processing that, I stared down at the pictures. So it could have been a triangle thing. Hazel got dumped for Joan, and Hazel wasn't going to lose Trent wrapped up in the half million dollars of drug money. I couldn't think of any more questions to ask. What more did I want to know? Gathering up the pictures, I said, "Thank you, Carrie. You have my card if you think of anything else I might need to know."

How could I have been so stupid and blind? My husband was out tom-catting around town, skimming drug money, getting ready to dump me and the boys, and I had been clueless.

No wonder I didn't know what Gabe wanted. My track record was dismal. Letting the door shut behind me, I headed for my car.

Rossi was leaning against the driver's side, his blue eyes watching me.

I slowed my pace, trying to sort out my life in the five seconds it was going to take me to reach my car.

"Sam, I see you got your car back."

"Rossi." I glanced at his white Camry parked next to my car. "What are you doing here? How'd you know I would be here?" Could be he was driving by and spotted my car. Weren't too many restored '57 T-Birds in Lake Elsinore.

"You okay, Sam? You look . . ." His eyes went to my hair, then back to my face. "Sort of humid."

I reached a hand up to my frizzy hair. "Sprinklers came on while I was getting my car from Gabe's house." That lie slid out with no thought.

The words hung between us. Rossi tilted his head and regarded me with a cool, interrogating look.

Bringing my arm up, I stared blankly at my empty wrist. No watch. I'd left it in Gabe's bathroom.

"You had your watch on when I left you at your house," Rossi noted in a level tone.

Ignoring his accusation, I asked, "What time is it, Rossi? I have to pick up my kids." Leaning forward on my toes to peek at his watch, I lost my balance in a wave of dizziness.

Rossi uncrossed his arms and caught me by my shoulders. "Jesus, Sam. Did the doctor say you have a concussion? What's the matter with you?"

Bubbles of laughing hysteria popped in my throat, but I kept my mouth tightly closed.

"Have you eaten anything but those donuts?"

Don't answer that! My brain screamed. He meant food, of course. I shook my head no, and found my wits. "I'm fine. It was just a moment of dizziness. I'll get the boys, then eat." Stepping back, I looked at him. "Did you find out anything about Hazel?"

"She didn't register the Mustang at the DMV. I ran her through the DMV files with her Social Security number, and she's not at her last known address." He glanced down at his watch. "It's one-thirty, Sam. Let's go get something to eat, then you can pick up your kids."

Shaking my head, I said, "No, I need to—"

He cut me off. "Sam, we have to talk about tomorrow night. The deadline? Do you have the half a million to take to the arcade?"

"I could write a check."

"Funny, Sam. You'll have to write two checks, remember? One for Luke, and one for the other person after you—unless Luke's been behind that too."

"He's not. Luke's not that smart."

Rossi's gaze sharpened. "You're probably right. We can walk to the Italian place on the other side of the hardware store."

But I already had Italian today. Mentally shaking my head, I fell into step beside Rossi as he headed back up on the sidewalk and strode down to the small restaurant. Rich smells greeted us as we went inside. A dessert case was the first thing we saw, with fat pastries, sinful cheesecakes, and decadent chocolate cakes. We chose a booth by the front window and sat down. The scent of tomato sauce and spices made my stomach growl. I ordered angel hair pasta and Rossi had lasagna. I desperately wanted a beer or some wine, but passed on that.

When the waitress left, I looked at Rossi. "What's this about?"

He leaned his elbows on the table and folded his hands. Giving me a grave look, he said, "I can't arrange for any kind of surveillance for you tomorrow night."

I sat back in the red vinyl seat. "I'm not going tomorrow night."

Surprise flickered in his eyes. "Every time I think I have you figured out . . . why not?"

Putting my chin in my hand, I looked out the window. "I'll be watching over my kids and Grandpa. I have to keep them safe. Trent put his sons in danger." I was wising up. Slowly, but it was happening. Gabe had tried to tell me to form a plan. I was going to form a plan. I was going to spend the afternoon figuring out where the hell Trent would hide half a million dollars. Tonight, I was going to Bunko to find out what Joan knew, and to figure out who was stealing the homemade sex videos of married couples.

Then tomorrow, I was going to make damn sure no one got near TJ, Joel or Grandpa.

But even if I found the money, then what?

"Rossi, if that money turns up, what happens to it?"

"It's drug money, Sam. You don't get it. It will be seized under the Asset Forfeiture laws."

The waitress brought our food. I kept quiet and watched her set down the plates. The scent of warm olive oil, basil and oregano wafted up. She set a basket of fragrant garlic bread in the center of the table and left.

"Eat, Sam," Rossi urged.

I picked up my fork and said, "So I would turn it over to you?"

"Yes, then Luke and the rest wouldn't have any reason to be after you anymore."

I made a dent in my plate full of pasta. Spearing an olive, I thought about it. "I don't know where the money is."

Halfway into his lasagna, Rossi stopped eating. "Do you think the money is keeping you alive, Sam?"

Maybe. Who knew? Sure enough, no one was going to kill me while they thought I might know where the money was. But would they kill one of my kids? Sighing, I set my fork down. "What time is it, Rossi? I've got to get the boys." Taking out my wallet, I began scrounging for money to pay for my half.

"What's this?" He reached across the table and using one long finger, slid my card toward him. It must have come out with my wallet. "Your business card?" His gaze scanned the card, then pinned me. "Getting pretty involved with this rent-a-cop, aren't you, Sam?"

Could he be jealous? "It's business." I fished out a ten-dollar bill and laid it on the table. Slinging my purse over my shoulder, I stood and smoothed my skirt down to the tops of my thighs.

Rossi leaned back in the seat, his blue gaze flammable as he watched me adjust my skirt. "Business, huh? I did a little checking on Gabe Pulizzi."

I stopped fussing with my skirt. I didn't want to know. Giving Rossi my best clean-your-room-and-do-your-homework glare, I said, "Why are you wasting time checking out Gabe? Shouldn't you be trying to find Hazel?"

"Which brings me to the point. Gabe Pulizzi, according to the Los Angeles Police Department, was married."

Married? I was immediately thinking murder. My gaze dropped from Rossi's eyes to the slight bulge beneath his jacket. Too bad I didn't know how to use a gun. Then I gave up that idea anyway. Gabe was too good for me to walk up and shoot him. No, I was going to have to throw the plugged-in, turned-on blow dryer into the shower while he was in there. Now that was a plan.

"Sam?"

Over the buzzing in my head, I lifted my gaze back to Rossi. "There's more?" Of course there was.

"His wife's name was Hazel."

Strangely steady on my high heels, I blinked while letting my mind work that over. Hazel. Trent's Hazel? The missing Hazel? Maybe she wasn't missing after all. Maybe a certain private detective knew exactly where Hazel was.

My stomach squeezed, threatening to give back my Italian lunch. In my head, I saw Gabe's face watching me panic and leave his house. His patient expression that made me think he believed I'd get it right. Could it all be an act?

Who was I kidding? I'd lived with a man whose whole life was an act. The boys and I had only been window dressing to Trent.

"The boys!" They were at school and I had to pick them up. I looked at Rossi. "I have to go." I turned and walked out.

My boys. They were my reason for living and getting stronger. My reason for wanting to be as tough and smart as a heroine in a romance novel.

A man, not even a man like Gabe, would be my reason for living. If he was after the money, if he hurt my kids, I would teach Gabe Pulizzi, the street-smart ex-cop turned PI, just what a betrayed and pissed-off mom could do.

More centered, I got in my car and headed toward the middle school.

12

"Mom, what happened to your head?" TJ asked as he climbed into the car. His face was grim with worry, which explained why he didn't grumble about having to sit next to Joel. The two-seater T-Bird had a few drawbacks.

"Whatever it was, did it do that to your hair?" Joel pointed around his brother to the frizz falling to my shoulders.

I pulled the car out of the middle school, turned right on Grand and headed up to our house. "I had an accident with a filing cabinet." I gave TJ a sideways glance to see if he believed me. "It's only two stitches and a lecture from the doctor to be more careful."

"How come the bandage is falling off?" TJ didn't miss a thing.

Forcing a grin as I braked for a stop sign, I answered, "I wasn't careful enough in the shower."

"Hmmm."

"Hey." I chanced taking a hand off the steering wheel to ruffle TJ's hair. "It's not that big a deal. It's just a cut and bruise. It'll heal."

"What about the money, Mom? Have you found that?

Those guys still want it, don't they? What if they kidnap you to force you to take them to the money?"

My heart seized up in my chest. Beneath the budding man, the little boy in TJ was afraid of losing his mom the way he'd lost his dad. I slowed the car and turned into the dirt path to our house. "That's not going to happen."

" 'Cause you got Gabe to help you, right, Mom?" Joel piped up.

I glanced over at Joel. "Well, he's helping." I shifted my gaze to park the car—and caught sight of Gabe sitting on the front porch with Ali's head in his lap. He had a beer in his hand.

Ali got up and bounded down the steps to greet the boys. Both TJ and Joel dropped their backpacks to pet Ali. They always saved her something from their lunches each day. She was not disappointed. Joel had saved her an Oreo cookie, and TJ had grapes. They were throwing the food up and Ali was catching it.

Leaving them to play, I stalked up to the porch. Grandpa's Jeep was parked in its usual spot. Now I noticed Gabe's truck next to it. Grandpa was probably resting on his bed and reading. The magic shows wore him out more than they used to.

Stopping on the porch, I glared down at Gabe. He looked good. Damn good. His hair wasn't frizzy, but sleek and straight. He had a Bulls basketball jersey on, leaving his arms bare. Shorts and flip-flops completed his outfit. His dark sunglasses hid his eyes. Dammit, he was sneaky-good-looking. Rossi was blatantly, young-Harrison-Ford handsome. But Gabe was devious; his thin mouth and slightly drooping eye should have ruined his looks. Instead, they added to his sly seductiveness. The kind that had women taking a second look. And a third.

He lifted his beer bottle up to me. "Cool hair. Sexyrumpled. Works on you, babe." Then he drank from the dewy bottle.

Hearing the boys still playing with Ali, I kept my voice low. "I could kill you with my blow dryer."

"Been thinking about it, have you?"

I wished I could see his eyes. "Will you leave?"

"Nope."

Somehow I didn't think he would. Who was Gabe? Why was he here? What did he want? All questions that I had to sort out. I couldn't hide from this. I had to figure out who was my friend and who was my enemy. But the flat truth was that I felt safer with Gabe here.

But then, I'd felt safe married to Trent.

"Stay away from me, Gabe. Just stay away." I turned on my heel and stormed into the house.

Once inside, I leaned against the wall and heard the boys talking to Gabe.

"What'd you do, Gabe?" Joel asked. "Mom's real mad at you."

"Does it have to do with whoever hurt her head?" TJ added.

My heart twisted at the fear and anger I heard in the voices of my children.

"I'm here to make sure no one hurts your mom anymore. If she's not happy about that, too bad," Gabe answered.

Shock lodged in my chest.

Gabe's voice held the same hurt and anger as my boys'.

The detached two-car garage sat on the south side of the house. A bare bulb hung in the middle and cast a brutal light on the interior. One side had all of Grandpa's magic stuff neatly lined up on shelves, all well packed and organized. In the middle was dust-covered furniture that I had kept after I sold the house. Couches, chairs, entertainment center, the usual stuff. The beds, desks and dressers were in our bedrooms in the house. The lumps beneath the covers looked a lot like I felt—abandoned.

On the other side of the garage were Trent's things, boxed and stacked. Wiping my hands on my cutoff denim shorts, I went to the boxes and just stood there looking over Trent's life. He'd wrestled in high school and college. There was a dusty box of his trophies, yearbooks, jackets and assorted memorabilia that I thought the boys might want someday. There was a box of carefully packed wines he had bought from various winery visits, both business and personal. Why had I packed those up? Why not drink them? Moving on, there were his books, mostly on wines and cigars, that kind of thing. Trent was just getting into cigar parties when he died. He'd even invested in a large, locked light-walnut display case—I think it's called a humidor. It was under all the sheets with the other furniture. Oh, and Trent's models of classic T-Birds and Mustangs.

I narrowed my eyes in a memory. The Post-it notes from the panties—for some reason, I'd stuck them down the side of that box of carefully packed wines instead of burning them with the panties. Angel and I had been pretty blasted on margaritas and I had no recall of the liquid reasoning that went behind that particular action. I decided to ignore that box.

Getting to work, I pulled a box of old CDs, tapes and books out. I needed the work. I needed to think. I decided to finally sort out Trent's stuff.

And maybe find the money?

Opening the first dusty box, I sneezed and got to work. I don't know how much time passed as I worked in a dust-pondering fog.

"Sam?"

On my knees, I put my hand over my heart to hold it in

my chest. How long had I been in here? I glanced at my wrist and remembered that my watch was still in Gabe's bathroom.

Gabe was standing over me. Tilting my head back, I looked up at him. He had taken off the sunglasses. His eyes caught the glare of the bare bulb overhead, making him look uncertain.

Gabe uncertain?

Swallowing down the dust, and something else I couldn't identify, I said, "You were married. Or are married."

His whole face turned to stone. "Were."

So he wasn't screwing around on a wife. I was able to breathe a little deeper. "Divorced?"

Gabe dropped to his haunches. "Widowed. We need to talk."

"We are talking." My nerves skittered and danced beneath my skin. Trent's things were all around me. I'd come across so many things I had forgotten about. Gadgets. Why had I kept three kinds of coffee grinders? Each one more expensive than the last. Trent had always been willing to throw away me and the boys for the newer, more expensive model. "Why didn't you tell me you were married? Do you have kids?"

"You never asked. No kids."

"What happened? How did she die?" I hadn't missed the hesitation in his voice when he said no kids, but I was focusing here. Trying to get coherent answers.

"Sam, we have other things to worry about right now. My wife is dead. Leave it." That street thing rode hard in his dark eyes.

Standing up, I dusted off my hands. "Let it go? I had sex with you! Then I find out that you were married to a woman named Hazel, and I didn't find it out from you!"

His jaw tightened and his hands curled at his side. "Who did you find it out from?" His voice was deadly soft.

I paused. Danger flew like static electricity. I could feel, but couldn't quite grasp, it. Danger to me? Or someone else? "Rossi. He's been investigating this case, you know that."

"Choose up sides, babe. I don't have time for your insecurities now."

I felt like I'd been slapped. "You sure had time to coax me out of my clothes." Why did sex have to make it all so complicated?

"I'm not going to answer that. You're the one that ran scared today. Not me."

He was mad. Hurt. Angry. Like a lion with a thorn in his paw. I turned away, looking at the boxes. "How did you know that Rossi had spilled coffee on me?"

I heard the long sigh before the words. "You were wearing white jeans this morning. When you showed up at my house, you had that skirt on. Your legs had the scent of coffee on them. Rossi's been after a taste of your thong from the first day he laid eyes on you. It wasn't a big leap, Sam."

"You're scaring me, Gabe." There. I was a chicken and a rotten judge of men.

"I know."

He didn't move. I wanted him to come take me in his arms and reassure me. Instead, he gave me space. "I don't want a relationship. I don't want the heartache, the betrayals. You must want a family, a young wife, babies of your own."

"No."

The word was sharp and quick. Turning around, I stared at him. "Why not?"

"I had a young wife. She was so dependant on me that she couldn't save herself, or our child that she was carrying."

"Oh, God." Bringing both my hands up to my face, I asked, "How?"

"Couple punks banging on the apartment door. She called me at work. They patched the call through to the car I was in. She didn't call 911, but me. I called it in, told her to get my gun. . . ." Gabe trailed off, but his gaze never wavered. "She wouldn't go to the goddamn closet and get my gun. She just kept begging me to save her. I was thirty miles away. I couldn't get there fast enough. I called it in, but the other squad cars were too late."

Horror washed up my throat. I forced it down. Vomiting would not change the past. It wouldn't change Gabe's long minutes in that car, begging the wife he had loved to get his gun and save herself and their baby—it wouldn't change his helplessness, guilt or grief. I could say the words, *I'm sorry, it wasn't your fault, you're not to blame,* but none of those words mattered.

I went to him, putting my arms around his waist. I expected him to reject me, but instead, he wrapped me in his embrace. I could feel the steady thump of his heart beating against my body. Very quietly, into my dusty, frizzy hair, he said, "I want a partner, babe."

Into the curves and ridges of his muscular shoulder, I said, "How about a temporary, limited partnership?"

"Mom? Where are you?" Joel's voice called.

Gabe let me go, and I stepped back, smoothing my hair down. "In the garage." My voice didn't sound right.

Joel appeared in the door. "Mom, Grandpa wants you. Says he found something on the Internet."

I looked up at Gabe and shrugged. With Grandpa, who knew?

I stared at the computer screen. It was like a really gruesome accident on one of California's finest freeways—I just couldn't look away. "Uhmmm, yeah, it's Linda and her husband. I recognize . . . their faces." Ohmigod. The image was grainy, but I could make out the act. They were having sex. "How did you find this?"

Grandpa slid his glasses back up his nose. "I didn't find it. TJ and Joel were telling me about rumors at school about sex videos on the Internet. I remembered you said you were looking for the missing videos of your PTA friends." Grandpa's gaze slid back to the computer. "I think we found them."

I was a little slow. "You have to pay to get into this site?"

"You'll get the charge on your credit card," Grandpa confessed.

My mind was trying to believe this. "Linda and Molly both said their videos were missing. Do you think their husbands did this without their knowledge? Or were the videos really stolen? Who stole them? How would some-one know that they were videotaping themselves . . ." I couldn't even say it. Sheesh, I didn't really want to tell Linda and Molly where their videotapes had ended up. In the back of my mind, memories were stirring, court cases I had read about in the newspaper about some guy putting hidden cameras in women's dressing rooms, then plastering them all over the Internet.

Men were dogs.

But I knew Frank pretty well. He was always involved in his kids' soccer games and stuff. Obviously, he'd video-taped himself with his wife, but that was their business. I didn't think he'd sell the tapes, though.

"Can we track this to who owns this web site?"

Grandpa stretched his nimble fingers out in front of him. "I'll give it my best shot. Take a while, though. These guys bury themselves good."

I had to smile. My grandpa, the magician and Internet

sleuth. Besides magic, there was nothing he liked better than snooping and gossip. I heard the boys' voices and Ali barking at the back door. "Quick, get rid of that," I whispered.

Grandpa did a couple of moves and the writhing images of copulation disappeared.

My shoulders slumped. Gabe was standing right behind me. He'd been looking over my shoulder, but hadn't said anything. As the boys and Ali spilled through the door, I looked at Gabe and whispered, "What am I going to tell Linda and Molly?"

"Hey, Mom, what's for dinner?" Joel shouted out.

"The truth, Sam," Gabe said, "but not tonight. We'll see what we can find out at Bunko."

Turning my gaze to my children, I mentally searched the fridge and pantry. Dinner. I hadn't given it a thought. I think I had some eggs and cheese. "Omelets?"

"Can I make biscuits?" Joel asked.

"Don't burn the bottoms this time, dweeb," TJ offered his opinion.

"Mom! Tell him to shut up!"

I sucked in a long breath. "Both of you stop it now. Go wash up. Then, Joel, you make the biscuits, and TJ, you set the table and grate the cheese for me."

Both boys pushed and shoved each other to the bathroom.

Ali went to the refrigerator and barked.

"No, Ali. You have guard duty tonight. You can have a beer when I get home."

She stuck her nose into the seam of the refrigerator and whined.

I saw her point. Walking to the fridge, I said, "Tell you what, girl, I'll split one with you. Deal?" I opened it up, brought out three bottles of beer and gathered up eggs, cheese, milk and butter to make the omelets. When I set all the stuff on the cracked Formica counter, Ali barked her agreement.

Gabe came into the kitchen, grinning at me. "You pass out the drinks, I'll make the omelets."

"You?" Popping the top off the one beer, I went to Ali's dish and poured half of it in.

"I can cook, babe."

His voice was low and throbbing. Standing up, I met his hot black gaze and was hit with a ferocious hunger.

I didn't think the omelet was going to fill the need, but it would have to do.

Archie and Linda's house was in a track of fifteen- or twenty-year-old-homes built on what used to be a walnut grove. It was still light when we pulled up in Gabe's truck. The grass was freshly mowed. The house had been painted in the last couple of years, white with blue trim. The tree in the front yard had a tire swing hanging from it.

Linda was one of the original Kool-Aid moms. I didn't know Archie real well, although I now knew him better than I used to. I had to halt my thoughts to cleanse my mind of the images of him and Linda having sex.

How was I going to face them? .

"Don't think about it," Gabe suggested as he took my arm. We walked up the driveway. I could hear country music and laughter floating out of the house.

"I just don't want to see their bedroom."

Gabe glanced around the street. It was house- and tree-lined, a few kids out riding bikes in the last hour of daylight. "You're investigating the theft of the tapes. Don't you think she'll find an excuse to show you where they were stolen from?"

"We already know more about those tapes than we want to," I muttered.

"Judging them, Sam? Remember, they were just a married couple having a little fun, maybe spicing up their sex life. They never planned to have their private life splattered all over the Internet to amuse perverts."

"You're mad," I said, more than a little surprised. Hadn't Gabe already seen it all?

"Damn straight."

Well, yeah, I saw his point. I was getting mad too. It was an obscene invasion of privacy to steal tapes like that, to feed the perverts, as Gabe called them, then make money off it.

"Let's go." I marched up to the front door. I was on two missions tonight. Find out what Joan knew about Hazel and my dead husband, and find out who was stealing the sex tapes.

I was going to kick some Bunko butt tonight.

"Sam!" Linda flung open the door. "You made it! And this is . . . ?"

I hadn't introduced them that morning. "Linda, this is my—uh, Gabe. He works with me."

Linda might be married and fond of tent-like dresses, but she fastened her gaze on Gabe as if he were a triple-layered chocolate cake. She'd seen him bare chested this morning, and I could see that memory in her hungry eyes.

"Nice to meet you, Linda."

"Oh, yes—well, come in."

Her gaze shifted back to me. Or more specifically, my bust in my halter-cut royal-blue shirt that I had paired with a knee-length white skirt. Balancing on strappy white sandals, I flashed Linda a wide smile and went into the house.

There was a lot of dark wood and tole-painted country-type stuff sitting around. It looked cozy and damn hard to dust. We went into the large family room that they had built onto the back of the house. There were three card tables set up that would be used for Bunko later, but right now everyone was hovering around the tables with drinks in hand. I smelled chili. I almost smacked my forehead, but remembered my stitches. Dinner.

There were firm rules to Bunko. Everyone took a turn hosting. Hostesses provided dinner, dessert, munchies and lots of wine, maybe a batch or two of margaritas. One could not get into the proper Bunko mood without alcohol.

"Molly, Frank, look who's here!" Linda was dragging us from group to group to make sure we knew everyone. A glass of white wine, probably Zinfandel, was pressed into my hand.

"Sam, how nice to see you," Molly said cautiously while Frank briefly turned from talking to Hugh Crimson to smile at me.

Wait a minute! *Hugh Crimson?* I said something to Linda, grabbed Gabe's arm and dragged him to the food laid out on the long counter. I pushed a bowl into his hand and started serving chili while eye-searching the room.

"What's up?"

I dumped a load of onions and cheese on top of Gabe's chili. "Hugh's here. That's Angel's ex-husband."

"So?"

"His wife, bimbo-Brandi, is over there talking to Archie, who is Linda's husband."

"Hard to recognize him with his clothes on." Gabe dug a spoon into the chili. "What's the problem?"

I had visions of explosions. "Angel's never really gotten over Hugh dumping her for brainless-Brandi."

"Babe, Angel's not here, so what's it matter?" He had a smirk on his face.

I scanned the backyard through the sliding glass door. No movement. I wondered if Linda had a guard dog. Turning back to Gabe, I had to take a minute. A minute looking at his pale green shirt stretched across a muscular chest, tucked into a pair of sinful black jeans. The man was fine. Frowning, I just knew these women were going to fight to partner with Gabe. If Angel didn't drop a full beehive down the chimney before we got started, that is. Getting back to the problem, I said, "She could be here. Out there"—I flung my hand into the air—"somewhere."

His mouth quirked on one side. "Angel stalks her ex-husband?"

He caught on quick. "Well, that term's a little harsh. More like she sort of keeps track of him." With state-of-the-art surveillance equipment, if you want to get technical, I added to myself. No sense in blowing things out of proportion.

"Hugh ever file a complaint?"

"Once, but the cops were sort of . . . unsympathetic."

"Why's that?" He dropped his gaze to my untouched bowl of chili. "You gonna eat that?"

"You kidding? This stuff's laden with fat. You put extra cheese in the omelet," I reminded him primly and handed him my bowl of chili. "The cops don't really like Hugh's former profession, but they do like Angel."

Gabe's spoon paused halfway to his well-cut mouth. "Yeah, Angel's hot. What was Hugh's former profession?"

"You think Angel's hot?"

He grinned. "Sizzling."

"Humph. Can you focus here?" I snapped my fingers in his face. "Hugh worked for his father's law practice in Temecula. His father's a pretty well-known defense attorney. That's bad enough, but Hugh could never pass his bar exam, so his time was spent behind the scenes finding dirt on the cops to destroy the cases that the DA and police built against the criminals the cops arrested."

Gabe stopped eating altogether. "Ass."

"Don't be so hard on yourself." I stuck my nose in the air and turned to go find Joan. And keep a lookout for Angel.

Linda swooped down on me. "Sam," she whispered in my ear, "do you want to see my bedroom?"

"No!" The images that splattered on my brain! I turned and saw the worry lines around her eyes, like a road map of her very real fear. When I was in the PTA/soccer mom business, I used to hear the barely concealed remarks about how we just let ourselves go after we were married and had kids. But that was far from the truth. It was a way of life. The women who stayed home and did the gym thing were the cheerleaders and manhunters, and the women who stayed home to do the PTA/soccer thing were the brains and were supposed to get the most respect. No one crossed over, or those who did were under suspicion, like me. Life outside high school was no different really. I felt true sympathy for Linda. Her whole identity was wrapped up in the success of her children and her role as PTA president. All of that was threatened by this videotape out there.

A videotape that I knew had already surfaced on the Internet.

Putting my hand on the sleeve of her country-blue dress, I said softly, "First I would like to talk to Joan. I don't want to raise any questions by investigating your bedroom."

"Oh, that makes sense. Uh . . ." She looked around. "There she is, over there with Gabe and some other women."

I followed her gaze and saw the cluster of females hovering around Gabe.

"Where'd you meet him, Sam?"

"We're . . . uh, business partners. Limited partners." He was just as bad as Rossi. Good-looking and charming the women. I was beginning to wonder if he had a panty collection.

Sighing, I knew that was unfair of me. I followed Linda back to the food. Gabe hadn't even made it two steps before he was surrounded. I recognized Molly, Brandi, a girl who looked exactly like the picture of Joan and . . . Oh dear, that was Nettie. Her husband was on the school board.

I lifted my chin, and in the process my breasts, and marched into the middle of the women. "Hello, Molly, nice to see you." I turned to Brandi and nodded—it was the best I could do considering she was the woman who slept with Angel's husband—then smiled at Nettie. "Been a long time, Nettie. How are you?"

"Samantha Shaw, what a surprise. I thought this was *Couples* Bunko."

My insult radar was screaming for revenge. "Are you lost, Nettie? Weight Watchers is all the way downtown in the Community Center—or at least, that's what the newspaper said."

Nettie was the Mack Truck of women. About nine inches over the five-foot mark, she tipped the scale way into the two-hundred-pound area. Her eyes widened in a surprise that took seconds to travel down to her full set of chins. "At least all of me is real." Beneath the thick streaks of gray in her wiry brown hair, she glared at my bust line.

Okay, I felt kind of bad about the Weight Watchers crack, so I changed the subject. "Have you met my friend, Gabe?"

"Your friend?" Nettie's gaze went over me like I was a piece of artificially flavored meat.

I hadn't done this for a while, but once you master female cattiness, it never goes away. I opened my mouth when Molly's voice cut in. "Sam, what happened to your head?"

Damn. Think fast. Can't use the I'm-so-clumsy line with these women, or they'd use it to skewer me over a barbecue of hot, bitchy coals.

"Did it have something to do with that body you found?" Brandi piped up.

I glanced over at Brandi. She had bottle-blond hair down the middle of her back. The straight kind that I had longed for in my high school career. Big brown eyes, cute little nose and possibly one quarter of a functioning brain buried beneath that smooth skin.

Hate her. Probably not just because of Angel. Really, Angel was more stunningly beautiful, but Brandi had that bobby-socks and pigtails, schoolgirl thing that made men wanna come out of their caves and get educated.

"I cut it while chasing down a . . ." Hell, suspect? Nope, that was police. Uhmmmm . . . "investigative lead that was uncooperative." Bingo! I gave them my most professional smile.

"Jeepers! It's true, then, you're really a private eye?" Brandi exclaimed and grabbed Gabe's arm in her excitement.

My professional smile grew ice. "Yes."

"So you're not doing that vile dating-service nonsense anymore? Mac and I—" Nettie looked around the tight group and said, "Mac's on the school board, you know, and we think that place should be shut down."

I silently thanked Nettie, who had no idea that she'd just given me the opening I'd been waiting for. "Heart Mates is a wonderful place, Nettie. I'm thinking about adding some social mixers to let my clients get to know one another." I purposely turned from Nettie to Joan, who was hanging on the opposite side of Gabe. "Did you ever have mixers when you worked at Heart Mates, Joan?"

Joan had put on a little weight since her picture, but she had her hips stuffed into a pair of skin-tight jeans, and a stretchy white top. Her hair had been cut and styled to a flirty chin length. Right now, her brown eyes had that doe-in-the-headlights look. "Excuse me?"

She had suddenly forgotten about Gabe. Now if I could just pry bimbo-Brandi off him. "Didn't you work at Heart Mates?"

"No, whatever gave you that idea?"

Gee, could it be the name, Social Security number and picture in my employee files? But I knew I had her. Now that she was mixing with respectable folk, she didn't want them to know about her sordid past. Which was my sordid present since I owned Heart Mates, but I no longer cared what these people thought. Much. "I don't know, Joan. I was going through my files and thought I saw you mentioned in there." Shrugging, I added, "It must be a mistake."

She recovered and waved her hand. "No problem, it happens." She reached into a tiny purse strapped to her waist and pulled out a business card, then handed it to me. "My husband and I own our own business."

I took the card and read it. *DJ's Carpet Cleaning*. I stared down at the card, my head spinning with the possibilities. In the background, I heard Linda announce that it was time to begin playing Bunko.

"Sam? What is it?" Gabe was at my side.

I looked up into his face. "I think I just cracked my first case."

13

There were twelve of us, six couples spread out over three tables. Each table had three dice and a tablet for one of the players to keep score. Points are accumulated for rolling sixes, with each six being worth one point. A Bunko is rolling all three sixes, and all the players at the table scramble to pick up the dice to get an extra point. A wipe-out is rolling all ones, and the team loses all their points. When a team reaches twenty-one at the head table, the game is over.

I started out at the loser table, leaving me back-to-back with Gabe, who was seated at the winner table with Brandi, Donny and Joan. I had Nettie, Hugh and Archie at my table. Nettie was my partner for this round. *Oh, goodie.*

Nettie grabbed the pad of paper and pencil. "I'll keep score," she announced. She was careful to align the pad next to the paper plate piled with fudge.

Tossing the dice, I got the game rolling.

"Wipe-out," Nettie said in disgust, then popped a piece of fudge in her mouth.

"Better luck next time." Hugh gave me a rat-eyed glance and snatched the dice off the table.

"I saw Angel today." I smiled at him. "She was in a fantastic mood. I wonder why? Did you get a job and start paying her the alimony you owe her? Bet that makes Brandi real happy. Is she still a manicurist?"

"Bitch."

I leaned back with my glass of wine. "Me or Angel?"

"Both," he muttered and tossed the dice. A six, a two and a three.

A vein throbbed in Hugh's large forehead, but he turned to Nettie and said, "Your turn."

"Have some fudge." Nettie shoved the plate towards Hugh with her thick elbow and took the dice.

As much as I enjoyed tormenting Hugh, I had a job to do. I turned to Linda's husband. "Archie, I love this family room. How do you keep the carpet so nice with the kids running through here?"

"Donny and Joan—they do our carpets every four months. They cut us a break. It's a great deal. You should talk to them."

Nettie tossed the dice. "You lost your house, didn't you, Sam? Aren't you living with relatives or something? What would you need a carpet-cleaning service for?" She inhaled a few more pieces of fudge while examining her throw. She snatched up the pencil. "Two sixes!"

"Need help with the math?" I didn't expect an answer and turned back to Archie. "Actually, I could use a good carpet-cleaning service for Heart Mates." Could use some decent carpet too, but that wasn't the point.

"Donny and Joan have been giving all of us the same deal, Sam. Talk to them."

"I will." It was hard to hide my excitement. I was pretty sure who was trafficking in couples' private sex videos, but I did wonder how Donny and Joan knew those couples had those videos.

"Bunko!" Brandi trumpeted from Gabe's table. "That makes us the winners, Gabe!"

I turned around to look. Brandi was bouncing up and down in her seat, looking adorable. I still hated her. Leaning close to Gabe, I whispered, "Find out anything?"

"Three sixes are a Bunko." He had that damned grin on his face.

I stared at him. "Anything else?"

Swiveling around in his chair, he said loudly, "You got a camcorder, Sam?"

I blinked. "Uh, no. Or maybe in Trent's stuff. But I don't think so."

He turned back to the table. "Damn shame."

Brandi and Joan both giggled. I glared at the back of Gabe's head, trying to figure out—*camcorder?* Videotapes. Sex. So he had found out something!

"What do you need a camcorder for?" Hugh leaned into our conversation.

"Same thing we need it for," Brandi yelled back, eliciting more laughter.

I was betting that Hugh and Brandi were going to be getting their carpets cleaned real soon. They'd be stars on the Internet and wouldn't even know it. Angel would love that! Looking around the tables, I took in the downcast gazes and flushed necks of Linda and Molly. Their two husbands, Frank and Archie, looked normal. Either they hadn't noticed the videos were missing yet, or they did know and were in on it.

"Excuse me." I stood up and headed down the hallway to the bathroom.

I took care of business and glanced in the mirror. The fresh bandage did little to cover the bruises on my head. I had a slight headache. I hadn't touched my wine. When this mess was over, I was going to sleep for a week. But right now, I needed to talk to Joan.

She'd been quite the busy girl. Opening the bathroom door, I was not a bit surprised to find Joan lurking in the hallway.

"I want to talk to you."

That was blunt. There was no one else in the hallway. "Why'd you lie about working at Heart Mates?" I asked her.

"Trent always said you were dumpy and boring, but he never said you were stupid."

He should have. I *was* stupid, and proof was standing right in front of me. Wishing that I had my stun gun with me, I settled for getting some answers. "I want to talk to you about Trent. And Hazel."

She looked impatient beneath her smooth blond bob. "I don't care about them. I don't want you messing things up for me, for us. Donny and I got a business and we need to be respectable."

I had a pretty good notion just how respectable a business they had. "If I were you, I'd be worrying about Hazel. You took Trent from her, and the money Trent had."

For such a lush figure, Joan had gaunt lips. She thinned them now in disgust. "Hazel always thought she was too good for everyone else. Losing Trent was her own fault. He liked sleazy underwear, and I gave him what he wanted. But there was no money."

Huh? No money? Then why were people slamming me around, using stun guns, and sending my kids threatening candy? "You must have thought there was money once to have gone to all the trouble of taking Trent from Hazel." To say nothing of the boys and me.

Those thin lips twisted into a sour expression. "Seemed like he had money. Trent was a big spender and all, but he kept claiming that he was rich and was going to take me to the Bahamas. He said that we might have to move fast and that if ever I needed to get the money for him, the key would be in the Mustang. How would Trent have hidden all that money he said he had in a car? Besides, you would have found it by now."

Maybe if I hadn't sold the Mustang to Hazel. It seemed likely that Trent had fed Hazel the same line, which explained why she had bought it from me. "He said it was in the Mustang?" I repeated myself. Joan was right, in her conniving, bitchy way. How would Trent hide five hundred thousand dollars in a car? Cashier's check?

"He said the key to the money and plans, or code . . . something, was in the Mustang. After a while, I started thinking he didn't have the money at all. He was getting more and more paranoid, and—" Her gaze eyes fixed on me. "Anyway, it doesn't matter now. Trent's dead."

"Thanks to Hazel," I said. "And who's to say she's not after you for messing things up for her?"

Her mouth slackened. "Hazel killed Trent?"

I was pushing hard. I did think Hazel killed Trent, but I also needed to scare Joan into giving me any information she had on Hazel. Self-preservation was a big thing for Joan. "Oh, yeah, she poisoned him with his own peanut allergy. And now she's looking for the money. If she thinks you have it . . ." I left the sentence hanging.

"But Hazel got herself a new boyfriend. Some cop. That's what I heard . . ."

I lost the rest of her babbling. Cop? Hazel had a cop boyfriend? Cripes-a-mighty! The hallway was lined with pictures in heavy wood frames. The faces in the photos blurred as panic exploded in my head. *Cop. Rossi. Ex-cop. Gabe.*

"Listen, I don't want no trouble. I don't know anything about that money. I got a good thing with Donny."

That reminded me of the videotapes. I pushed past Joan and headed back to the family room. Everyone was taking a break, getting drinks and snacks. I barged into the middle of the food swarm. Shoving Brandi off Gabe, I said, "I think I'm sick. Can you take me home?"

In Gabe's truck, I leaned my head back against the headrest and closed my eyes. My thoughts boiled and bubbled. "I have Donny and Joan's business card. We should take a look at their house while they are still at Bunko." I didn't open my eyes. "I need to get some stuff from my house first." And make sure Grandpa and the boys were all right.

"What'd Joan say to you?"

I opened my eyes. Gabe had been right earlier when he'd told me to choose up sides. I chose. "That Hazel took up with a cop. I think you're right, Gabe. Rossi could be . . ." I shrugged.

"This is getting really dangerous, Sam. I'm going to put you and the boys someplace. Barney too." He reached for his cell phone on the dash.

I caught his hand. "No."

He cut his gaze sideways.

"I think I know where the money is."

Letting go of the cell phone, Gabe took my hand in his. "What does that have to do with the videotapes?"

I was surprised that he didn't demand to know where I thought the money was. "It was something Joan said about the key, or code, to money being in the Mustang."

Gabe kept his eyes on the road. It was full dark, but we were almost home. My stomach tightened and I leaned forward as Gabe made the turn onto the dirt road that led to the house.

"Sam, you're trying to do too many things at once. We should let the videotape thing go until we make sure you, TJ, Joel and Barney are safe. It's time to draw out all the players in this mess."

The house came into view. Lights blazed in the front

room window. Loosening my grip on the seat, I acknowl-
edged that what Gabe said made sense. But . . . "No, I
want to get over to Donny and Joan's tonight. I want to
find those tapes and get them off the Internet." Taking my
gaze from the house, I looked at Gabe. There was enough
light from the windows that I could see his face.

"Why?"

"Because I have to get it right. Get something right."
How could I explain it?

"Prove something to the town?"

"Maybe to me. Besides, Donny and Joan are really piss-
ing me off. First Joan went after Trent for the money.
Then, when he died, she moved on to the next easy mark.
It's personal in a way."

"Okay." Gabe reached across me and unlocked his
glove compartment. He pulled out a gun. "We'll go just as
soon as we see what Barney's found out. He might be able
to tell us how to erase those videos already on the
Internet. What time do you think Bunko will end?"

"Uhmmm . . ." I glanced at the truck clock. It was fifteen past eight. "I doubt it will break up before ten."
Surprised that Gabe hadn't argued with me, I decided to
test my luck further, "I was sort of thinking that you could
stay here with TJ and Joel."

The glove compartment slammed shut. Still leaning
across my body, Gabe turned his head and looked at me.
"Were you? And how were you going to get into Joan and
Donny's house? Break a window?"

I could almost see the leaping electricity between us.
Hear the sizzle. A shiver went up my back. "Maybe the
door's unlocked?"

He put a hand on my thigh. "We'll take Barney, TJ and
Joel to my house and lock them in. I have an excellent security system that, combined with Ali, will keep them safe."

He understood. "Thank you." Frowning, I said, "Why are you leaning over me like that?"

Bad-boy grin. "I can see up your skirt."

Coming out of the bedroom with my black, multi-pocketed vest on, I headed down the hall toward the kitchen. Grandpa and Gabe were too intent on their discussion to notice me.

"It depends on the setup, Gabe. I checked the domain and it is registered to DJ Entertainment Group. Probably that is Donny and Joan since they use D&J for their carpet-cleaning business. I should come with you and Sam—I have to physically be at the computer where the data is stored to get those videos off the Internet site. Then there's the whole thing with going through the directory and passwords."

Gabe brushed his hand through his hair. "No way, Barney. You need to stay with the boys. Besides, we don't even know if the setup is at Donny and Joan's house. I'm sure they are the ones taking the tapes and broadcasting them over the Internet, but they could have the equipment anywhere."

Taking my cue, I walked in with the solution. "We can call Grandpa from my cell phone." I pulled it out of the inside pocket of my vest. I had on skin-tight black jeans, hiking boots, a spaghetti-strap black T-shirt and the vest. I'd bunched my hair up under a black hat.

Gabe turned and grinned when he saw me. "Central casting?"

Unzipping my vest, I pulled the edges apart to reveal my stun gun peeking out of another pocket. "What did you say?"

"You look cool, babe," Gabe amended. Then turned back to Barney. "Sam's got a good idea. We'll call you from the house if the equipment's there."

Grandpa rubbed his hands together gleefully. "Right. I'll access my friends in the magic community on your computer, Gabe, then wait for your call. If I don't know how to do the job, one of them will." He sobered. "But you two be careful. I don't wanna have to come out there and save your hinnies."

Zipping up my vest, I went to Grandpa and hugged him. He'd been with me on almost every adventure in my life. I loved him more than I could have ever loved a bio-dad.

"We'll be careful." I kissed his weathered cheek.

Donny and Joan's house was on a road where the blacktop ran out into dirt road. Only a single street light flickered; the rest were broken from either rocks or bullets. There was an assortment of shabby apartment buildings and jerry-built houses. Tract homes didn't exist here. We passed the house we were looking for and drove around the corner into a darkened alley.

I didn't want to be here. Gabe set the brake on the truck and glanced at me. "Okay?"

"Sure." It came out a squeak. Gabe looked comfortable and confident. He opened the door and got out. I followed him, more afraid of being left alone in his truck. We walked quietly back to the house. It looked like a square box of maybe four rooms. I was guessing it had a kitchen, living room and two bedrooms. "How are we going to get in?"

"Let's hope they don't have a dog." He took my hand and tugged me down the garage side of the house until we came to a warped fence. "Get your defense spray out."

I pulled the canister out and followed him through a creaky gate. No dog. Sighing, I looked around. Dirt. The back area was dirt and weeds. All the windows had bars on them. Not exactly fire safe.

I shuddered and followed Gabe to a door that had a window in the top half. "Shine a light on the lock, Sam." He dropped to his knees, pulling out his set of lock picks. Getting the heavy flashlight out, I aimed the beam at the doorknob.

The lock clicked. We were in. I was doing my first breaking and entering. Or was it robbery? Wait, Gabe had a gun, so that made it . . .

"Sam, come on." He took my hand and tugged me into the house, shutting the door quietly behind me.

"It's official. I'm a felon."

Gabe reached out and took the flashlight from my icy-cold fingers. "You're more of an accomplice."

We were in a small kitchen. There was an ice cream table with two chairs in the middle of the room. An olive-green refrigerator rumbled in one corner. A brown washer and dryer was against the far wall. I spotted a coffeemaker, blender and toaster. "No computer in here. What time is it?"

"Nine. Come on." There were two ways out of the kitchen—to the left of the refrigerator it led down a hallway, the right opened onto a living room. Gabe did a quick survey of the living room, shielding the flashlight with his hand so the beam was muted. Couch, TV, stereo, but no computer.

"Ouch!" He backed up into me.

"Don't you dare spray me," he muttered and went down the hallway.

I still had the defense spray in my hand. We passed a bathroom, then a bedroom with a double bed and TV. They were both on the front side of the house. We came to a closed door that led to a room on the back side of the house.

My heart swelled in panic and cut off my breath. "Is someone in there?"

"One way to find out," Gabe whispered and reached for the handle. Nothing happened. "It's locked."

Locked. Either someone was in there, or . . . bingo! My excitement edged out my fear. "Can you get in there?"

"Hold the light." He handed me the flashlight. "It's a keylock dead bolt. Pretty heavy duty for an interior door."

I held the beam of light on the doorknob, fully expecting Gabe to drop to his knees and do his lock-pick thing, but instead, he stretched up high and was feeling around the door frame.

"Here we go." He pulled a key down with a good deal of dust. Grinning, he explained, "Most people hide keys in the same places."

"Seems stupid to me," I muttered as he slipped the key into the lock and opened the door. He left the key in the deadbolt to secure it when we left.

We were in an office, with a big computer on a folding banquet table shoved up against one wall. Different kinds of scanners, printers and other fancy accessories filled the table. Shelves made out of plastic crates held videotapes. The overhead light snapped on and I blinked. "This is it, isn't it?" I turned to look at Gabe.

He had moved from the light switch to browse the videos. "Oh, yeah, this is it." He pulled a tape out and handed it to me. The title read, *Archie and Linda*.

"Can you find Molly and Frank? I'm going to call Grandpa and see if we can pull the cyber plug on this porn business." I pulled out my cell phone, dialed and pushed "send." Then I glared at the computer. I knew how to turn on the computer at work. Blaine had only had to show me twice. Okay, maybe five times, but then I never forgot after that. "I wonder where that big machine part of the computer is?" I muttered as I listened to the ringing in my ear.

"The hard drive?" Gabe bent over and pointed. Beneath

the table was a tower of plastic that was likely the hard-drive thing. Using his pointer finger, Gabe pushed a button on it, then leaned across me to turn on the monitor.

A voice rumbled in my ear from the cell phone. "Hello? Sam, Gabe?"

"Grandpa? We're inside and found the computer. What now?" I looked around for a clock. On the bottom right hand of the screen, the time read nine-sixteen. We should still have an hour.

"Can you find the program files?" Grandpa asked.

I stared at all the pretty icons in neat rows on the screen. "Program files?" I leaned down to read the names below the icons. Gabe slipped into the chair, leaving me staring over his shoulder, and started clicking the mouse. "I found the directory," he announced. "Ask Barney what to look for."

"What do we look for?" I glanced at Gabe to repeat the instructions as they came over the phone, "Look for DJ Entertainment Group. If you find that, open it."

I listened to Grandpa breathe while watching Gabe go through files. "Got it!"

"Really?" I leaned forward and looked at the screens that Gabe was going through. "Oh. *Oh!*"

"Give me the phone," Gabe said. "I didn't find Molly and Frank's video on the shelf—why don't you look while I finish up here?"

I handed the phone to him and went to the shelves. Donny and Joan had quite a setup. There were at least thirty videos lined up with their spines out on the yellow plastic crates. I wondered how much money they made off sleezebags who paid with their credit card to watch other couples having sex. Gathering up all the videos belonging to my clients, I set them in an empty computer-paper box and brushed my hands off. Gabe disconnected from Barney and said, "Done."

"Linda and Molly are off the Internet?"

"Yep." He was closing files.

I was feeling really good. Successful. Pretty awesome. Damn, was I a good private detective or what? Well, I wasn't a private detective actually, more like an associate or perhaps a consultant... "What was that?" It sounded like a car door slamming.

Gabe stood up from the computer. "Could be a car pulling up at another house." His voice was low. He pulled his gun out of the waist of his pants. "Stay in here, Sam."

"No way." I was right behind him at the doorway.

He looked back over his shoulder at me with dark, hard eyes. "Stay in here. Get out your stun gun or defense spray and hide. I can move better alone and besides, this gives you the element of surprise if someone comes in and spots me."

I could hear movement outside in front of the house, but it was indistinct. It could have been the house next door.

Or it could be this house. "Think it's Donny and Joan?"

"If it was, they'd be coming right in, not skulking around."

Fear shot through me. "Who?"

He shook his head.

I understood the problem. We were trapped down the hallway in the last bedroom on the back side of the house. We couldn't go out the window unless we could pry the bars off, and that noise would alert whoever might be coming into the house. I shivered, then settled into a hard tremble. "Someone knows we're here?"

Gabe was in the hallway, his head slightly cocked to one side, listening. He had his gun pointed down at the floor, and he moved lightly. "Go back inside the room, Sam. Close the door."

"No! I—"

"Do it."

I blinked at the order. Gabe was fully cop right now. He knew what he was doing and would have a better chance of handling things if I stayed out of the way. Stepping back and easing the door closed, I had to force myself to wait.

If Gabe got into trouble, I was going to save him.

"Please," I whispered, "let it be nothing."

I leaned my ear against the door, barely able to make out the sound of Gabe moving down the hallway.

And the sounds coming from the kitchen end of the house. Did we leave the kitchen door unlocked? Maybe it was open and the noise was just the wind blowing it? I ran past the computer to the barred window. It was so dark that I couldn't see anything.

But I felt watched.

Sweat prickled under my arms. Icy-cold fingers of terror clawed at my chest. I was panting. What did I do? Gabe was in danger! I was sure of it.

Why had he suddenly wanted to take Grandpa and the kids to his house? The question slammed into my head. It was important—relevant to what was happening.

"Freeze—police!"

Police? Oh, God! Silent alarm? But Gabe would have known if the house had a security system—he was a specialist in security. Had someone seen us? A neighbor?

"You're not arresting me, and we both know it. Wanna bet on who can shoot faster?" Gabe answered.

Huh? I turned toward the door. I had to get out there and stop this. Gabe sounded calm and confident—he wouldn't shoot a cop, would he? There was a slow thump, then nothing. My pulse was pounding in my ears. I went to the door, put my hand on the cold knob and heard the lock turn.

Staring at the door, I blinked. Everything slowed down.

This wasn't happening. Gabe wasn't out there with someone who had shouted police. Gabe didn't threaten to shoot a cop and someone had not just locked me into a room with bars on the windows.

And I didn't smell smoke.

14

No way in hell was I going to die. I wasn't leaving TJ and Joel behind to join their dad as worm food. Trent was a worm, but I wasn't. I hailed from good old-fashioned American Trailer Park Trash, and there was no way I was going to let the fact that I was locked in a room with bars on the window in a house that was on fire kill me.

"Dammit, Trent, you really made some enemies."

Staring at the door, I didn't see any smoke curling in from underneath it. I could still smell smoke. Reaching out, I laid my hand flat against the door. Cool. Okay, now all I had to do was open the door. And me without Gabe's handy lock picks.

Wait! I ran to the computer desk, grabbed the chair and dragged it to the door. Getting up on the chair, I ran my hands over the door jam. Two dead flies and a key! Leaping off the chair, I kicked it away and shoved the key into the lock.

I was halfway out the door when I remembered the videotapes I had stashed in the box. Rushing back into the room for the tapes, I tried to reason out my situation. Where was Gabe? Had the police really arrested him?

Or had Gabe planned this whole thing?

What about the fire? With the box under my arm, I got out my defense spray and ran down the hallway. Seeing the flickering light of flames, I followed them into the living room fireplace. *A fireplace.* Someone had lit the fireplace to scare the hell out of me.

I didn't waste any more time. I ran out the back door and hauled ass to where we had left Gabe's truck. If it was gone—that meant that Gabe had betrayed me. But I didn't think he had. I was doing my best to think clearly and consider all the possibilities.

The truck was there. Locked. I stood in the shadows from the apartment building where we had parked the truck, beset by mounting frustration.

Someone had arrested Gabe. A cop? Rossi? And why? I had to find Gabe. I needed his truck to do that. First, I would go back to Gabe's house and make sure everyone was okay there. Then I would figure out where Gabe was and how to help him.

I had to face the fact that I knew the voice that had yelled "Police—freeze."

I stared at the truck. I could find another way back to Gabe's house or I could hot-wire the truck. How hard could it be? Of course, I'd have to break a window to get into the truck. Setting the box of videotapes on the gravel and rocks scattered on the ground, I selected one of the plastic cassettes and lobbed it hard at the driver's side of the truck.

It bounced off the window and landed on the ground with a defeated thud. *Damn.* How hard was it to break a window? TJ and Joel had done it with alarming regularity.

The flashlight! Taking off my vest, I pulled out the heavy flashlight, emptied the pockets of cell phone, defense spray and stun gun into the box of videotapes and wrapped my hand and arm with the vest. Then, turning my head away, I whacked the window.

The vibration rattled down my arm, but the window stayed intact. It never looked this hard on TV! I drew my arm back and swung again.

The impact set off the loud screaming of the car alarm, but didn't break the window. "Shit!" I dropped the flashlight into the box and reached down to pick up a jagged rock that was about half the size of a soccer ball. The car alarm was throbbing violently and I looked around, expecting all the tenants of the surrounding apartment buildings and cracker-box houses to spill out and stop me. Or call the police. But so far, no one had even come outside. I took three large steps back and heaved the rock into the middle of the driver's-side window.

The glass cracked like a layer of thin ice and spilled out of the frame. The rock hit the passenger-side window, causing a spider crack, then landed on the seat. The same seat that was now covered with small pieces of safety glass.

I looked around once more. No one was paying any attention to the car alarm. I ran up, reached in the broken window and unlocked the truck. Keeping my vest wrapped around my right arm, I swept the glass off the seat onto the ground. Then I picked up the video that had bounced harmlessly off the window, dropped it in the box with the rest of the stuff, scooped that up and shoved it inside the truck and crawled in after it. Slamming the door closed, I fished my cell phone out of the box and dialed the first mechanically inclined person I could think of.

"Blaine?" I screamed over the pulsing sirens of the alarm.

"Sam? God, is that my head or are you in a police chase?"

I clutched the phone tightly to the side of my head and

tried to concentrate over the noise. "Blaine! It's Gabe's truck. I had to break a window to get in. I need to know how to hot-wire it."

Blaine's silence was as loud as the blaring security system.

"Blaine?"

"Boss, where's Gabe?"

"Don't know! I've got to get the truck started to find him!" Panic had me screaming as loud as the alarm. I peered out the windows, but no one was coming. Didn't they hear the car alarm? Weren't the residents going to check it out? Call the cops?

"Okay. Calm down. No one hot-wires anymore, boss. These new trucks have electrical systems that make hot-wiring almost impossible. Even if you got it started, the steering wheel will still be locked."

"Blaine, I'm kind of in a hurry here." I tried to scream calmly.

"Do you have pliers and a screwdriver?"

I looked in the box of videotapes that I had tossed my spray and stun gun into. The siren was making my head pound. "No."

"Sam, Gabe might have a hide-a-key. Look under the wheel wells and around the spare tire in the truck bed."

Spare key? I turned to look at the broken window. Guess I should have thought of that first. Getting my flashlight, I got out of the truck, ran to the tire in the front and dropped to my knees. "How do I find it?" I yelled into the phone.

"Use your hand, slide it inside along the wheel wells."

I was going to ruin more clothes. At least I was wearing black. Quickly, I aligned my fingers on the inside of the wheel well and slid around, feeling for a magnetic box. "Nothing here," I said into the phone.

"Try another one, Sam."

Running to the passenger side of the truck, I wondered how long these people were going to ignore the alarm. It had only been a couple of minutes, but it felt like hours. Gabe was in danger, and maybe Grandpa and my kids too. If someone, Rossi, had kidnapped Gabe, what was to keep him from getting my kids? On my knees again, I was searching the inside of the wheel well.

My fingers hit a cold metal bump when the question that had been teasing me finally materialized. How had Rossi known where Gabe and I were? It was Rossi's voice I had heard—I had to face that. It scared me. Rossi was a cop, a detective and very smart. Had he turned bad and decided he wanted the half a mil for himself? That had to be it.

Yanking the little box off, I stood up and ran with my prize to the driver's side door. Once there, I slid open the case and pulled out the key. Climbing back into the truck, I jammed the key into the ignition and turned over the motor.

Blessed silence! The alarm turned off! "Thank you, God!" I prayed, put the truck in gear and roared down the street. Into the cell phone, I said, "Blaine I know you're still recovering, but I need help."

"Bring the money to Main Street park at midnight, or I'll kill the rent-a-cop. Next will be your kids."

Gabe's answering machine snapped off. "Rossi, you bastard." We were all standing in Gabe's office adjacent to his living room. Blaine was already at Gabe's house when I got here, waiting inside with Grandpa and the boys. He had two buddies with him. One was a guy I recognized from the garage that Blaine used to work at, and the other was a gun.

I accepted his help and the gun. My kids were more important than my dislike of guns.

"Mom, you don't know where the money is!" TJ was white, his eyes huge in his face. I reached out to him, putting my arm around his shoulders. Ali woofed once from where she lay next to Joel, who was kneeling on the floor with his face buried in her fur.

"I think I do know where it is, TJ." I glanced up at Grandpa. He was behind Gabe's desk, his nimble fingers flying on the keyboard. He had somehow accessed his own Internet Provider account through Gabe's computer. "Do you have it?"

"Sam, give me a minute. Cops keep their addresses and info very secured. Even the DMV doesn't have it. But if he's ordered something off the Internet, like a book, me or one of my friends, we'll find it."

Grandpa was typing and reading, his balding head bent to study the screen. He had linked with several of his friends from the Triple M magic society. The lines in his face looked tighter, but he seemed okay. "I know where the money is, Grandpa," I repeated myself.

He glanced up. "What are you going to do, Sam?"

"Blaine, take the boys in the kitchen and see if they want something to eat or drink."

"Mom!" TJ protested.

I looked down at my son. "I will be careful, TJ, but I'm not going to let Gabe get hurt. I have to go after him."

"Can't you call the police?"

And tell then that I think one of their top guys, a detective, had just kidnapped my friend to extort half a million dollars out of me? "No, I can't. I don't know who to trust."

"Mom's right, TJ." Joel stood up, his face splotchy from crying. "Gabe would save her. Besides, she's got all that stuff we got her, the stun gun and all. And Ali."

I hugged both boys. "I'll be okay." They went off with Blaine and I turned to Grandpa. "I'm going to get the money, then go to Rossi's house. He's probably got Gabe there."

"Why'd he take Gabe? Why not the boys or me? How'd he know where you were tonight?"

That answer had come to me when I was looking for the hide-a-key. "I think he had the house bugged. And I think he's in some kind of pissing contest with Gabe. A cop thing, maybe."

"Over you?" Grandpa's gaze was sharp.

"I don't know. All I know is that Gabe would help me. If I hadn't been in that house, they wouldn't have gotten him."

"You think he went with them to protect you?"

I did. He didn't want me killed in a shoot-out. "Maybe, but right now I have to concentrate on the money and rescuing Gabe."

"I'll help you."

I whirled around. Angel was standing by Blaine, who must have let her in the house. Her long hair was caught back in a long ponytail. She had on black spandex pants and a black T-shirt. "Blaine called you?"

"Yes."

"Got it, Sam!" The printer chugged out a sheet of paper. Grandpa picked it up and handed it to me.

I glanced at it. "It's up in the hills, of course. Probably isolated. All right." I looked up. "Thanks."

"That's why Gabe wanted us to come here, right, Sam? He figured our place might be bugged?" Grandpa asked.

"He didn't say, but yeah, I think he was getting more and more suspicious of Rossi. Especially after Rossi tried to imply that Gabe had been married to Hazel—he had been but it was another Hazel, who is dead."

"You got two experienced cops against each other. This is dangerous, Sam, and we don't even know where the woman is." Angel was up to speed, which meant Blaine had filled her in.

"Yeah, and Luke's out there too. Time for me to go. Ali, you're coming with me." I reached for my newly packed vest and slipped it on.

"I'm coming too, Sam. I mean it." Angel fixed her green eyes on me.

I was heading toward the door with Ali pacing me. "You said yourself that it's dangerous, Angel."

"Only makes it interesting." She was right behind me and I knew I couldn't win this one.

Gabe's truck fishtailed when I turned it onto the dirt road that led to Grandpa's house. Ali whined low in her throat from where she sat between Angel and me. Stopping the truck, I pulled the lone key out.

"Sam, there's someone sitting on your front porch."

We had left the porch light on. I glanced around Ali to see a man slumped in a chair with a baseball cap on. Ali's whining got more insistent. "What is it, girl?"

She stepped over Angel and nudged the door.

"Let her out," I said. Ali leaped from the truck and ran up the porch to the man in the baseball cap.

He never moved. Quickly, Ali returned to the truck. She was fussing and turning in circles, insisting on some kind of action from us.

I was scared. The baseball cap. "Oh, God, I know who that is." Staring at the man, I knew he was dead.

"Who?" Angel slid out of the truck.

I opened my door and got out and followed Ali and Angel. "Luke, Perry's brother. I'm sure he's dead." I got my stun gun out, while Angel took a real, bullet-shooting gun from her purse. We both followed Ali up onto the porch.

Luke had a small black hole right between his eyes. I turned away, my stomach heaving up into my throat.

"Do you think they're still here?"

Tearing my gaze from dead Luke, I fixed it on Angel's tight, grim mouth. Listening, I didn't hear anything except my breathing and Ali's toenails clicking on the porch boards as she shifted around restlessly. Did that mean no one else was here, or were they hiding and waiting for me? But Rossi needed me alive and to do what he ordered on Gabe's message machine. What purpose would there be for him and Hazel to hang around after they killed Luke and left him for me to find? A little message to scare me into doing what they wanted. And to get rid of their competition for the money.

God, I had no idea what I was doing. Who was I kidding? The panic circled my chest and cut off my breathing.

Ali sat down beside me and stuck her head beneath my shaking hand. Ali the dog who was police-trained, the dog who knew right away that the man on the porch was dead—wouldn't she know if someone alive and dangerous was still here? Forcing a full breath into my terrorized lungs, I got control and shook my head at Angel. "If someone was still here, Ali would know."

Still stroking Ali's head, I leaned back against the porch railing. The damn money. Trent had started this whole thing—hiding drugs in condoms, then not being happy with that and skimming money from Perry. But it wasn't Perry who killed him, but girlfriend number one, Hazel, who was peeved about girlfriend number two, Joan. How and where did Rossi fit in here? Had Rossi first shot Perry, and now Luke?

What would keep him from shooting Gabe? And why hadn't he gone after my kids?

Because Gabe had put my kids where Rossi couldn't get them—in his house with his high-tech security system. Rossi had gotten really pissed off when he'd heard that on the listening device that was probably right now in the kitchen.

I pulled myself together. My kids and Gabe were depending on me. Putting my finger over my lips, I motioned to Angel to follow me to the freestanding garage. Ali kept pace with me, every now and again whining low in her throat. The dead man being on the porch was freaking her out.

She wasn't the only one.

Once in the garage, I flipped on the light. Had Rossi put a listening device in here? Angel and I had been friends for a long time; we didn't need to talk. She and Ali flanked me as I looked down at the box of Trent's wine.

Joan had said it—the key or code to the money and plans was in the Mustang. Hazel had killed Trent and bought the Mustang from me. What a shock that must have been for her to find the money wasn't there.

I now knew the money had never been in the Mustang. But the directions to the money had been. I'd found the directions with the panties on the Post-it notes. Only Trent would keep information like that on Post-it notes with panties he had collected from his conquests. The box of wine was on the floor by itself. I opened it up and reached down the side to pull out the stack of Post-it notes.

Angel watched without comment. Ali sniffed the wine bottle with canine interest—or was it alcoholic interest?

On another box, I laid out the notes, discarding ones that said obvious stuff like "Ari—great ass—eight." I was left with eleven Post-it notes. Each one had a small number up in the left-hand corner that ordered them one through eleven. All laid out in order, they read: Hum

Nine, Hum Seven, Hum Eight, Date Eight, Date Eleven, Dep Five, Dep Zero, Dep Six, AA One, AA Seven, AA Seven.

Angel studied them at my side, then looked up at me and shrugged. She and I had both thought that the Hum, Date, Dep and AA were abbreviations for the name of the panty-wearer and the number was the rating. That was how the other Post-it notes read, something like "Rach—nine—big tits."

I whispered into her ear, "The first three with the Hum are a combination lock number on Trent's humidor, the second two are the date they were leaving, the next three are the time of departure and the last three are the airline initials and flight number."

She looked again, her perfect mouth tightening in a thin line. "Sicko."

I smiled in agreement, leaving the Post-it notes. Going to the pile of furniture in the middle of the garage, I pulled the sheet off one of Trent's last purchases, a humidor for his cigars. It was a light walnut, about as tall as the top of my thigh, and more than three feet wide. I never had known the combination and hadn't given it a thought. Trent had stored his cigars in there, and why would I want those?

"It was here all along," Angel whispered, "in Trent's humidor."

I knelt down and worked the lock Trent had special-ordered. Nine, seven, eight. Then I undid the latch and opened the doors.

The scent of Spanish cedar hit me first. Then the realization that I was staring at piles of money carefully rubber-banded and stacked on the slotted shelves.

But no cigars.

"What now?"

I could barely hear Angel. We both kept our voices low to avoid being detected by any listening device Rossi might have planted in the garage. Or so we hoped.

Indeed, what now? Looking around the garage, I got up and went back to the boxes of Trent's belongings. Stuffed in with his wrestling gear from high school was a coach's soccer bag that the boys had bought him one year. They had wanted him to coach their team.

Trent refused and forgot about the bag.

Pulling it out, Angel and I stuffed the money into the bag. At least Trent had gotten a lot of hundred-dollar bills, making our job easier. What if he'd decided to get all ones and fives?

God, I was losing it. We quickly finished and left the garage, the three of us and the money, piling back into Gabe's truck.

Rossi lived up in the hills that surrounded the old country club. It was condemned now, but had originally been built to lure the rich and famous to Elsinore as a kind of resort.

Didn't quite work out that way. But right now, I had to concentrate on the web of roads, many of them no more than a dirt path, that wound up through these hills.

"Sam, do you have a plan?"

I knew where I was. My mother had sold many of these homes to unsuspecting folks. I pulled the truck into a small dirt turn-out and parked it. "Oh, yeah, I have a plan. To rescue Gabe and kick Rossi's butt. By the way, Joan told me that Hazel had taken up with a cop boyfriend. Any guesses as to who that cop might be?"

"And he was so cute, too. Damn."

I laughed. Angel would be Angel in the middle of an eight-point earthquake. She couldn't help herself. "Yep, he's handsome all right. But then, so was Trent. And he's still managing to screw up my life, even while dead."

"What now, Sam? We just march up to his house, hand him the money and ask him to let Gabe go? Maybe even ask him to go back and get rid of the body he left at your house?"

Rossi's house was just up the road. On a clear night, his backyard would look out over the lake and the Ortega Hills that loomed up in a rugged beauty behind the lake. I could see the two-story structure a couple of houses up from where I parked. "We need to find out where they are keeping Gabe. I'm assuming that Hazel is there with him."

"The same Hazel that Rossi was supposedly looking for?"

I flushed in the dark. "This private investigating stuff is almost as hard as Tae Kwon Do," I defended myself. "Besides, who would have suspected a cop was trying to get into the action?"

"Gabe suspected."

"Shut up," I snapped, feeling stupid. Even though I myself had suspected Rossi, I hadn't wanted to believe it.

"Ah, been sampling our security consultant's goods, have we?"

I ignored her. At the moment, I didn't want to examine my feelings for Gabe. We were friends. We'd had sex. He'd told me about his dead wife and baby. Gripping the steering wheel hard, I forced myself to focus. "I don't think Rossi's expecting me, or us, to show up here. He figures I'll find the money and bring it to the park."

"You sure?"

I remembered the conversation in the Italian restaurant with Rossi. "Rossi made sure I had every reason to show up. First he figured out that Gabe means something to me, then took him so I'd be motivated to bring the money to him. Second, he eliminated the competition for the money—Luke. But in doing that, Rossi is unintentionally warning me that he's playing for good. He has every intention of killing Gabe and me tonight. Probably set us up for a crime that he is going to solve with our bodies in the park." Like the murder of Luke on my front porch.

"He believed that you had the money all along?"

Had he? Probably. He'd investigated me as fully as he could. Rossi believed he had a good handle on who I was. But I was changing. Rossi wasn't banking on that—he believed I was still head-in-the-sand Sam who'd bought Heart Mates without having a CPA audit the books because I had a dream. "I'm going to get Gabe out, Angel. Ali here's going with me. Do you have a lighter?"

15

The house was a narrow two-story set back on a hill. The front yard was landscaped in green slopes and bushes. All there was in the back was a deck on stilts built into the hill. No one was escaping that way, unless they knew how to fly.

Angel and Ali guarded the soccer bag stuffed with money while I prowled around the house. The only way out was the front door, through the interior door to the garage or the smaller door on the far side of the house. There were matching brass outdoor lights on either side of the garage and a porch light by the front door.

Not knowing who was in the house, I could only assume that Rossi, Hazel and Gabe would be in there. Gabe would be incapacitated. I shut down that thought.

I had the lighter in the pocket of my jeans, and my stun gun, pepper spray and cell phone in my vest. Angel had her gun. Ali had her teeth. Quietly, I returned to Ali and Angel crouched down by the shrubs. "Okay, give me the bag. You sure you know what you're doing with that thing?" I looked at the gun Angel was holding.

"I could shoot Hugh's balls off from across the street.

Don't worry, Sam, you and Ali go hide up there by the front door. I'll do the rest."

"He's dangerous, Angel. Be careful. Wait until I unscrew the front porch light before you start shooting."

Angel nodded. Ali and I went up the short driveway, past the white Camry, around the garage wall of the house, passing the hose neatly wound up on a reel. The front of the house had a window covered in tightly closed wood shutters. Beneath the window was a flower-and-bush garden. Keeping low, I led Ali over there and told her to get down and stay. Her amber eyes remained fixed on me.

Wrapping my hand in a long scarf that Angel had had in her purse, I clamped my jaw tight, reached up into the glass casing of the porch light and grabbed the bulb. Pain seared my fingers through the scarf, but I forced myself to twist the bulb. Plunged into darkness, I yanked my hand off the bulb. Panting from the pain in my burned fingers, I made my way to the bushes, where Ali was hiding and crouched down, trying to be one with the shadows. When Rossi opened the door, the back lighting would let me see him easier than he could see me.

I hoped.

Okay, Angel, I thought, do your thing. Ali edged up on her belly close to me and licked my burned hand. The two lights on the garage cast enough glow for me to see Angel's shadow down on the bottom of the driveway. She raised her gun.

Pop! The first gunshot exploded. Glass shattered, and one of the lights on the garage went out, the one closest to me. Angel's shadow disappeared in the gloom.

I jerked, but it didn't faze Ali. She was trained for this kind of thing. Holding my breath, I waited to see if the front door would open. Behind me, I heard the wood shutters move. Then nothing.

Again, Angel.

Pop! The second gunshot hit its mark, taking out the second light on the garage. Over the pounding of my heart, I speculated on Rossi's next move. What was Gabe thinking? That last thought almost made me smile. Gabe would know it was me. Grabbing up the soccer bag of money, I waited.

The door opened. Crouching low, I watched Rossi. He had his weapon out and was looking around. No sign of Gabe or Hazel. Light poured out from the house.

Rossi stepped out, keeping his back to the wall. "Police! Who's out there?"

I could feel his eyes scanning blindly over where Ali and I were hidden. Rossi was smart, damn smart. But he also knew that I didn't have a gun.

Angel fired again, straight through the window of the white Camry parked in the driveway. The factory-installed car alarm began honking a rude tattoo.

"Fuck!" Rossi exploded. Then nothing. He was moving silently. I sensed more then saw him slide along the garage wall of his house, heading toward the car.

Come on, Rossi, I screamed in my head, go around the corner to the front of the garage where your house lights and car are being used for target practice. Angel should be across the street now, heading back to the truck.

Rossi went around the corner. Along with the car alarm, I heard the sound of a set of keys being fished out of his pocket. Getting up, I moved as quietly as I could and slipped into the opened door of the house. I had the soccer bag slung over my shoulder, and my defense spray out. My stun gun was in a zippered pocket and Ali was at my feet. "We have to find Gabe, and be on the lookout for Hazel," I told her.

No one was in the living room on the left. Blue-carpeted stairs opened up from the front door. I went right, ignoring the dining room just ahead of me to turn left into a kitchen. A family room lay just beyond that. No Hazel. Was she upstairs? And where was Gabe?

Panic was pouring adrenaline through my body. My thoughts were skipping frantically. Rossi would be back any minute. I looked at Ali. "Find Gabe!"

She gave me a pitying canine look and headed right around the kitchen wall, deep into the family room. She stopped at a door. It had to lead to the garage. *Shit.* If Gabe was in there, Rossi could open the big garage door from his car and catch us. The honking had stopped at least thirty seconds ago. Please let Angel have gotten away.

Ali was scratching at the door to the garage. Sucking in a lung full of air, I reached out and turned the knob. It was dark inside.

And it smelled. I recoiled and Ali emitted a low, vicious growl. "Shhhh." Hanging on to the pepper spray and juggling the heavy bag on my shoulder, I fished out my flashlight. Flicking the switch, I shined the beam into the garage.

Blood. "Oh, God." The garage floor was littered with car parts, blood and—a body. A woman shot in the chest and still draining blood. Was she alive?

Ali stopped growling and walked into the garage, her toenails clicking. "Ali," I whispered and followed her. She went to a corner by an outside door that must have been the far side of the house. Playing the light in front of us, I saw him just as Ali reached him. Gabe was handcuffed to a pipe coming in from the bottom of the wall and lying exposed against the unfinished side of the garage as it fed gas into the house from the meter on the other side of the wall. Gabe was sitting down, his mouth duct-taped. His dark eyes watched me.

Time was running out. Rossi would be here in seconds. "Sorry," I muttered, reached down and ripped the tape off.

He didn't flinch. "Babe, hurry, you've got to find the key to the handcuffs."

"No time! Rossi'll be back." I raised the flashlight over my head. "I'll have to break the pipe."

"No, Sam, it's a gas pipe. You'll kill us for sure."

I brought the light down and aimed it around the garage, landing on the woman. "Is she . . ."

"Hazel's dead. With my gun. Rossi's setting us up."

"Yeah. Where's the key, Gabe?" Ali had planted herself next to Gabe and was giving me an impatient look.

"On Rossi." Gabe got his legs under him and slid his handcuffed arms up the pipe to stand up. "He might have a spare around somewhere, but Sam, there's no time. You have to get out of here."

"I'm going to go look for a key." I hated seeing Gabe handcuffed and helpless. It was like caging a powerful cat. I put my hand on his arm. "I'll be back."

I turned away and hurried back into the house. Ali followed me, crying low in her throat. "I know, girl," I said as I stepped into the family room and paused to listen. No sound. I turned left and headed for the kitchen. Didn't everyone keep their extra keys in the kitchen? The soccer bag was weighing down my right shoulder. Ali sat down and watched me.

The kitchen was a walk-through, and pretty small. I began opening drawers at the family room end. I could see the edge of the opened front door. The first drawer had silverware. I slammed it shut, and found sharp knives in the second drawer. I moved to the drawer between the stove and refrigerator, wrenching it open and glancing back toward the front door when I spotted the keys hanging on a set of hooks magnetized to the white refrigerator.

A small silver key hung on a piece of white string. I grabbed the key, turning to run into the garage, when I heard the sound of footsteps on cement.

Rossi! He must be on the porch, coming inside. My gaze locked with Ali's—she was backing out of the kitchen. Not knowing what else to do, I tossed the key-weighted string toward her, but she turned and trotted around the corner, leaving me.

The key sailed over the tile to land on the carpet. Now what? The hairs on the back of my neck stood up. Rossi. He was behind me. With a gun. Chances were good that he was pissed.

But I had what he wanted.

I grabbed the lighter out of my front pocket and turned around.

He'd already seen me. His gun was up, aimed right at my face. "Sam."

"Rossi." What did I do now? The key to the handcuffs was on the floor behind me. Gabe was handcuffed in the garage, and Ali was probably searching for beer. Questions and prayers screamed in my head. "I brought your money."

"Did you fire those gunshots?" His blue eyes traveled over me expertly. He was all cop now.

I didn't bother lying. "No, Angel did. By now she's long gone and calling for help."

Amusement flickered. "Nice try, Sam, but I already called the station from my car phone to report vandalism on my car and to assure them that I would file a complaint tomorrow. I expressly wanted to let them know not to bother with any other worried neighbors that called the incident in."

He had all his bases covered. I was an amateur up against a pro.

"What were you looking for in my kitchen?"

I was shifting from foot to foot. Terror made my hands shake and my voice wobble. I didn't want to die. Besides, getting shot probably hurt even more than the slamming around I'd taken lately. *Think!* I couldn't tell him I was looking for the key, but staring down the barrel of a gun made my brain—*that's it.* "A gun. I was looking for a gun. Gabe's gun."

His handsome face watched me, then swung away to search the kitchen. "Any bombs in here? Listening devices? An accomplice in the cupboard or broom closet?"

I shook my head, feeling the weight of that small key on the carpet burning into my back. Jesus, what did I do now? The only thing I could think of was, "I wore my thong."

Male interest flared in his gaze, sizzling the color to an electric blue. "Why don't you put the soccer bag down on the table"—he waved the gun to the kitchen table on my right—"and we'll talk about your thong."

How could I get that key to Gabe? Slowly, I hefted the bag up and walked the few steps to the table. Even if Rossi somehow won, I had no intention of letting him get the money. Setting the bag down on the brass-and-glass table, I unzipped the bag. I needed to get Rossi turned around, facing the table. That way I could see the key. I had one shot, one slim chance of distracting Rossi, then running for the key and trying to get to Gabe.

Odds were good that Rossi would shoot me in the back before I got to the key.

He was behind me now, his chest to my back. He was not one of those cops who let themselves go. I could feel his flat stomach against my back. "Where'd you find the money, Sam? Or did you have it all along?"

"It was in Trent's humidor in the garage, and I only found it tonight." He hadn't realized that I had the lighter in my hand.

"Turn around."

"You're too close, I can't turn around." And I didn't have enough room to run.

He stepped back. Frantically, I thought about yanking

out the pepper spray and zapping him in the eyes. Carefully, I turned around.

"Time to get naked."

I was staring past him, searching for the key. There it was, gleaming off the blue carpet next to the black leather couch. "What?" I heard what he said, but couldn't take my eyes off the key.

"Naked. You've got weapons stashed in your vest, and God knows where else. One thing about you, Sam, you have the damnedest luck, and you are smarter than your stacked blond-streaked looks suggest. Now get your clothes off. You can leave on the thong."

I heard him. Heard every word, even as I saw Ali belly-crawling toward the key. Could she do it? She'd stolen my beer that night—surely she could steal a key and take it to Gabe.

Naked could work. I forced my eyes away from my key-snatching dog and looked up at Rossi. Into his handsome face and piercing eyes. Then I slipped off the vest, holding the lighter in my closed fist. I pulled off the black T-shirt. I had on a black sports bra. Leaving that, I unbuttoned my black jeans and cast around for something to say. "You can see that I don't have anything stashed in my bra."

He did a slow grin.

Men, they were all dogs. Even good-looking, murdering cops. Did he think I wanted to do this for him, or was he really checking for weapons? Likely, he thought I'd be easier to control naked, or semi-naked.

Rossi was a murderer, but not a rapist.

Unzipping my pants, I wiggled my hips to slip them down, catching sight of Ali. Her nose was an inch from the key. She was silent and intent. But I had to keep Rossi looking at me.

I pushed the pants past my black thong to my knees, then looked up. "I have to take my boots off."

Rossi's eyes were locked on my thong. I wasn't dumb enough to try any sudden movements. His gun was in his right hand, hanging at his side. Besides, I wasn't running anywhere with my jeans around my knees. A bead of sweat formed on his forehead. Then he reached out and grasped my waist, lifting me up onto the table. "Take the boots off."

He backed up a step and started to turn around.

"Rossi!" I grasped at one hiking boot, trying blindly to snag the lace while staring at Rossi. The thick lace scraped across my burned fingers, wrenching a groan from me. Ignoring the pain, I frantically thought, *Oh, God, don't turn around!* I didn't dare look at Ali.

Rossi stopped turning and reached for my right hand. He looked down at my fingers, then slow-climbed his gaze up my sports bra to my face. "Unscrewing the light bulb in my porch light?"

Using my left hand that still held the lighter, I got the laces undone and pulled off the hiking boot. It landed on the tile. Rossi let go of my burned fingers. I had to think of some way to keep his attention so he didn't turn around and see Ali. "That story you told me, about the girl who died from drugs that you said came from Heart Mates—was that true?" I got the other shoe off. It thunked on the ground. I cut my gaze to Ali.

She had the key! The white string with the silver key was hanging from her mouth. She was scooting around to head for the garage.

"It was true. We were dating."

Sorrow coated his words. Forcing a breath of air into my lungs, I said, "That's why you're doing this? Some kind of revenge?" I kicked my pants off. I was sitting on the table in my thong and sports bra, with the bag of money snuggled against my right hip. But Rossi had my attention.

His gaze rolled over me, slow and hot. "I worked my ass

off for damn near twenty years trying to put scum like your husband away. The law protects them more than the cops or the victims. I got tired of it. I'm taking the money. Why should the dealers get it all?"

"But you murdered Perry, Luke and now Hazel!" I slapped my lighter-free, burned hand over my mouth. Would I ever learn to shut up?

"They were all losers, Sam." His voice gentled slightly, growing husky. "You have to understand what I see on the streets every day. Perry and Luke, they were both small-time drug dealers who would sell dope to your kids. And Hazel—she killed Trent."

"So you used her?"

His smile had no mirth or sexiness now. "Cops, especially detectives, use informants all the time."

Part of me was buying time for Gabe to get free of the handcuffs, but another part of me was truly saddened by the waste of what had been a good man. The system had beaten him down until he fought back by becoming one of the very element he was supposed to protect society from. "Rossi, do you really think you're going to get away with all this?"

"It's too easy." He reached out a hand to cup one of my breasts.

Revulsion spread through my belly.

"You are an intriguing woman, Sam. Sexy and smart-mouthed. Too good for that rent-a-cop."

Suddenly I was scared again. So scared, my hands were numb and my fingers ice cold. I shivered, my nipple hardening beneath his hand. Pushing with my hands, I slid off the table. My socks slipped a bit on the tile, but I caught myself.

Rossi grinned. "Too bad I don't trust you."

"You're going to kill me." I stated the fact. I could feel the plastic throw-away lighter against the palm of my hand. The money would catch fire. I closed my eyes and prayed silently, *Please let Gabe have freed himself and help me!* He didn't have a gun, but he would have the element of surprise.

But I was pretty sure Rossi was going to get off a shot at me before Gabe could do anything.

"I'll make it easy for you, Sam."

That snapped open my eyes. He was looking right at me. "Is that supposed to make me feel better?"

Rossi stiffened. His whole posture went on alert. I had heard it too. A clank from the garage, the sound of metal hitting metal. *Like a handcuff hitting a pipe.* He turned and looked toward the garage.

Now! Switching the lighter from my left to right hand, I flicked the lighter on and stuck the live flame into the bag of money. It caught. Jerking my hand out, agony seared my already burned fingers. I shoved the pain away, thinking only about what I had to do. I prayed I could remember everything Gabe taught me.

"What are you . . ." Rossi swung his head around, bringing up his gun hand. I used the outside edge of my left arm to knock the gun arm away from my body, and aimed hard for his nose with the heel of my right hand. The jolt of contact was shocking, but in my head I was chanting, *All the way through all the way through.*

Rossi's head snapped back and he stumbled. I could hear the money crackling in the flames and smelled smoke. Pivoting on my sock-clad foot, I turned my side towards Rossi, clasped my wrists and rocked my arms back and forth. Before Rossi recovered his balance, I slammed my right elbow into his gut, pushing through to his solar plexus the way Gabe had taught me.

Rossi went down and I ran like hell. Praying I could stay on my sock-clad feet, I raced around the leather sofa. Rossi was swearing and moving behind me.

He had a gun.

I expected a bullet to slam into the back of my head, exploding it like a cantaloupe. I tried to run faster, heading for the garage door.

Eighty pounds of pissed-off German shepherd came barreling through the door. Her black and tan fur stood straight up in a marching line down her back; her lips were pulled back from her teeth in a vicious snarl.

I had to jump onto the end of the black couch to avoid a collision with Ali. My socks slid on the leather, and I landed on my thong-bared butt. She never stopped, her growl ripping through the air. Time slowed. The door to the garage was still four feet in front of me. I was turning my head back even as I heard the gunshot.

Ali's growling stopped.

I blinked in horror. "No!"

Rossi was staring at the silent, bleeding dog lying halfway between us. He was as shocked as I was. He hadn't known the dog was there. Ali had leaped up and caught the bullet meant for me.

Oh, God. Poor Ali. My throat filled with raw pain. It was in a strange trance that I turned from Rossi and scrambled off my butt, got to my feet and leaped over the end of the couch. When my feet hit the carpet, I spun to the right and ran through the door.

All I could think about was getting to Gabe. He would know what to do to save Ali.

An arm hooked around my waist as I shot through the door. Gabe literally lifted me off my feet, throwing me past him into the wood and black paper that passed for a wall. His whole attention was focused on the door.

"Ali . . ." I had to save her.

"Shhh."

Leaning my head back against a piece of wood, I

squeezed my eyes shut. Over and over I heard the gunshot. How would I tell my kids?

The thought hit me—I *wouldn't* tell my kids anything if I didn't live through this. I opened my eyes and looked around. Gabe had a tire iron in his hand. It didn't take a detective to know what he was going to try and do.

But Rossi was a cop. He was trained for doorways and dark places. And he had the gun that he had shot Ali with.

I still had the lighter in my left hand. Looking around, I saw the unfinished workbench covered with car parts next to me. From a Mustang. Rossi and Hazel had ripped apart the car looking for the money. A dry gas tank lay on the ground, next to a bucket seat.

And Hazel.

I tore my gaze away from the dead woman. The workbench held cans of paint, motor oil, rags, a toolbox . . . My eyes caught on a blue can with a four-inch red stray tip attached. It was sitting next to the toolbox on top of a rag.

A spray in a can that lubricates, cleans, protects and is flammable. Quietly, I slipped along the wall to the workbench and snagged the can. It was cold against my twice-burned fingers, but my wrist screamed in pain. Probably from trying to smash Rossi's nose into his brain. I slipped next to Gabe's side.

He glanced at me. I showed him the WD-40 and the lighter.

His dark eyes moved up to my face. Our gazes locked. He had that expression on his face—could I do it?

Could I?

Damn right I could. Rossi had killed Perry, Luke, Hazel and probably Ali. I nodded.

Breaking the eye lock, Gabe rolled carefully around, took a quick peek, then slipped across the door opening and resumed his position on the other side.

Rossi was coming. Through that door. Gabe had turned off the garage door opener at the site of the inside button. He'd locked the side door. There was no other way. I sucked in a breath and heard the squeak of shoes.

Gabe looked at me and held up a hand. He'd give me the signal.

We waited. Sweat rolled down my chest, pooling at the bottom of my sports bra between my cleavage. The skin covering my spine prickled. My ears ached from trying to listen. How badly had I hurt Rossi? A cramp bit hard between my shoulder blades.

I heard it. The sound. Rossi was there, in the doorway, getting ready.

Gabe's hand went down in a signal, then returned to the grip on the tire iron. I aimed the four-inch spray tip at the door, stiff-armed to keep the contents as far from my hair and face as I could reach. Flicking the lighter, the flame caught.

Rossi's gun slipped through the door.

I depressed the spray on the can of lubricant. It shot out in a forceful spray, caught the lighter flame and flared in a wicked hiss.

It took all my willpower to hold the spray tip down and not let go.

The burning lubricant hit Rossi on the arm. His scream was vile. The gun dropped and the fiery spray hit his shirt, catching him on fire.

Gabe swung with the tire iron, but missed. Rossi disappeared back into the house. Gabe snatched his gun off the cement floor and followed.

I ran after them both. Rossi had grabbed an orange and brown afghan off the couch and was trying to beat the flames out on his shirt. His hair caught fire, then the afghan caught and burst into flames.

"Rossi! Stop! Drop and roll!" I screamed at him while running to the kitchen. Throwing the soccer bag of burned money out of the sink where Rossi must have put it, I turned on the water and shoved the coffeepot under the stream. I had some vague notion of throwing the water on Rossi and putting out the fire.

Rossi ran past me and up the stairs. He was fully on fire now. Jesus! "Rossi!" I screamed, gagging at the horrible smells.

Gabe flew past me, trying to tackle the burning man. I abandoned the half-filled coffeepot, grabbed up two dish towels and ran to Ali. Dropping to my knees on the carpet, I thought she was too still. Her eyes were closed.

"Ali?" Her right flank was bleeding profusely. Putting my head down to her face, I said softly, "Oh, Ali, please be alive."

A pink tongue licked my face.

She was alive! I stroked her face. "Shhh, Ali, lie still," I coaxed, laying a towel on the wound and pressing. "We'll get you help."

"Sam! We have to get out of here!"

Gabe ran into the family room, still holding the gun. "The house is on fire! Rossi set everything on fire as he ran!" He stopped and looked down at Ali. His face shifted into a mask of pain.

"She's alive! Help me! I can't lift her!" I would not leave her. She was my hero dog.

Without another word, Gabe bent over and scooped Ali up into his arms. I kept the pressure on her wound and we hauled ass outside.

Flames were coming out the upstairs window. I stared up at the sight. Rossi had to be dead. Why? Why didn't he fight to live? Why had he done all this? So many whys.

"The whole afghan went up, Sam. Rossi was a madman,

fanning the flames as he ran to the master bedroom. He fell on the bed. I think he was trying to get to his backup gun. I couldn't save him."

By the time the police and firefighters arrived, the whole house was burning.

16

There was a ringing in my head when I woke up.
No, wait, that was the doorbell. Glancing at the green
numbers on my digital alarm clock, I groaned. It was six-
fifty-five on a Saturday morning. "Who could that be?"
Throwing the covers back, I almost stepped on Ali. She
was sprawled on a blue blanket by my bed. "Sorry—no,
don't get up." She'd had surgery on her right hip to get
the bullet out and repair the damage. But she would be
her beer-drinking self in no time.

The doorbell rang again. Grandpa must not be up yet,
and only the scent of breakfast cooking wakes up the boys.
Trying to avoid slamming into walls, I headed for the living room. I already had enough bruises, burns and
sprains. My right wrist was in one of those elastic bandage
things. The blistered fingers were left to heal on their
own. Padding to the front door, I glanced down at my
Storm team baseball shirt, shrugged and opened the
door.

The alarm system screamed and my mother stood in
the doorway. "Shit." Leaving the door open, I went to the
system on the coffee table and punched numbers. The
racket stopped.

"Samantha, you're not dressed!" My mother glanced at the slim gold watch on her blue-veined wrist. She was wearing a cream-colored suit today with a rose blouse.

Stopping halfway back to the door, I tried for innocence. "Dressed for what?" Maybe she'd cut me some slack.

"The real estate class! It begins promptly at eight." Mother breezed into the house, her expensive leather purse smacking my sprained wrist as she glided past me to the hallway. "I will pick out something for you to wear. Your taste is . . . questionable."

"Mom!" I didn't think it was my injuries that were making the sleep-swollen skin beneath my left eye quiver. "I could be arrested today! I don't have time for classes."

She paused at the hallway. "Well, you surely don't want to be arrested looking like that." With her mouth pursed in motherly disapproval, she added, "Besides, I'm sure those nice policemen are not going to arrest you."

"Mom, one of those nice policemen tried to kill me and I set him on fire!"

She waved her frost-tipped nails at me. "All the more reason to have a respectable career. These things don't happen to real estate agents, dear. Now come along." She pivoted around and disappeared down the hall.

I closed my eyes and slapped my good hand onto my forehead. Then I remembered my stitches. "Ouch!"

"Hey, babe."

Snapping open my eyes, I tried not to look at him. But I did. He was leaning on the door frame, dressed in a pair of butt-hugging jeans and a dark green shirt. His ebony gaze rolled over my sleep-ruptured hair, the Storm T-shirt, and traveled down my bare thighs to my toes. "Gabe."

"So you're taking up real estate?"

"Ugh!" That summed up my feelings on the subject. He slow-smiled. Shoving off the door frame, he went past me into the kitchen, saying, "What are you going to do about your mother?"

"I'd run away, but I'm not safe on the streets with all the cops I've pissed off."

Gabe pulled a can of coffee out, found filters and started measuring out crystals into the coffeemaker. He ran water into the carafe. "There's nothing like setting a local cop on fire and burning down his house with a murdered woman and a half-million dollars inside to get the undivided attention of the local authorities." He poured the water and set the coffeemaker to brew.

Gabe in my kitchen brought up questions that I didn't have the answers to.

Uneven paw tread saved me from my romantic problems. Ali limped into the kitchen and found her spot by the sliding door at the end of the counter. She curled up and looked at Gabe expectantly.

He went over to the dog and hunkered down by her to pet her. "Hey, girl, you feeling better?"

Curling my good hand into a fist, I stared at Gabe's back. He asked the dog how she was doing, but not me. I was jealous. Of a dog. This was why I thought Gabe and I should keep our relationship professional. Thursday night had been spent at the vet's, then the emergency room for my wrist, and finally I saw the dawn from the police station as I explained the events with Rossi over and over.

Gabe and I were kept apart.

Friday, Gabe went home to get some sleep and I spent the day scrubbing down the front porch and going through Trent's things in the garage. I didn't want any more surprises. I never told TJ or Joel about Luke's body on the front porch, but I did tell them what their dad had done.

I had to focus on my family, not my hormones.

Voices were raised in a heated argument. "Katherine, leave Sam alone!"

"I've left her alone and look what she's done!"

"What she did was save Gabe's life and her own. She's doing fine, and she loves that dating service. You just mind your own business!"

"Samantha is my business. She's my daughter!"

"Grandma?"

I heard Joel's tired voice in the hallway and jumped up.

Grandpa, Mom and Joel came straggling into the kitchen. I met Joel a few steps from the table and hugged him. "Morning, sweetheart. It's early yet if you still want to get some sleep."

His big blue eyes lifted to mine. "I'm hungry, Mom."

My heart eased. He was hungry. A good sign considering all that he had learned about his father.

Grandpa said, "Wake up your brother and get dressed. Your grandma and I are taking you boys to breakfast."

"Dad, I'm taking Samantha to the real estate class," my mom reminded everyone.

Grandpa gave me a wink over my mom's head. "Sam can't write with her sprained wrist and burned fingers, Katherine—doctor's orders. Besides, she's too tired to concentrate."

"But I paid for that class!"

Gabe walked over and handed me a check. It was drawn on the Pulizzi Security and Investigation Services account. "What's this?" I forgot about my mother and real estate.

He grinned. "I returned the videotapes and collected your fee. Just to keep everything kosher, since you've told the authorities you were working with me, I deposited the money in my business account and wrote you a check. Congratulations, Sam, you are officially a part-time employee."

So this was why Gabe had come over. "Thank you," I said dryly and turned away. "Mom, I will pay you back for the class. I'm not going to become a real estate agent. I'm a businesswoman and I run Heart Mates."

"A businesswoman would not be on the front page of the local paper in her underwear and a blanket." My mother's gaze slid over my bruised and stitched forehead, her lips thinning at my bandaged wrist.

I winced at the memory. Angel had come through in spite of Rossi's belief that he had covered his bases. The police, paramedics and firemen came to the rescue. Someone threw a gray blanket around my shoulders. But it was all a shock-numbed blur. Killing Rossi still made me ill, but I had taken control of my life. I wasn't going to let go now. "I'm not going to the real estate class." That was final.

Before my mother could respond, Joel raced back into the kitchen with TJ trudging behind him. "We're hungry—can we go to McDonald's?"

"Sure," Grandpa said.

Grateful that my sons had diverted my mom's attention, I said, "TJ, do you want to go to breakfast?" He looked tired and worried.

"You coming, Mom?"

"Your mom's going to stay home and rest, TJ," Grandpa answered.

"Oh. Yeah, I want to go." TJ came over and hugged me. I brushed the hair off his forehead. "You okay?"

He gave me a grin, his gaze roving over my bandaged forehead and wrist. "I look better than you, Mom."

A lump filled my throat. My serious son had just made a joke. Hugging him closer, I said, "I love you."

"I love you too, Mom. Later." He turned to follow the rest to Grandpa's jeep.

I was left alone with Gabe and Ali. "Thanks for the money, Gabe." I shuffled to the table and laid the check down. "I'm going to take a shower."

"Don't you want to hear my news?"

Sucking up my torn and shredded courage, I turned to face Gabe. He was pouring coffee into two mugs. A deep throb in my chest overrode all my other aches and pains. He looked so damned good. Picking at the logo on the front of my T-shirt, I said, "What news?"

"Sit down, babe. I don't bite."

A flush crawled up my neck. Lowering my protesting body into the chair, I tried to smooth down my hair. Somehow I don't think it helped. I looked like I had just rolled out of bed.

At least I had full-sized panties on.

He sat down, his denim-clad knees touching my bare ones. Carefully, he reached out and covered my bandaged hand resting on my thigh. "The police have cleared us, babe. They found all the listening devices in your house, and Rossi had left some of the tapes at work and they heard what was on those. It appears that Rossi had sought out counseling with a police psychologist after his girl friend's overdose. Since then, he's been under some suspicion."

I stared at Gabe's face. "What about the money? It burned up in the fire, didn't it?"

"The IRS has forensic accountants that will do their magic with what wasn't burned, and if they are convinced it's all there, you're off the IRS hook too."

A huge weight tumbled off my shoulder. I dropped my gaze to my lap. He was gentle with my injured hand. But I still didn't really know Gabe. All I knew was the horrible, blinding fear that I had felt when Rossi had Gabe, and the terror that Rossi had already killed him. I tried to stay focused. "You didn't tell me that Rossi had put bugs in my house."

Shrugging, he said, "I suspected after Bunko when you said that Hazel was dating a cop. Suddenly it dawned on me, but I didn't have time to do a sweep for bugs before we went to Donny and Joan's house in search of those videotapes. So I moved Barney and the kids to my house."

I looked back up into his eyes. "And sent Rossi a message. He took up the challenge and came to get you instead. Why did you go with him?"

"Hazel and Rossi both had guns, Sam. If you'd heard gunfire, you would have come running out of that room. Hazel had her gun trained on the room. She's the one who locked you in."

I shook my head. "You could have been killed."

"Sam, I couldn't let TJ and Joel's mom get killed. They already lost their dad. But we're both alive," he said, then leaned across our laps and kissed me. The kiss seared my mouth and turned my brain liquid.

When he stopped, I said, "What was that for?"

"Saving my life. You are one hell of a resourceful woman, babe."

Was that a compliment?

"And a damn sight more coordinated in your underwear than when dressed."

I was on a high wire without a net. "I do my best work in a thong."

"Oh, yeah?" He gave me a look hot enough to bleach my dark roots. "Businesswoman by day, thong-wearing PI by night. I like it."

"Hmmm." I didn't know where Gabe and I were going together. In some ways, he still scared the hell out of me. But I did know one thing—I was becoming one of those women depicted in romance novels. The kind who went out and faced the very things that scared them the most.

"I think I'll put that on my business card."

	DATE DUE		